For my Dad...

Acknowledgments

As my mind developed SEAL Team 7, I liked playing around with the concept of where I would go in Book Two. There were certainly many directions but this particular storyline seemed to call to me more. As always I think I should thank a few people.

My husband, my number one fan! I love you more and thank you!

My family, as always I love you all.

Those who didn't get to see my dreams come true...or did they?

To the fabulous Kathleen and Lori for all you both do.

To the amazing people who left me wonderful reviews for Book 1; I thank you from the bottom of my heart and hope you enjoy this installment just as much ☺

And lastly, to the two women who are in essence the female characters for this installment. I love you both and cherish your continued support and friendship. Elisabeth and Kris, I hope you enjoy this one!

SEAL Team 7

Elisabeth's Story

<u>PROLOGUE</u>

Lightning flashed through the small hotel suite like a knife illuminating the sparse space. The French doors to the patio were open allowing the swift wind to billow the sheer drapes that had earlier been tied back by the maid, the only thing stopping the rainfall from coming inside was the large covered balcony area that during the sun soaked days held a positively amazing view of the waterfront and the tourists coming and going on boats from other islands.

The room's occupant had spent most of the day down on those docks gathering information while posing as another ignorant American tourist who couldn't see past their own being to what this paradise in the middle of the Caribbean Sea could offer. Now with his room in total darkness aside from the sporadic natural illumination from outside, he stood below the harsh spray of the shower savoring the cool water as it washed away the salty air and sunscreen film that had been covering his lean body.

His thoughts were going over the data he had collected since his arrival a few weeks ago. He had been Island hoping for a couple of months in search of his target, the handful of people who could ever detail him in any kind of investigation would remember him as an early thirties American business man looking to open a restaurant on one of the islands because as he had explained to them he was looking for someplace sunny and relaxing to start over after his wife and two kids had been taken from him in a plane crash eighteen months before. It wasn't the truth but if anyone suspected him as anything else and checked him out they would find a lot in the Boston Herald about the restaurant owner who lost his high school sweetheart and two angel faced children.

Turning off the stream of water, he reached out a tanned arm and grabbed one of the fluffy and soft towels delivered that afternoon and wrapped it around his narrow hips as he stepped out and walked over to the mirror wiping away the cloudy sheen from the fogged up glass. Resting his hands on the edge of the white, cool porcelain sink he stared at the face before him. A few days of beard growth covered his jaw and his brown eyes glared back at him mocking him for being such a coward and accepting the project two years ago instead of sticking around to deal with the breakup he had seen coming like a freight train at full speed and with headlights brighter than the sun. They had wanted different things, their worlds were so completely polar opposite and like always his absence due to his job had killed whatever trust they'd had because he just couldn't confide in her what he did the weeks he had been gone.

Sighing aloud he pushed himself off of the sink and walked in to his room the thunder had subsided in to the distance but the wind was still blowing fiercely and the lightning made his still wet torso glisten every time when the flash would slice through the room and hit him lengthways. He picked up the loose cotton sweat pants from the edge of his bed and threw the towel to the floor before pulling his crisp white t-shirt over his head. Clicking the muscles in his neck he was about to bend over to retrieve the towel as another flash came through all the glass windows and for a split second he swore he had seen a figure standing out on his balcony.

Not wanting to break from his cover he looked over to the wardrobe that held his gun in the lining of his suitcase and figured that if there was someone out there he'd have no chance to get his only weapon before whoever it was lurking could strike. Instead he eased back towards the wall and as the sky lit up again he knew for certain that someone knew who he was and was coming to take him out.

He remained standing, back to the wall as the dark figure boldly made its way in to the room through the balcony doors. He held his breathe watching as the person's eyes scanned the room, not seeing its occupant to the side of the entertainment center. The figure came further in to the room as the light from the bathroom spilled out and cast everything towards the room's main door in a brighter light. Thinking this was the chance to get out, the rooms occupant made a slow walk towards the door but halfway there the unknown stranger turned from the bathroom obviously sure it was empty and the two of them came face to face just feet from each other.

Even with all the training he had, without the gun he had hidden he was defenseless against this hulk of a being standing before him decked out in black from head to toe. It was like being inside a bad Hollywood movie with nowhere to go. The two of them stood there surveying each other and as the hulk went for something in the back of his pants he knew it was time to strike out with his fists. It had been one hell of a long time since he had to take anyone on by bodily force and he hoped his training as a rookie a decade before wasn't lost.

In the beginning he had the upper hand and quick jabs to the hulks stomach and a right hook had caused some disorientation not to mention a slight crippling in his hand from the blunt force. The stranger regained control of the situation before he could do anything but surrender under the steady hold of the gun pointed right at his head. Within moments he was roughly shoved to the floor and his hands bound and a crude strip of unknown material was shoved in to his mouth to render him unable to call for help before having the awful strip of duct tape slapped over his partially open mouth to ensure he couldn't spit it out. The last thing he saw of his hotel room was the feet of the bed and thinking if only he hadn't been so gutless back in the states he wouldn't be doing this mission that more than likely had just written his ticket to hell.

Coming too on a boat he had the rain and the salt water from the spray of the waves in his face and he was lying on the crafts back seat near the roar of the propellers under him. He could see three men up near the controls and couldn't make anything but the occasional word out and that was in the islands French and mixture of their slang language he had a hard time translating. He had a headache to boot that was going to take more than a bottle of aspirin to cure.

One of the men, not the one from his room because this one was at least fifty pounds skinnier came over and pulled him roughly so he was sitting, a quick scan from the corner of his eyes and he knew he was off somewhere to the east of an island, the shore lit up on the horizon like a magical sea beacon.

"You asked the wrong question." The man's voice said, his voice had that sharp island twang to it. "I don't know what you mean." He answered, his tongue felt so dry and his lips dry and sore probably from when they'd ripped off the tape. "I know you do, and you aren't going to get a chance to tell anyone anything Mr. Walsh." The man laughed and pulled him again but this time to his feet. A harsh push and he was facing the ocean on his feet, the boat slowing slightly before he felt a hand on the middle of his back. "This is where we let you off." He was told as he was severely hit over the head with what felt like a baseball bat and blacking out seeing the crashing waves come closer as he fell, bound with his hands behind him, face first in to the chilling darkness of the moonlit ocean.

CHAPTER ONE

The rain was falling with as much intensity as it had during the night and it added nothing to qualm the hurt and anger that had been simmering close to the surface for the last day and a half. The sky was as grey as a Massachusetts winter and the air only whipped near the water so for now the little heat and warmth remained encapsulating the grounds of the villas thirty feet from the waters edge.

Elisabeth had been a fool to believe her life was finally going the way she had always planned. There had always been something that would come along and knock her on her ass the moment she was feeling settled and comfortable, the latest was just another in a long line of emotional let downs.

At twenty-six, she was seriously pondering the long running joke of becoming a nun for real. Surely living without the material items and male scum she fell for would be nice, but as she walked along the wet sand outside of the large villa she had hours before day dreamed of sharing with her latest mistake for the next two weeks she laughed at herself, because she knew if she didn't she would emotionally crumble inside and spend the next few weeks wallowing.

The beach was deserted because for the most part the neighboring villas who shared this private beach were unoccupied. She hadn't slept much during the night, half from the noisy storm and the other because of her high strung emotions. She appreciated the quietness now as she walked further towards the water. Her Capri pants and BU sweater keeping the biting wet rain from her as much as they could and her long brown hair was pulled into a ponytail and threaded through the back of her Red Sox cap to hang between her shoulder blades.

At the waters edge she let the wet salty mist from the waves and the drops of the rain mix with her own salty tears, wrapping her arms around herself she fell to her butt and let the anger filled tears fall all the while watching the horizon through blurry eyes.

Off to her right about sixty feet away was a set of rocks that marked the edge of the private beach before the islands natural vegetation sprung out and cut the beach off from the rest of the islands shoreline. The ocean was pounding the rocks and she became enthralled by the highness of the spray. A movement caught her eye and she strained through her wet eyes towards the largest of the set of rocks. Some sort of animal, something that looked like a mixture of a fox and a coyote was interested in something on the rocks and for a split second Beth's breath caught in her throat as she realized the thing the animal was sniffing around was a person.

XXX   XXX

"Well?" The older man asked as he came in to the study of his very opulent house, the three younger men, two of which were his own flesh and blood rose to their feet with respect to the man they considered even more powerful than the fictional character of the Godfather. He moved his generous girth around to the large leather seat behind his impressive mahogany desk and the three men watched as the two hundred and fifty pound mainly muscle man made the chair groan under his weight.

"We dealt with him." Miguel the oldest son said as he sat back down and reached inside his suit jacket taking out a gold cigarette case and snapping it shut before lighting the small thin cigar. He was the older of their fathers four children, two of which were off in the states attending the best boarding school and his younger and more foolish half-brother Luis who was still naïve at nineteen worked with him for one of the many businesses their father owned on the group of islands that fifteen years ago had become home after their father fled America for fear of prosecution in one of the country's biggest Mob takedowns.

"He's swimming with the fishies." Luis said in his best Marlin Brando impersonation, which made everyone including Vince a thirty something retired Special Forces goon from New York even roll his eyes. "Luis." Miguel snapped hating that his younger sibling was related in any way only different mothers but completely different in looks too. He had lighter skin with their fathers strong almost black hair color whereas Luis tanned very easily. "We did as you asked and took care of the spy. We took him out and dropped him offshore about three miles out." Miguel explained. "Good. You made sure he was dead before right?" Their father asked.
"There's no way that fool made it anywhere but the bottom of the ocean." Luis told his father. "He was tied and unconscious." The three of them watched as the older man's face unchanged emotionally but the tell-tale twitch in his jaw and forehead told them he was far from happy.

"So, you're telling me you don't know for sure that he's dead." His voice seethed through gritted teeth but you could still hear that New York accent perfectly, there was no way of missing it. "He has to be; no one could make it to shore alive in his condition." Vince tried to reassure the older boss who he had admired since the day he had started working for him and would take a bullet for him without question. "In my experience, unless you see him dead with your own eyes it still aint good enough. I should have been more specific in my orders." He sighed in frustration. Instead of the problem going away for good, there was a good possibility that it would come back and bite him in his well-rounded ass.

"I want you all to keep a look out in case he surfaces, I don't want him coming back now that he knows we wanted him gone he'll have a new sense of strength to take me and all of you down." "Yes boss." Vince said and the boys knew that was their cue to leave the room and go on about their daily routines. "Can you stay a minute?" The father asked Vince, which caused the always suspicious Miguel to look back before Luis shut the door behind them. "What is it boss?" Vince moved back over to the front of the desk and placed his hands together in front of him waiting for whatever his boss may have for him. He had been the right hand man to this marvel of a God for sixteen years and would do anything, he knew which side of his bread was buttered on and had seen what happened to those who couldn't be loyal. "Tell me. Is Miguel's wife still up to her tricks?" "She is Boss." Vince looked at his feet. "Luis spent most of yesterday afternoon with her over at the Sands Point hotel." "So blazon and in public, have they no respect for me and Miguel?" "I don't think Miguel knows anything" "We need to take care of this whore Vince. I can't have a woman coming between my two sons. They already despise one another. I blame myself. Luis hates Miguel because he doesn't understand how much his older brother reminds me of Charlotte. She was my love you know."

"Yes boss."

"Charlotte was an angel from heaven who loved me when I came here with nothing and she stuck by me even though the feds wanted her too. My heart broke the day she died."

Vince remained quiet, it was rare the boss ever talked about his first wife and he knew very little about the private woman whose face adorned many surfaces throughout the mansion and he had worked for the man when Charlotte had been alive. Even wife number two and three had never compared to his Charlotte, sure they had given him three more children but they never stayed around long and became distant memories that even their own children no longer wanted anything to do with.

Now at the age of fifty-four, the boss was as handsome as he had been, maybe a little bigger around the waist but the ladies still loved him. There was a few of the local girls who would come over regularly and keep the man sated and happy, and when the boss was happy, everyone else was happy too.

CHAPTER TWO

Pulling in to the familiar driveway of his San Diego house that he shared with his wife and three-year-old baby girl, Lieutenant Commander Mathew Taylor relaxed for the first time in over a week. He had been gone for what felt like an eternity and was restless to see his two favorite girls. Like always his job took him from his family way too often and this time it had been on the other side of the world as he and the rest of team seven had dealt with another of the world's notorious scum.

His usual short hair was longer, curling at his neck and a weeks' worth of beard covered his boyish face and he knew for a fact he smelt bad in the gear he'd been wearing since he had boarded the transport because like him, the rest of his male family in the squad too smelt like week old garbage. He was looking forward to a long hot shower, fresh clothes and more than that to hold his wife and daughter for as long as he could.

He got out of his truck and pulled his pack out of the bed in back, walking over to the familiar front door, just quickly stealing a glance at the house next door that they had finally sold to another young couple from the base just starting out. It had once been his haven, a bachelor pad. He was glad the walls now held a family that would grow and bloom within.

"Hey, anyone home?" He called dropping his smelly bag inside the door and closing the wooden door with his boot. "Mathew?" A female voice called back, not the one he had been hoping for but it was close. His wife's twin sister came out of the kitchen, an apron tied around her waist; she was looking for a change less high strung as she dried off her wet hands on a dishtowel. "Hey Mel." Mathew gave his sister-in-law a brief hug. "Where are the girls?"

"Jamie took Izzy over to the base for her checkup." She saw his frown before it formed and had to laugh a little. "They should be back in a bit."

"How's my favorite sister-in-law?" Mathew said making his way in to the kitchen she had just left, Mel close on his heels. He stopped short when he saw all the food she had prepared for what looked like a large feast on the kitchens large island counter top. "I'm doing fine." She said going back to the cucumber she had been slicing.

"How's the new place?" He asked grabbing a cold beer from the refrigerator and twisting the cap off so he could take a long soothing drink, feeling the coldness of the fluid sliding down his throat. "It's great, it's peaceful and I'm close to my favorite niece."

"She's your only niece."

"For now maybe." Mel waved the long knife around in his direction as she gave him a sly wink.

"What does that mean?"

"That I'm sure the two of you will be having more kids the way you both go at it like rabbits." Her words made Mathew almost spit his drink out before he could swallow it. "I knew there was a reason I didn't want you so close." Mathew joked, knowing Mel wouldn't take offense to anything he jested about.

"Speaking of being close brother-in-law dear, you really should take a shower before your wife and baby girl get back. Don't want them to smell you like that; they may put you out to sleep in the backyard." She joked back.
"Hmm. I guess you're right." He put the cold beer down and saw her quick glance at the condensation covered bottle. "Before I go, I gotta ask. What's with all the food?"
"It's so you and Jamie can have a nice dinner together."
"How did you know?" He stopped mid-sentence and realized he knew the answer before she could tell him. "Steve called you."
"He sure did. Don't worry, I didn't tell Jamie or Izzy. They have no clue unless they run in to anyone who knows on base."
"How thoughtful of you."
"That's not the best part. After you spend a little time with your daughter I'm going to take her to my place for the night. Her uncle Steve's going to come over to play for a while."
"So you and Steve?"
"Are just hanging out." She replied not looking up from her new vegetable she was cutting in to strips.

Mathew left her to the salad she was preparing, he had seen a couple of steaks and some other items out but he knew Mel would do nothing but prepare them with marinade or mixing. She wasn't the best cook but she could prepare better than anyone. He walked with beer in hand upstairs, stopping at the door to his daughter's room and inhaling the sweet smell that came out of it, the mixture of Jamie's own perfume and baby powder. He didn't know before they had Izzy that such an innocent smell could be such a huge memory trigger.

Shaving fast with first his beard trimmer and then electric razor he stripped quickly and not caring how cold the first moments of clean water was he stepped under the jet of water and using the fresh wash cloth from the towel closet he thought about how far his sister-in-law had come in just the last few years.

When they had first met she had been a complete screw up that her twin, his wife had covered for their entire lives but she had hit rock bottom, pulled herself up and since then tried her damndest to ensure she never made anyone suffer from her actions again. She had been involved with a man from her sister's past, someone who had loved his wife Jamie uncontrollably at one time. But after Mel's stint in rehab and of living with a man who had more secrets than the CIA he worked for she had walked out, not looking back and moved to California and in to his old house before recently buying a place down on the coast about twenty minutes away.

Turning around under the now hot spray he saw the fuzzy image of someone sitting on the counter through the showers fogged up glass door. Even with the amount of distortion he recognized the female body. "Why don't you get undressed and join me?" He shouted over the noise of the water. "I'd love to baby but I'm waiting to see your bare wet body get out." The voice joked.

"Come on. Your sisters down stairs what will five minutes in here matter?"

"Only five minutes Lieutenant Commander, that's disappointing." Jamie thrust the door to the walk in shower open and he feasted on her like he hadn't seen her in years. She had a wicked smile on her face that turned to sheer pleasure at seeing him.

"I can wait until we're alone tonight." She said holding out a towel to him. He turned off the water and moved towards her pushing away the arm with the towel and grabbing her close for a very wet hug. "I can't." He said as he bent his head slightly and captured her lips, the lips he would never in a million years forget the feeling of, all feathery light and beautiful. "You'll have too. Izzy knows you're home and wanted to race in here and get you. I had to bribe ice cream on her to make her wait."

"Bribery? My, my resorting to sneaky tactics huh." He teased her, letting her go and enjoying the sight of her standing there in her white now see through tank top and DKNY sweat pant Capri's. His wife may have been worried about losing her figure after childbirth but she could still look perfect in that old black bikini he wouldn't let her throw away.

Mathew had just tied the towel around his waist when the soft sounds of approaching footsteps came towards them and the sound of Izzy's voice calling for him. "Daddy." The little girl's voice shouted even louder on sight as she launched herself at him and he caught her midair, giving her the biggest bear hug he could without her sliding out of his wet arms. Her face was covered in chocolate sauce and ice cream, her light brown hair in the cutest little ponytail and she wore one of her many little girl dresses that she loved so much at such a young age. "Hello cupcake." Mathew said kissing the top of her head. "How's my favorite little girl?"
"I got an owie." She said holding out her little finger that was covered by a small Winnie the Pooh band aid. "Ahh, what happened?" He asked walking her in his arms to the bedroom where he sat down on the edge of his bed so he could inspect the finger closer. "I got blood taken." She pouted. "Isabella is perfect as always though." Her mommy said sitting next to them. "She's right on chart for everything."
"Don't like doctor." The little girl pouted again.
"Doctor Peter is nice baby." Mathew told her.

"Mommy what does bonking mean?" Izzy asked looking at her parents, who both looked at each other and blushed simultaneously. "Where did you hear that?" Jamie asked sure she knew the answer already. "Aunt Mel said it to Uncle Steve downstairs."

"I bet she did." Mathew laughed. He kissed Izzy's head again and handed her over to Jamie so he could get dressed, pulling jeans and a t-shirt out of his closet and retreating back in to the bathroom for privacy. "How about we go down and see your Aunt and Uncle." Jamie said carrying her precious daughter out of the room.

"Can I have more ice cream?" Izzy asked.

"Sure, you can have as much as you want. After all you're staying with Aunt Mel tonight." Jamie laughed wickedly.

CHAPTER THREE

"Damn it." Beth swore under her breath as she ran around the villa looking for anything that looked like a first aid kit, after searching the two bathrooms and the kitchen she gave up and went back to the main bathroom where she took a handful of clean washcloths and wet them all before heading back in to the only bedroom.

The still body of a man lay on the clean white sheets as she returned to the bedroom. As far as she could tell there weren't more than a few bumps and scrapes across his body and a somewhat large looking bruise on the back of his head. He was covered in sand and after having to haul his unconscious ass from the rocks to her villa; she no longer had the energy to hold his dead weight in the shower to wash away the sandy grit that covered him.

She had stripped him down to his underwear on the back porch, feeling a little voyeuristic and actually felt the blush rise up her face as she pulled his damp and dirty sweat pants from his legs. With his clothes drying in the machine in the mud room after she had washed them quickly she went to work cleaning him up the old fashioned way with the cloths.

Having finished with his long tan legs, and equally colored chest and arms she moved on to his face, she mentally compared it to the men she had been involved with in her life and came to the conclusion that this man was the perfect male specimen. His hair a little too long and a few days of beard covering a strong jaw, she knew there had to be someone out there missing him, a loved one, maybe a wife.

As the wet cloth cleaned some of the grit off she wondered how he had come to be lying out on the rocks. Obviously he had washed ashore during the storm, the waves having enough power to carry anything. But as she looked closer she knew something more had transpired. There was faint bruising on his wrists and the bump on the back of his head, also his split lip made her imagine awful things. Had someone purposely tied this man and

thrown him from a boat out at sea? It was
something that made her body shake. She had seen
all the signs of abuse before. In her line of work,
she saw it every day, never before though on a
male.

 After she could do all that she could she bundled
up the man with the spare blankets she had
collected and also lit a fire in the room to increase
the warmth. Even with the heat rising back outside
the villa she wanted to make sure he didn't suffer
from the cold too much.

Taking a seat in the chair across from the large
king sized bed, she wrapped her own body under
the softness of the chenille throw and as her
breathing regulated to the normal pace she felt her
eyes get heavy from sleep she hadn't realized she
had so plainly missed last night. With visions of
the unknown male dancing in her eyelids, she fell
asleep.

XXX   XXX

"I think she's fine now." Steve came up behind Mel
and wrapped his arms around her waist, it was a
little before dawn and Izzy had been up for a while
with a stomach ache and then she missed her Mom
and Dad. When the little girl had fallen asleep
between them both on her little bed in the spare
room Mel had decorated just for her niece it was
mostly from complete exhaustion from crying than
anything else. Isabella definitely had the stubborn

Buchanan gene all of her relatives shared.

"I knew there was a reason my sister let her eat all that ice cream." Mel turned around and rested her head on Steve's shoulder, wrapping her own arms around him and lightly running her fingers up and down. She felt his chest move with his shallow laughter. "Jamie wouldn't do something like that."
"Oh yes she would. I should have called her and ruined her night of wild married sex. After all she ruined my night."
"But I was here."
"Not that we got to do anything." She looked up and in to his eyes. Their relationship was easy and uncomplicated. She had been warned by Jamie that Steve was a love 'em and leave 'em kind of guy but he'd spent every night he was in town in her bed.

"Did you get any sleep?" He asked resting his chin on the top of her head.
"Not a stitch. You?"
"I got a little combat nap in."
"You really have to teach me that trick." She joked as she moved out from his arms. He followed her towards the living room and fell beside her as she sat slouched down on the overly stuffed couch.
"So, how was your week?" Steve asked, her head resting on his shoulder and he hadn't realized that their hands were tracing each other's fingers until he saw his hand actually moving with hers, the feeling feather light and sensual. "Slow. I didn't do much."

"I thought your new boss would be booked out this time of year."

"So did I." Mel sighed. "Seems he doesn't like to have his artistic eye rushed."

"Artists." Steve jived, pulling Mel even closer.

Steve was glad for the moment of silence between them; he had been trying all night to not think about the situation he was in. For the first time in his adult life he was falling in what he could only comprehend as love. Although Izzy wasn't biologically theirs, he had felt tender pulls at his heart as he had laid out holding Izzy between him and Mel. Sure he hadn't slept a lot but he had felt a peace that he wondered why none of his friends with kids on the team had told him about. If he'd known about what coming home to a family could feel like he may never have become the one-night stander, but then he would never have been able to be with Mel. That wasn't something he was willing to give up.

The silence was going on longer than he would have figured and he moved Mel on his shoulder slightly and saw her closed eyes and felt her even breathing. He relished in the sight of her, the feel of her and when they were apart especially when he was away on missions it was Mel his heart ached to be back with, the person that he stayed safe and alive for. He had talked with Mathew before they had shipped out about making something more permanent and he had heard what he had wanted to hear, something that would gain him access to the family club within the squad.

XXX   XXX

His head hurt like someone had run it over, in fact he felt like his whole body was on fire, something was making it so hot. His eyes hurt and he didn't want to open them, because then he would have to face whatever had become of him. He had a dreadful feeling he was in hell, burning for all his past sins. Surely the feelings of what he associated with a week's bender worth of alcohol drenched days like he had experienced as a young teen were real and he would forever suffer in this torment.

He remembered how he had been alone in his hotel room during the storm and how someone had come in and attacked him and taken him to their boat where he had been knocked out again. Once from a right hook to the jaw and one with an unknown instrument to the back of the head. He knew who the men had been. He had seen only one of them from the hotel and the same one on the boat but he knew they were the men who worked for the guy he had been working hard to get intel on for his bosses.

He moved his arms and he felt constricted by something heavy and soft, it smelt good too, almost definitely feminine. He breathed in more through his nose and he was sure there was a scent in the entire place that was foreign but absolutely female. As his hands moved with a smidge more force and strength he felt around as the cool air hit his skin that was now in the open and realized he was covered by what seemed to be a great deal of blankets. Using his other trained senses, he deduced that he was also relatively safe, there was an occasional crack and pop from what could be described as a fire burning along with the faint smell of burning wood.

Feeling a little more together, he opened his eyes and was hit by the blinding light from all directions. The room was mainly white and the sun was coming in and hitting him square on. He rolled over on to his side away from the sun and he took everything in. There was a closed door and a set of doors that looked like closet doors and also a tall green bushy plant that he recognized from somewhere else. His eyes wandered towards his feet and he took in the fire place that had almost nothing left to burn as the embers popped and sizzled away, and there on the whitest couch chair he had ever seen was a dark haired female fast asleep.

Where was he? He couldn't understand it for the life of him. He knew he had been thrown from that damn boat and he had a vivid recollection of the freezing chill the ocean had set in to him as he had descended deep below the dark water, struggling to get free from his restraints. The sound of the propeller cutting up the water above him as his attempted murdering men had sped away. He knew he had loosened the rope enough to wriggle his hands out and had surfaced the water just as the burn deep in his lungs had started to feel close to dangerous. But he didn't know how he had ended up here or even who this female was.

Maybe they came back to check I was dead? He continued to think. Maybe this is the boss's house and this female was the person made to ensure he didn't die before they got a chance to kill him properly. He knew as he continued to look towards her that his mind was getting carried away.

Finding the strength and the adrenaline to block out the severe pain at the base of his neck he sat up completely and shucked away the mountain of blankets he had been covered with. He had to smile. No wonder he had thought he was roasting in hell. The fire and blankets were enough to slow cook a frozen chicken in an hour.

It was when a blast of the central air hit him that he noticed his lack of clothing, he pulled more blankets away and felt relief that he still had his underwear on, but they looked grimy and on touching them, they felt like he had rolled around in a mountain of sand. Interesting he thought. He had absolutely no idea how he got to where he was and he was only wearing his skivvies and they had a coat of sand on them.

Putting his feet on to the wooden floor he got to

his feet and had only taken one step when he swerved slightly and his second step had him coming in to contact with a leg of the bed with his little toe. He let out a "shit" before he could stop himself and the sound of his curse woke the female fast. She jumped up and looked as if she were the one stuck like a deer in head lights.

CHAPTER FOUR

"Commander, those test results you wanted are in." Jamie's nurse came in to her private office holding a manila file. "Did you look at them?" She asked the young petty officer. "No, Ma'am I didn't." She handed over the file and stood at attention. "You can go Largo." Jamie dismissed her and waited for the door to close behind her before she opened the file.

Scanning the papers inside she saw what she had dreaded from the first day of taking the assignment in Coronado as the main physician for the SEAL teams. In her hands she held the one thing that would end a career, and to make it harder it was someone she knew very well. She just felt relieved it wasn't for her husband but he would feel the ramifications of the results none the less. "Largo." Jamie said in to her intercom. "Yes Ma'am."
"What do I have on the schedule for this afternoon?"

"You have Chief Jordan coming in for a follow up at three."

"Okay, thank you." Jamie got up from her desk and grabbed her hat from the coat stand behind her desk where her lab coat was hanging.

"I'll be back in a few hours." Jamie said to Largo as she came out of her office.

"Is everything okay Ma'am?"

"Unfortunately no." Jamie kept walking towards the elevator and once on the ground floor and in the noon time sun she took out her cell phone and pressed the pre-programmed number for her husband. He picked up on the third ring. "Taylor." His deep voice said. "Hey honey it's me. I wondered where you are."

"Missing me already?"

"Always."

"We're over in the classroom. We just finished a training class."

"Is Daniel there?"

"He went to his office a few minutes ago with Cooper and Chris."

"I have to talk to them but would you like to have lunch after?"

"Sure, is there something up?"

"I'll talk to you about it over lunch, bye honey." She disconnected before her very astute husband could figure out something was up.

Jamie made her way over to the separate building monopolized by the SEAL teams for training and offices for the senior ranking men. The building was relatively clear and she saw very few men as she made her way to Commander MacCafferty's office, once outside she heard their laughter over something and wished she wasn't about to ruin their day. She knocked and waited for her invite in.

"Commander." The three men said simultaneously, standing together for respect.
"Please, sit."
"What can we do for you?" Daniel asked getting back to his comfortable position behind his big desk covered in more paper than she would have thought for a man that was so meticulous. "Here." Cooper offered her his seat, knowing there wasn't enough seating for everyone, there were purposely three seats. "It's okay, please I'd rather stand."
"This can't be good." Senior Chief Chris Polanski said.
"I'm afraid it's not." Jamie could feel all the emotion she had boiling up inside of her. She fidgeted with her hat under her arm and the file she was carrying in the other. It took her a minute to regain her composure before she could tell them why she had come.

"I received some test results for one of Team Seven and I'm afraid it isn't good." Jamie told them. "What is it?" Daniel asked leaning back in his chair and looking up in to the badly tiled fake ceiling. She could tell he knew the emotional ramifications of this coming out. "Chondrosarcoma, its Cancer I'm afraid. Stage Two."

"Where?" Chris asked.

"The top anterior portion of the tibia."

"In English?" Coop asked

"Just below the knee, in the top section of the lower leg bone."

"Damn, who?" Daniel asked.

Jamie took a deep breath and waited a second. "Schlome."

"Steven Schlome?" Daniel asked for clarification.

"Yes sir."

"Has he been told yet?" Chris asked.

"No, I just got the results in ten minutes ago. He came in before you all went wheels up, his knee started hurting more and he wanted me to run tests."

"Are you absolutely positive?"

"I'm afraid I am, I had the lab run the tests twice and I had a fellow doctor look at the x-rays yesterday, I was hoping I had jumped the gun."

"What are his options?" Coop asked.

"I'm afraid it will end his SEAL career. We'll have to remove the affected bone and tissue and even then we may have more reconstruction than just the replacement of the bone we remove; we may have to give him an entirely new knee. With rehab and subsequent surgery's, it will be a year before he'll even be able to walk again."

"Wow." Daniel let out a long sigh. "I have to ask again Jamie, no offense but are you a hundred percent sure?"

"I wish I wasn't but I am sadly sure the results are

right."

"He's a good man, are you sure after?" Cooper began but Jamie stopped him.

"Even if he comes through the operation one hundred percent, after that year of rehab he may never be able to maintain the strength in his knee to do what you all do. There is such a slim chance he will I can't even tell him because if I give him one spec of hope and he fails I can't let him down that bad. I'm afraid the best he may be able to achieve is a teaching post on base, his days of going wheels up are over."

"This will kill him." Chris stood and looked out the window, there near the 'O' course with his team mates was Steven. "Well, he's dating my sister; this will be hard on everyone." Jamie told them. "I would rather have you here when I tell him, I think he will need your support and guidance also I think you may want to have my husband and Lee here."

"Good idea." Daniel reached for his phone and dialed a few numbers. "They'll be here in a minute." He said replacing the receiver.

XXX   XXX

"Who's beeping?" Ryan asked coming to a stand with a few of the men, drinking down some refreshingly cold water after the jog around the base that had made none of them break a little more than a minor sweat. "Me." Steven said taking the beeper out of his back pocket. "I'm buzzing."

33

Mathew held up his.

"This makes three." Lee said turning his off.

"Seems the Commander wants to see us."

"I hope it doesn't take long, I was going to go and grab a bite with Jamie."

"Were you not going to invite us?" Steven asked.

"Don't you have Mel? Ask her down for lunch." Lee suggested.

"I don't know."

"Don't know what?" Mathew wiped his forehead with the bottom of his t-shirt and replaced the sunglasses he had taken off before their jog.

"Things are pretty simple with me and Mel; I don't want to rush her and make a big deal out of stuff."

"Rush her? Man what happened to you?" Lee stopped and frowned, half kidding with his friend.

"I guess I see now what you two love about married life that's all. When we have Izzy over to Mel's it's like this neat little family where there's only laughter and none of that bad stuff."

"I think she may be the one for you." Mathew patted Steven's back.

"But how do I know? I mean, she's been through so much."

"And she came through fine; she's as tough as his old lady. You'd be mad to pass her up." Lee told him, opening the door to the building and letting the other two go in first. "I know but how do I know it would be the right time to bring it up?"

"It's always a good time; women like to know they are desirable enough to marry." Matt laughed and knocked on the Senior Officers office door.

"Come in." They heard MacCafferty yell, and Matt turned the knob and saw at the same time the other two did who was in the office. Mathew had known his wife was on her way to the CO's office but he was confused as to why he was called in there with Lee and Steve. The looks of the four higher ranking officers stirred something in his gut and he knew his two friends were thinking the same thing. Something was up, and whatever it was it wasn't good.

"What's going on?" Lee was the first to ask.
"We called you here because we have some bad news." Daniel explained and then looked at Jamie.
"Steve, please sit down." Jamie patted the chair opposite to the one she herself was now sat in.
"What is it?" He sat down and his friends stayed close by.
"I'm sorry Steven; I got the results back from the tests we ran on your knee."
"It can't be that bad, I have it taped up and I did the jog fine." He squinted as if not understanding.
"Steven, the results showed you have a form of bone cancer at the top of your tibia, the tumor is what has been giving you discomfort the past few months."

"Cancer?" He said almost inaudibly.
"Stage two; it's going to require immediate surgery and a long recovery."
"And the Team?"
"You won't be able to perform active duty again."

"Then I don't want the surgery."

"It's not an option, if we let it go then the cancer can metastasis to other tissue and organs, this will kill you if it is left untreated, you will be able to do everything you do now but the high stress of the SEALs job is too much."

"What am I meant to do? I'm a SEAL. I don't know how to do anything else. Jamie." He took her hands within his own big ones, Jamie's entire being lodged in her throat as she knew this was going to be hard but this was worse. "Please don't tell me I can't be a SEAL anymore."

"I'm very sorry." Jamie said and a tear slid from her eye. Mathew came over and put his hands on her shoulders, that was as much comfort he could offer his wife in front of his team leaders.

"You can still be a member of the SEAL team." Daniel leaned on the desk and looked down at a hopeful Steve. "You would make a great teacher and I think you will be a great asset for years to come."

"You can give those recruits hell." Chris said.

"When will I have to have the surgery?"

"As soon as we can schedule it, before the week is out I expect."

"That soon?"

"It has to be."

"Will I have to go through that radioactive shit?"

"The surgery will be followed with a round of chemotherapy, depending on what we find when we go in you may need radiation therapy too."

"This is really serious huh?"

"Very."

"I need some time with this." Steve stood up and went towards the door. "I'll report to the medical building later this afternoon."

CHAPTER FIVE

"Who are you?" She asked; the blanket covering her slender form fell to the floor.

"Who are you?" He countered. His head throbbed and his mouth tasted salty but dry.

"I asked you first." She stood straight, her five foot one height gaining only an inch.

"I need you to answer first." He explained holding his hands before him palms facing her. "It's important."

"Okay, I'm Beth. Elisabeth DeVeuve from Boston."

"Are you here on vacation?"

"Yes."

"Alone?"

"Yes, I was meant to have my boyfriend here but he couldn't make it."

"Why not?"

"His wife didn't approve of him going away without her."

"Sorry to hear that." He said stumbling a little as he took a step closer. "I'm sorry if I seem strange but I can't tell you much, I'm an undercover agent. I can't blow my cover."

"I think whoever it is you were investigating may

know who you were already."

"What Island am I on?"

"Bequia."

"I was staying on Bequia but two days ago I moved back to St Vincent." He explained. "Last night a man came in to my hotel room and knocked me out, he took me out in a boat and dropped me off."

"Dropped you off is a good way of sugar coating it. Nice people by the way."

"Did anyone other than you see me?" Beth hated he didn't find her humor distracting because his bright blue eyes and dark hair were totally making her forget whatever it was...

Oh yeah, bad man, boat, ocean...

"No one; you washed up on the rocks down the beach but the other houses are empty right now, hurricane season and all." He took in her words and came to the realization that he had no recollection of walking to this house. That had to mean that this female that couldn't weigh any more than a hundred pounds when dripping wet had somehow dragged him back, while trying to absorb everything and whether or not to risk her life by explaining who he was further he became conscious of his state of dress. For some reason he was wearing only his light blue boxers.

"Where are my clothes?"

"Your sweats and t-shirt are in the dryer; they should be dry by now if you want them."

"Yes please." He said and watched her reach for

the fallen blanket before leaving the room. He took in more of his surroundings, the room was not as starkly white as the haze he had woken in had made out but subtler; the accents of pale blue and the many potted greenery made everything very clean looking.

He walked over to where the doors to the patio were closed, outside the waves came and went and what looked like the noon time sun was sitting perfectly in the sky where there was no one to enjoy it, like this female had said there was no one to be seen for miles down the white sand. Turning to look in the other direction he saw the jetty of rocks that went out in to the ocean, she had said that she had found him washed up out there, it had to be over three hundred feet from the back deck of this property.

Looking back in to the room he scratched his head only to find a band aid that was causing the itch, his fingers ran through his hair and he felt the remnants of sand and salt water, he must look worse than he felt. He ran through everything this Elisabeth had just said, he realized she'd mentioned a lover who was supposed to come to the island with her and didn't show, he wondered if maybe he could persuade her to let whoever needed to know that he was said love, just long enough for him to be able to figure a way to contact the states and get some back up.

XXX   XXX

39

"I know I've asked you this already but are you sure?" Mathew asked his wife. She was sat there on the bases ocean view picnic benches, a half-eaten chicken salad on wheat and a bag of chips unopened. "I'm afraid I am."

"I just can't get my head around it."

"It's hard for someone as physically fit and able to face this kind of obstacle, it's harder for them than someone who sits behind a desk at an office five days a week."

"Will he at least be able to walk after?"

"There will be no reason for him to not be able to run around the base with the rest of you Matt." She reached across the table for his hand, taking it and giving it a slight squeeze. "But will he be able to physically do a high altitude parachute insertion or be the base of a four man wall climb or do any of the things that strain a leg bone? I believe there is no way he will. I know he's our friend and we will help him through this but Matt, his life is now on a path far different from that of Team Seven."

"I hope he stays with the SEALs; I think he'd make a great teacher."

"Yeah, can you see the pent up hostility he could rain down on those hopeful to be him." Jamie joked trying to get his mind off the bad and focus on the positive. "I guess."

"I've heard some of his complaining about that senior chief you had here for BUD/S."

"Tanner."

"Yeah, you know I saw him a few weeks ago."

"Where were you?"

"In my office."

"He's a patient?"

"I care for those retired SEALs too." Jamie put the rest of her sandwich in the brown bag their lunch had come in. "All we can do is be there for Steven because even if he won't admit it, he's going to need all of our help and support."

"What do you think your sister will do?" Mathew asked and Jamie had known it would come because it had crossed her mind also. Bottom line was she didn't think her sister could handle this with everything else but then Mel had been doing so well. What she knew is no matter how new or old Steven and Mel's relationship, the strain was going to be great. "I hope she does the right thing."

"Me too."

"I have to get back to work." Jamie stood up, brushing off the back of her white uniform skirt. "I should too, we don't have much this afternoon but I wanted to get some language practice."

"Which one?"

"Vietnamese."

"And this would be how many languages now?"

"Nine I think." Mathew, one hand carrying their leftover lunch, the other holding his wife's hand as they crossed the grass back towards the SEAL buildings.

"Will you be involved in his surgery?" Mathew asked after a few feet.

"There's a specialist flying in later from Bethesda,

he's the leading go to guy in the Navy right now specializing in bone cancers but I did request to observe so I know first-hand how it goes. Steven's my friend but foremost he's a patient right now and I need to focus on having him stay positive and get back to the way he should be."

"Have I told you lately that I love you?"

"All the time."

"Well, I think I should do it more."

CHAPTER SIX

They parted ways at the parking lot and the stress of the past few hours weighed on Jamie's shoulders. There was so much to prepare for and so much to get ready, this surgery was going to take place ASAP and she wanted to make sure everything was checked before the specialist arrived.

"Any messages for me Largo?" Jamie asked her assistant upon entering the sterile office.

"Lieutenant Schlome is waiting in your office."

"He is?" Jamie opened her office door and stopped at the sight of Steven standing at the window, closing the door behind her she was the first to speak. "Steve, I was hoping you'd be here."

"I needed to ask you something."

"Sure." Jamie hung up her hat and came to stand behind her friend and patient.

"Why did I get this? I don't know of anyone in my family who had any kind of cancer, why me?"

"There's not really a way I can tell that. There are risk factors but no exact causes."

"Then what are the risk factors?" He turned and looked at her and she wasn't sure if it was fear or anger she saw behind his eyes.

"Let's see." Jamie turned away and went over to her desk, pulling out her chair, sitting on the front so her upper body was leaning forward enough for her elbows to lean on the cold wood. "Inherited genes from a family member, but you say no one in your family has had cancer, that doesn't mean none of them had the gene. A hundred years ago people would die without ever knowing the cause, it's possible an ancestor passed the gene through the chain and your cells decided to mutate the gene."

"Anything else?"

"In your case, you have Chondrosarcoma which is rare and I'm surprised there's never been any other problems until now but it can also be caused by an injury or infection to a part of the body and when cells have to divide then our main DNA usually proofreads the plan to make sure nothing goes wrong but sometimes those cells can be damaged and daughter cells form before the original cell has time to repair, by then it's too late to change the pattern and then the result is that new cell has a totally new plan for growth and cancer can develop."

She watched him, he was looking at her and she wasn't sure if he just didn't understand or if he was waiting for more. "I know from your records that six years ago you had a serious infection in that leg from some accident while on mission."

"A bullet nicked a chunk out, just meaty tissue, but we were in the middle of nowhere and by the time we got back state side it was all messed up."

"Then that's most likely the cause, but whatever the cause, just remember it is treatable."

"Yeah, treatable yet fatal to my career."

"Steve, I wish I could give you some hope, something, but ethically I can't because I don't know what your medical recovery will be to the exact percentage of strength you'll regain with whatever we may have to replace. What I do know is it will be a long road, a lot of therapy and strength on your part. What I can tell you is that I will be there every step of the way Steve, your friends will be there too."

"It's funny, after last night I thought everything was finally falling in to place with my life."

"How so?"

"This is hard." Steve shook his head. "Talking to you about this."

"Are you talking about my sister?"

"Yeah." He looked back to the window unable to keep his eyes on her obviously the resemblance between her and her sister was too much for his synapses. "I was talking to Matt right before we shipped out last. I was telling him how your sister made my life complete. I feel when we are gone she is the one I stay alive for."

"You're worried what she might do?"

"I wouldn't expect her to stay with me now. She's had her own problems. Forcing her to take care of a cripple isn't what she needs."

Jamie got up and walked over to him, she made him turn and face her, her hands on his upper shoulders. "True my sister has had her problems and she can be a bone head sometimes but she has come a long way in the last year alone, most of that is thanks to you and your relationship with her but Steve, at the end of the day the only person who can decide what she wants is her, let Mel figure out what she wants."
"I wouldn't want to make her feel she had too."
"You might think this is harsh but stop being selfish here." She shook him gently. "Mel is a grown woman and can make up her own mind. Don't think you know what's best for her when you don't. She may well love you and want to stand by you no matter what."

She let him go and returned to her desk seat. "There's some paper work I need you to look at and sign. The specialist will be here later and I would like him if he agrees to perform the operation tomorrow morning."
"It seems all rushed and soon."
"We need to get this now; the sooner we can get you on the road to recovery the better for you."
"You're sure?"
"I would never suggest something medically if it wasn't needed." She watched Steve move over to the other chair opposite her desk and take the

forms she had talked about in front of him.

XXX   XXX

Wearing his sweats and t-shirt he still felt rather naked these were what he wore lounging around not in the company of a female he knew nothing about.

After she had brought him his clothes she had told him she would fix something to eat in the kitchen if he wanted to join her, he had taken a fast shower and washed out his sand encrusted boxer shorts which were now hanging in the bathroom drying.

He stood on the living room side of the breakfast bar that separated the room from the kitchen and watched her fixing some sandwiches. "I hope you like turkey." She said not looking his way.
"Turkey's great."
"Mayo, lettuce, tomato?"
"Yeah, all of it." He paused. "I wanted to make sure I thanked you for helping me this morning."
"Don't worry about it. It seems I can rescue people a lot and help them find their way but when it comes to my own life it pretty much sucks."
"What do you do back in Boston?"
"I work for social services."
"What area?"
"Young mothers and battered women." She carried the two plates of sandwiches over and a large bag of potato chips, setting them down before going back and returning with two unopened bottles of

water. She took the stool next to his own and he wondered why she wasn't as afraid of him like she should, a strange man she had rescued who had told her so very little so far.

"You must see the worst side of humans in your job."
"Probably, what amazes me more is the stories always get worse not better, I very rarely have a day when the drama is getting better. The amount of women who go back to their battering spouses and boyfriends just because they know in their hearts they can change and that love will prevail."
"And it never does."
"No it doesn't." She went quiet as she started to eat her food.
"I work for a government agency back in the states; I can't tell you which one."
"How about your name?" She asked after hurriedly swallowing but he noted her small hand as she held it before her mouth as she chewed. "If I give you the undercover name and you use it someone might be led to me through you and I can't take the risk of you getting hurt. If I give you my real name that wouldn't be wise either."

"So what shall I call you?"
"What do you want to call me?"
"Well." She looked at him thinking for a moment.
"You look like a man with a strong name."
"I'd rather you didn't call me fluffy or moonbeam."
"How about John?"
"John is good, close to what it is anyhow."

"I don't understand."

"To you I'm a John Doe so I think John works perfectly."

"Good, so John, what is your plan now your cover was blown by the bad guys?"

"For now lay low."

"You're more than welcome to stay here."

"It might be a little suspicious."

"No, as I told you earlier my supposed boyfriend was meant to be here, if anyone asks you are he." Good he thought, she was smart and came to that without him having to suggest it. "The married boyfriend?"

"Yes, that one." She had finished her sandwich and he had still a half to go.

"I would appreciate you letting me stay here for a few days. I need to make contact with my office and get a new plan in to action."

"Truth be told I'd like the company."

"Then think of it as my payment on you rescuing me."

He watched her and did a mental list of her look. Her long straight brown hair pulled back in a ponytail, her fresh make up free face with the big blue green eyes and long eyelashes. Her small straight nose, full lips and high cheek bones. She was wearing a big BU sweater that confirmed her statement of being from Boston, but it hid what her body shape was like underneath and the cropped pants she was wearing told him she had lean yet short legs. Over all she was a very attractive woman and being stuck here with her was by far a lot more appealing than being fish food.

"What?" She asked noticing his looks, his eyes scanning her up and down.

"Sorry. The agent in me was just summing you up, I apologize, it was rude."

"Yes it was but I won't take offense, it takes a lot more than that to piss me off."

"Good to know."

"What else can you safely tell me?"

"Ask a question. If I can answer it I will, then again I may lie about it." She laughed and he loved the sound it was like flowing silk to his ears. "Is there someone back in the states that will worry if you don't check in?"

"There is." He smiled. "But it's a male colleague."

"No women?" She fished.

"I don't do well with women."

"Why, are you gay?" Her voice turned serious and softer as she turned her head slightly.

"I might as well be." He groaned inwardly.

CHAPTER SEVEN

Mathew had picked Izzy up from the base day care after what had become a mentally long day. Jamie had stayed behind to get everything ready for the specialist who was going to be flown in by transport to the base from Bethesda. He was grateful for the alone time with his daughter, he didn't get as many of those as he'd like and this was his chance to really spend time with her.

He had given his daughter the choice of what they could do. It had been an awkward few seconds when she had said in her little voice. "Daddy, we play tea set." He must have pulled a face that his daughter had caught and in her small astuteness had told him. "Uncle Steve does it." And he had tried very hard to keep from laughing out loud at the image of his friend sitting in a small chair sipping from the tiny china tea cup with his pinky in the air, thinking of Steve made him remember the bad news and he was glad to get in to the tea game to forget for as long as he could.

The two of them were in the pool when Jamie finally came through the patio door, she looked drained and tired taking a seat with her bottle of water in hand watching as Izzy tried hard to swim on her own but her body from the waist down was just too low compared to her top half to be of much use. The only thing keeping the small child's head above the water were her arm floaties. "I guess she doesn't have your frogman genes." Jamie joked. "Very funny." Mathew laughed as Izzy grabbed a hold of the wall and shook her head. She turned to wave and gave her mother a smile and Jamie stifled a laugh at the image of her daughter's fogged up goggles.

"How was the rest of your day?" Mathew asked. "All big words and surgical procedures. Did you two eat yet?"

"Izzy had some of that chicken and salad in the fridge."

"Daddy let me eat not cooked onion." Izzy had pulled herself from the pool and was walking around the pool towards her mother, her goggles now on the top of her head and her wet hair sticking out in all directions. "He did? Well daddy will get a telling off later."

"But I like them." Izzy whined.

"She ate like half an onion." Mathew laughed getting a towel and wrapping it around Izzy before she got up on Jamie's uniform. "You also like to eat dirt but we can't let you do that." Jamie gave her husband a scolding look that she couldn't hold for long and it soon turned to a smile. "Noted." Mathew said rubbing the water from his own head.

"How about I braid your hair so it looks all cute tomorrow for your big day?" Jamie asked her daughter and saw as the little blue eyes before her became larger. "Yes, yes, yes." Izzy jumped up and down. "Can I wear red dress too?"

"What's so special about tomorrow?"

"Yes you can." Jamie held her on her lap all wrapped up. "Nana and Papa Buchanan are coming in and taking Izzy to Disney for a long weekend."

"That's right." Mathew crouched before Izzy and took her goggles from her head. "You are so lucky."

"Papa gives big hugs and Nana has candy in her pockets."

51

"I think my father spoils her slightly."

"He's making sure Izzy knows he loves her." Mathew gave his wife a look and she knew what it was, her father was making up for how he had treated her when she was younger. It had been a mix of her keeping secrets and her Fathers willingness to believe them.

Jamie picked up her daughter from her lap so she could go in and change her; she also had to get out of her own clothes and in to something a little more comfortable. Mathew followed closely behind and was careful to make sure he didn't drip on the floor. "Can I take Mr. Buttons with me?" Izzy asked standing on the floor of the bathroom both her parents in there, Mathew was in and out as he went in to the walk in closet to dress, coming back in to hang his bathing suit up in the shower. "Why don't you go with Daddy and you and he can pick things out because Nana and Papa will be here at breakfast time, then you can come get me we'll do your hair and then we'll all snuggle together and read books."

"Okay." Izzy ran to her room wrapped only in her little towel.

"I need to call Steve and make sure he's set. He's having surgery at noon tomorrow and I gave him his pre-op instructions but I want to make sure he's mentally accepted it."

"Lee and I saw him before we left, he was cleaning out his stuff in the locker room, he didn't say much and to be honest, we didn't know what to say to him. He stopped by to see Daniel and I didn't see him after that."

The phone on the bedside table rang interrupting them and Mathew walked over to get it as Jamie began to undress in the walk in closet. "Taylor." He said in to the phone. He waited and there was nothing. "Taylor." He said again. He hung the phone back up and looked to see Jamie, she had managed to get her sweater on but her long legs were bare and even today he got a lump in his throat at seeing her body. "No one was there." He told her as he watched her pull her yoga pants on. "Probably a wrong number."
"I'm sure it was." He moved towards her as she came out and wrapped her in his arms, kissing her soundly. He missed his wife and daughter when he was away and when he was lucky enough to be stateside for a while he liked to make sure he let them know how much he missed them.

Again the phone rang cutting off their kiss. "I'll get it this time. You go and make sure Izzy hasn't begun pulling all her clothes and toys out in to a heap on the floor."
"Okay." He kissed her quickly on the lips and left leaving her to get the phone on its third ring. "Dr. Buchanan." She said.
"Jamie?" A male voice asked, it was a quiet and deep and eerily familiar.
"Who is this?"
"This line isn't secure." She was told and she knew with no other words that this was a call from the agency. Her mind started to swirl while her heart

pounded in her ears as adrenalin kicked in. There was no way this call could be good.

"Go to your front door, there's something there for you." The line went dead and she threw the phone on the bed in haste to get down stairs. Mathew had seen his wife run past the bedroom where as he had feared Izzy had pulled whatever she could reach in her room. He had brought out her pink and purple duffle and was on the floor helping organize some of the chaos.

Before opening the front door, she took a look out of both the front living room window and the glass in the door. Up and down the block as far as she could see was clear, no strange vehicles or people she'd never seen before walking their dog. Careful not to open the door too far she crouched down and saw the ominous legal sized envelope on the door mat and pulled it in. Mathew was at the top of the stairs when she had the door closed and was making sure it was secure and locked. "What's going on?" He asked knowing the look on her face. The same look she had gotten when she had heard her sister had been ambushed overseas and presumed dead just less than four years ago.

"I don't know, there was a man on the phone. He knew my name and said the line wasn't secure and then told me to come down here and get this." She waved the envelope slightly. "Did you recognize his voice?" He asked taking the steps down to her. "I don't know." She was dreading what could be inside this envelope. The CIA spook rumor that 'once in always in' ran through her mind. Shaking her fears off she opened the envelope carefully and tipped it so she was able to get whatever was inside. A cell phone fell out along with a picture of someone they both knew, knew very well but with different feelings on him.

In her hand she held a glossy image of Robert Wakefield looking less together as he walked down the sidewalk of some island country, boats to the right and white sand stone looking buildings, all with canopies and what looked like a restaurant had an open eating area so there were a lot of umbrellas in all the colors you'd expect to find. The man himself was looking rugged, his hair was a lot longer then she had ever seen him wear it and it looked as if he hadn't shaved in a few days, his clothes were what made him blend in. Long board shorts with a bright colored shirt hanging loose.

The sound of a car pulling in to their driveway made them both turn to see who it was. It was safe to say this cloak and dagger envelope was making them edgy. Mathew opened the door when he saw it was Steven's truck pulling in the driveway. He had just stepped out closing the screen door when he heard the cell ring, looking back he saw Jamie physically jump. "Hello." Jamie said in to the phone.
"Hey Jamie, remember me?" The male voice said and she did recognize it.

"Nick." Jamie felt her shoulders get lighter; the pending doom she had felt was lifted.

"Good girl." He laughed. "Sorry about that but I can't take the chance either you or I are being listened to."

"Why did you send me a picture of Robert?" She asked passing the picture and envelope to Mathew and with her now free hand waved to Steven.

"Who's she talking to?" Steven asked closing the screen door as he came in the house. Mathew showed him the picture and he recognized it from when they had spent hours on the USS Abraham Lincoln when Jamie had been bait for a terrorist leader and Robert had been the CIA agent in charge. "Is something wrong?"

"I don't know." Mathew put the envelope on the hall table. "Are you here to?" He pointed at Jamie.

"Yeah, I wondered if I could talk to both of you."

"I was helping Izzy pack. Do you want to help while we wait for her to finish up?"

"Sure." Jamie turned to see the two men going up as she continued to listen to Nick.

"'J' I don't know how to ask you this."

"Then why are you?"

"I need your help."

"I don't do that anymore."

"Not even for your oldest friend Robbie?"

"That depends."

"Can you meet me?"

"Where are you?"

"Can you meet me at Greenwood cemetery?"

"Give me thirty minutes."

"Done." He hung up and she threw the phone that would now be useless on to the couch.

She ran the stairs and stopped short when she saw the two men sitting on the floor, Izzy dancing around in one of her Disney princess nightgowns that Mel had bought her, the purple was one of her favorite colors. "Hi Steve." Jamie crouched down and Izzy came running in to her arms. "I need to run out for a while."

"Who was that?" Mathew asked as Jamie began brushing Izzy's hair and was pulling it in to two separate French braids as she spoke to the two men. "Nick."

"Is everything okay?" He was more than concerned, more for his wife knowing she would do anything to help her friends or family. It was one of the reasons he had fallen in love with her but if he had to relive the event that had happened a couple of weeks after they had met he may not be strong enough to deal with it.

"I have to meet him and I'll find out what is going on." She explained.

"You're not going alone."

"And Izzy can't stay here alone." Jamie countered.

"I'll go with you." Steve offered.

"Are you sure?"

"Yeah, I wanted to speak to both of you but I can help with this first and then Izzy will be asleep when we get back and we can do that talking."

"I'll get some dinner ready, you'll join us?" Mathew asked his friend.

"If it wouldn't be too much I'd love that."

"Consider it done."

"Are you going Uncle Steve?" Izzy asked leaving her mother's lap now both braids were looking cute and walking to stand in front of him. With him sat on the floor they were the same height. "I'll be back later but I hear you are going to have lots of fun up at Disney."

"Yes I will." She cocked her head to the side and then put her small hands on his cheeks. "I love you Uncle Steve." She said in her tiny voice and it touched him to his core. "I love you too Izzy." He wrapped her in his arms and saw Jamie slyly wipe a tear from her eye.

CHAPTER EIGHT

His head had started to hurt shortly after lunch and he had excused himself to go and lay down. He had gone to sleep with the sun shining brightly through the sheers on the windows but now there was nothing but moonlight coming in and also the faint aroma of something he didn't recognize.

He stumbled out of bed letting his equilibrium settle after God knows how long he had been asleep. He needed an aspirin badly and was hoping the house was stocked with some. Pulling his pants and shirt back on he was just getting his balance and noticed the pile of men's clothes next to him on the chair Beth had been asleep in when he had first woken up that morning. He wondered where they had come from and who's they were.

Beth was in the kitchen and that was also where the aroma was coming from. It was an amazing assault on the senses something very tangy and spicy was somewhere within. "Hey." Beth smiled as she turned hearing his footsteps on the bare wooden floor. "What time is it?"

"Just after six." She had turned back to the various pots on the stove and he came over closer. "Something smells really good." He peeked over her shoulder and she happened to turn her head as he was there in her personal space and for a moment it was awkward. It was he who moved back feeling bad he may have upset her. "I'm, um, making this chicken curry that has some tropical fruits in it."

"Sounds weird but smells great."

"Thanks. Truth be told I'm in my element. I love to cook and I love to cook for someone else."

"Does your boyfriend know what he's missing?"

"Of course not." She blushed and replaced a lid on one of the pots.

"I went to the store and got a load of food. I wasn't sure if there was anything you didn't eat or like."

"I'm a pretty easy guy when it comes to food. As long as I don't have to cook it we'll be okay."

"Then I'll cook but you have to promise to be on dish duty after."

"That's fine with me."

"There's some wine and beer in the fridge, choose what you want." He went over to the fridge and

found it full to the brim with food and different beers and wine. The counter next to the fridge had various red wines on it too. "You didn't have to go to all this trouble. You must have spent a fortune."
"Actually I didn't. You can thank Brett; he's the one that gave me his share for the vacation. I see it as my way of making both our bad situations better."
"Brett your boyfriend?"
"Not anymore."

"Can I get you something to drink?" He asked her as he tried to decide which beer he would have.
"Could you pour me a glass of wine?"
"White?"
"Yeah, any of them is fine with me." He went to his duty of uncorking the bottle and finding glasses so he could pour them both a glass while he watched her putting food in to serving bowls and plates. He hadn't even noticed the large dining table off in the next room all ready for them to eat, a salad sitting there waiting to be dressed and eaten. He offered to help her carry everything in but she pointed to the seat at the head of the table and told him to sit and rest.

Good thing, she tired him out walking back and forth from that kitchen carrying different bowls of food.

Finally, when everything was on the table, Beth took the seat set next to him and she took a long sip of her wine. "Did you find the clothes I left out for you?"

"The ones on the chair?"

"Yeah, I had packed some of Brett's clothes with mine. You're a little taller than him and if you don't mind wearing them you are free to use them. I was only going to burn them."

"Thanks."

"I also picked up a few toiletries for you at the store and before you freak out that I might be making myself some sort of target from getting male products, I made sure I gossiped to the local lady in there that you had lost your luggage in Miami and no one knows where it is."

"Wow. Can I hire you?"

"So I did good huh. That's thanks to all the years of reading those mystery books while commuting everywhere on the T."

"You live long in Boston?"

"For the last ten years. I'm originally from New York City." He noted that explained her jumbled East Coast accent. "Really, how do you deal with all that up and down weather?"

"When I was a kid the snow emergencies and the nor'easters were days off school and an adventure now as an adult they are like a part of everyday life; you deal with them."

He smiled and waited while she served her own rice and curry before he dug in. He watched as her delicate slim hands used the tongs to put a generous amount of salad on to a side plate and covered it with an oil vinaigrette. "You were definitely smart to make the lady you spoke to believe I was your boyfriend. Now if we have to go out most of the people will probably dispel seeing me before as someone else and that I just happen to look like a typical tourist. I've noticed since I've been here that gossip spreads like wild fire and the locals keep very close eyes on everyone."

"Small places are like that." She took a bite of her curry and he watched as she enjoyed the flavors, he had taken a hefty bite and it was as good as it had smelt, better even. "I know you can't tell me all the truth about yourself." She began "But I have one question I have to ask."

"Shoot."

"Why has no female snapped you up? I mean you're good looking, you seem nice and you have a great body." She winked and he felt the heat rise in the room, obviously she had seen a lot when she had undressed him after she had rescued him. "Is it work? The fact you are rarely around? Never found the right person? Got your heart broken and decided you're better off on your own?" She rattled off and it was his turn to laugh. "There was someone until about two years ago but I was gone so long and the secrets about where I had been and her never knowing when I'd be back killed it all."

Beth thought about this for a minute as she chewed and once her mouth was empty she had to interject. "I understand not being able to talk about your work. I can't talk about mine either so that wouldn't bother me but I can understand you being gone would be a problem."

"There were a mountain of other things too but it's

too much to get in to."

"Go on, I'll share some of my war wounds if you do."

"War wounds?" He asked and she shrugged. "Don't get me wrong. Mel, that's her name, she was a great person."

"But." Beth said holding her fork in the air for emphasis.

"There was a history for both of us."

"You knew her a long time?"

"No, I knew of her for a long time. I was very good friends with her twin sister for years, she went through a lot of stuff as a kid so she came to live with me in New York while I was at Columbia law school."

"Which one?"

"The sister, her name is James."

"A female named James?"

"We call her Jamie but her full name is James yes. Anyway, Jamie came to live with me because she and her father were not getting along. My father and hers were stationed together in San Diego."

"The navy?" She asked.

"Yep, both of them were SEALs. Her Dad didn't know where she had gone and when the police finally tracked her down they made her go back to him. I moved from New York and went to Chicago, she had made her father agree to send her to a boarding school near me and we remained friends. See, she was always covering for Mel as kids, Mel was a drinker and did various drugs but the father thought it was Jamie. She also had a hard time in rehab which she had been sent to because of those lies."

"Oh no, she didn't get hurt in there did she? I have heard some horror stories over the years?" Beth had guessed and hit the nail smack square on the head. He nodded not wanting to actually say the words.

"Jamie is smart and strong and held it deep down but she also knew she couldn't continue living with these lies and her father so when she got to boarding school she found herself graduating earlier and she decided to go to medical school and she had been closer to my father than her own and had listened to all his stories about the Navy so she did her first few years of pre-med and then he helped her get a position in the Navy to finish up Medical school and she served a few years while I went and joined who I work for now." He squirmed in his chair slightly trying to remember he couldn't say anything about who he worked for.

"What happened next?"

"I needed a female on an upcoming mission. I knew I could use Jamie because she was so strong willed; I trained her and then sent her in. I almost got her killed but one of my male team members saved her. I had hoped bringing her in would bring us closer but she wasn't in a place in her life to return the feelings I had for her. I knew she had once loved me and I had taken advantage of it and in the end hurt her and when I was ready she wasn't. After that mission I didn't speak to her for five years but I kept tags on her so I knew what she was doing."

"Did she stay in the Navy?"

"Yes and Mel had foolishly joined the Marines."

"That's a very butch life isn't it?"

"Not really, all the female Marines I know are strong independent women thanks to the core."

"All I can picture is those weird shaved heads they all have."

"That's the men and it's a high and tight cut they get not a shave." He laughed.

"Just over three years ago Jamie was mistakenly transferred to San Diego from the carrier she was a doctor on. She was a Commander and had become able to hide her beauty behind a pretty smart disguise of dressing down, thick glasses and baggy clothes. With her name and the pentagon thinking there should be doctors on missions with the SEALs to save more men who die when they are nowhere near a doctor or hospital they made a mistake and sent her to join the Team. Now normally these all male teams would have thrown a fit, no females allowed and all. She turned them around in a few weeks and when she had become comfortable and had proven herself she got a call that her sister's team in the Middle East had been abducted from their look out post."

"And that's when you saw her again?"

"It was a little complicated. The man in charge of the terrorist group had taken the team but Mel had never been caught and when another Marine team came through they found her dog tags and that's

when Jamie was told she was presumed dead. This evil man was the same man we had tried to take down in the mission Jamie and I had worked on together. He wanted Jamie so he could extinguish the shame she had brought upon his family."
"What did she do?"

He thought about if he could answer it for a moment and decided why not, it wasn't like she would ever meet either of the twins or their friends. "She had killed his son."
"She killed him?" He could hear the absolute shock in her voice.
"She'd had too; it was kill or be killed." He paused making sure she understood. "So now we have Mel presumed dead and this man telling us if we wanted the Marines back we had to give him Jamie."
"Which you couldn't have done because America doesn't negotiate with terrorists." Beth repeated the famous words she'd heard in a movie somewhere.

"That's what we like everyone to think but when it comes to our service men we do if there is absolutely no other way. We don't give them nuclear weapons but we trade, when Jamie found all this out she said she would do it, play the bait go in so they could come out."
"She has either balls of steel or a death wish." John ignored that.
"The plan was to insert her and then pick up the Marines from where they were being held and

then save Jamie too. Her SEAL team was acting as back up, the ones going in. The helo dropped Jamie off, we waited and when we knew it was time to go in the SEAL team did but when they got to the cell they found an extra marine who'd been beaten and next to a video tape."

"Mel?" She guessed.

"Yep, and the tape was the first of two we received from a man who now had Jamie and we had no clue where that was." He took a sip of wine and noticed he had demolished his plate of food the flavors playing on his tongue with the wine.

"That curry was good." He nodded as if surprised. "Thank you. So what happened next?" He noticed she sat on the edge of her seat completely engrossed in his story. "All we could all do when the SEALs returned was wait and try and figure out where they may have taken her, we thought we were smart and had put these very tiny little trackers on her but she had put them on Mel when they had found each other in the middle of nowhere that's how we found the Marines. The SEALs were all fired up and myself and the rest of my team were running around with our heads cut off, clueless and time was running out. One of the SEALs, a great guy named Mathew had fallen for Jamie and from what she had said to me before she had left she felt something for him too."

"That must have been hard on you?"

"Yeah, and then her father turned up. He's a senator and an ex-military man, I'd never met him and although he knew about me he never put two and two together. We got another video from the man who had taken Jamie. Now, the first had been hard to watch as they had beaten her but the second was worst, the image made us all sick to our stomachs and at that point I thought we were never going to get her back but a member of my team found some satellite pictures of a movement of suspicious trucks in a direction of an enemy base we knew had been used by them before so on a hunch the SEAL team left to collect Jamie."

He finished off his wine and watched her eat her salad as he continued. "Mel was back on board but she was in a complete state, see Mel had a long running drug problem and she had been missing from her team at base when they were originally captured because she was getting high, by the time she was back aboard the ship she was coming down and finding out her sister who covered for her for years was still MIA and her father was there. I had promised Jamie I would do whatever I could to help keep the secrets but Mel thought it was time to come clean. She was going to get a BCD-basically being discharged for conduct unbecoming a marine and possibly spending time in a military jail. I pulled some strings and as long as she agreed to a mandatory rehab stint she wouldn't do any time. Their father found out and didn't know how to mend the past."

"What happened to Jamie? Did she-?"
"Die? No, the SEAL team had been sent to the right place and although she had broken bones and

been beaten badly, had been tormented and was weak from dehydration she was strong enough to survive. He was about to kill her when she found the strength to make everything even and as the SEALs entered the room she shot him dead. She collapsed and came too on board safe. It was then I had to come to terms with her love for Mathew and he had been losing it the whole time but when he went in there he was not looking for the woman he loved but doing his job.

Looking back, I knew Mel was a bad choice but we had become close and in some ways I guess I saw her as being Jamie but the differences between them were so huge, I mean they're identical aside from a few details like eye color. She got treatment and is doing great but like I said my secrets and travel drove us apart. She needed more of my time."

Sitting back Beth took in the story, it sounded so scary and mainly very sad. She knew little about the military and any of the government organizations and it was ignorant to not. Since nine-eleven they had become our security and savors keeping life as we know it safe and comfortable while so many lost so much. These people he talked about were humans who had been through so much and they weren't alone, so many risked their lives every day. She needed to know more and wondered if he would tell her. "What happened to Jamie? Did she leave the Navy?"

"No, she did leave the SEAL team, well not really completely she's still their doctor, their main physician and for all the other teams and she works closely with her team still, they accepted her and once you're in they regard you as family for life. She went through a very intense psych debriefing straight after we left the ship and a month later she was back being a doctor."

"Did she and Mathew?"
"Get together? The night she got back he proposed to her and then moved in. They were living next door to each other." He explained from her frown. "They were planning their wedding and she found out she was pregnant. I went to their wedding, as did Mel and their father, it was a beautiful but simple affair and then six months later their first daughter was born."
"What's her name?"
"Isabella, Izzy for short." He had to take some more wine his mouth was getting dry. "It was the name of their mother; she died when Jamie was eleven. Izzy is a hand full and quite the character."
"So you keep in touch."
"First because of Mel and then because I was a Godparent but my work and the split with Mel has torn me away a lot, plus I live on the East Coast they live on the west."
"Do you still love Mel?"
"No, I don't think I ever really did."
"What about Jamie?"

CHAPTER NINE

"Thanks for doing this." Jamie said to Steven as he pulled the truck to a stop in the lot just inside the gates of the Greenwood cemetery. Jamie was about to get out when Steven's hand on her arm stopped her. "You aren't going alone."

"I'll be fine, it's just Nick."

"Yeah, I remember Nick and no your husband would never forgive me if I had to call and tell him I let you be taken by a spook."

"Okay." She reluctantly agreed not wanting to pull anyone else in to whatever mess this was. On the ride over there had been little talking, a few sentences here and there but whatever he had come over to talk about to Mathew and her had not yet been shared. It had also taken a bit of time for her to pull herself together after seeing her daughter touchingly let her Uncle Steve know she loved him.

The two of them walked down in to the cemetery the night was dark and there were very few lights illuminating any of the paths. Jamie was the first to catch sight of Nick as the burly man leaned against a tree, his cigarette giving a red glow as the embers got hotter from his inhaling on the thing. They knew he had seen her and he didn't look too happy she had brought someone along with her. "Wait here." She told Steve when they were close but not close enough for him to hear what Nick might say to her.

71

"What's with the SEAL escort?" Nick asked still sucking on his smoke.

"My husband didn't think I should come alone and he had to stay with our daughter so Steve offered to come."

"I don't want to hurt you, man; you scare the hell out of me sometimes." He laughed.

"What's happening with Robert?" She cut to the chase.

"He's gone missing."

"Okay."

"He's on an undercover assignment and he has called in every day to a contact only known as 'mother' giving updates. As of two days ago he hasn't called and we're worried."

"Who's we?"

"Okay I am." He threw his smoke down and stood straight towering over her; she heard Steve take a few steps forward and watched Nick keep an eye on the man behind her.

"I'm sure he's fine." She said.

"He was pretty broken up over his break up with your sister and throwing himself in to his work. He took this assignment to get her out of his head."

"So because he has a broken heart from a relationship that ended two years ago he messed up and got caught by whoever he was trying to infiltrate and because of that he's gone missing." Jamie made it sound so light hearted.

"I think we should take this seriously, have you ever known Robbie to not make a call in just because he was caught? Man, he has to be either dead or stuck and he needs our help."

"Then why are you here?"

"I can't go to where he is, I would compromise any mission."

"No." She shook her head. "I can't, I have things going on here."

"It would just be for two or three days."

"I said no Nick."

"You know I expected more from you, he's always saved you and you can't repay him?"

"Fuck you." She shouted so loud Steve was by her side faster than either she or Nick could imagine someone moving.

"I can't go Nick I have things I can't just drop. I have a daughter and a husband to consider now."

"She's not going anywhere." Steve stuck in, yeah like Nick wouldn't listen to her.

"I heard you I just can't believe you wouldn't." Nick shook his head making her feel even worse. "There has to be someone else who can go." She said.

"Unless you can suggest someone we have no one who can go."

"What about Mel?" Steve said almost quietly.

"My sister."

"Her sister." They said both at the same time.

"Well you want Jamie to go and she's unable too she has a really important surgery tomorrow and her days of being a super hero are over since Izzy came along but Mel isn't doing much and she's now doing really well. She's also a trained ex-Marine."

"She has no CIA training." Jamie couldn't believe

she was hearing this especially from Steve, he was dating her sister after all.

"I'm with Jamie." Nick crossed his arms.
"Is this your idea of how you can make sure Mel's not around to know what's going on with you?"
"What's going on with you?" Nick asked before Steve could reply.
"No it's not, but if she's just going down on the premise of finding out what happened to Robert then why not send her, it's not like you're asking her to go to Cuba and kill Castro with her bare hands."
"It would be her decision." Jamie didn't like this.
"Look, I need to figure something out and fast before it may really be too late. Ask your sister, see if you can look in the mirror guilt free whatever, let me know. The phone I sent you has my number programmed in it. Use it and call me."

They watched as the hulk of a man walked away in the other direction disappearing behind a mausoleum. Not saying anything she just turned around and whacked Steve in the arm, it caught him by surprise and it left a stinging sensation where she had done it. "What?" He couldn't help smiling and knew it would piss her off more.
"Offering your girlfriend up so you can get out of telling her about your surgery?"
"No, it was just an idea to get you out of it."
"Sure."
"It was, look, I came over tonight to ask you and Matt something."

"Which was?" She butt in.

"Whether you thought tonight would be the wrong time to ask her to marry me."

Jamie was holding her breath from the shock she knew but couldn't seem to get her lungs or diaphragm to work. "Are you kidding me?" She finally said.

"No."

"You don't mind asking her and then shipping her off?"

"It would be a couple of days and it doesn't sound dangerous."

"But it could be."

"And she may want to go running when she hears about the surgery, give her the choice she was complaining about her job and I'm sure she would do it."

"Do you have your cell handy?"

"Of course." He took it from the thigh pocket of his cargo pants.

"Call her, tell her to meet us over at my house and there you will first tell her about this surgery even if I have to strap you down and then we'll ask her but I know she'll say no when she hears about you."

"Robert is her ex."

"Yeah, he is but she never loved him like she loves you."

XXX   XXX

He had gone an hour earlier leaving her there to

finish what they had all started. As usual the man had ideas and an appetite that bordered on the extreme kinky and she loved it.

Her husband was quite the missionary man, never changing the style, place or design that he made love to her. Always in the bedroom and always the same way. She didn't doubt he loved her, he said it enough and showered her with all the material items she wanted and allowed her to make her trips back state side to buy whatever new fashions the designers had come up with and the jewelry was always given in his attempt to keep her sated and it worked to a degree.

But her real passion and life lived with another man, a man who was a dangerous drug to her if anyone found out she would be punished in any of the many ways she could manage to conjure up in her imagination. Her husband believed she was at a girlfriend's house at a weekly card game night with a bunch of other close friends, instead she had met her lover and he had brought a new item in to this hotel room, another woman.

The female she had done things with had left with him, making anyone who may have seen him enter believe he had taken her there not herself. She had washed up, removing their scent from her body, fixed her hair and reapplied her make-up, getting dressed and looking back at the bed the sheets completely strewn everywhere and ready for a maid to come and fix.

Having left her car with the valet she waited just outside the lobby of the hotel while they brought her car around. Her eyes skipping all over the place as she had the most unnerving feeling that someone was watching her. She tried hard to shake it off, it was stupid, even her husband or his over bearing family wouldn't stoop as low as to follow her.

Would they?

Getting in her red flashy BMW convertible and pulled out in to the shore front road of the Island she had grown to love after months of despising its backward features, that had been partly due to Luis her husband's brother who had flirted and flirted with her telling her constantly that he could make her so happy, happier than his boring half-brother. He was right and he sure did make things easier to get through, these few hours every week and whenever Miguel was away on another Island or in the states or even doing things for their father a man she most definitely was scared witless of.

The shore front road left the main hotel drag and above the noise the air made as it rushed through her head the sounds of the night were only a chorus of the bugs singing their melodies in the darkness of night. She stepped on the gas the feeling of being watched was getting worse and with only the beams from her headlights it made a shiver of fear run down her spine.

Her knuckles were white from the grip she had on her steering wheel and her speedometer read she was over the thirty mile per hour speed limit and up to sixty-five. She was taking the badly laid road the best she could and had driven them a thousand times before she anticipated each curve, every pot hole but she was having a harder time from the speed so she took her foot gently off the gas.

Rounding the second of three tight curves in the road between town and the house she shared with her husband she was startled by the bright set of head lights seemingly stopped in the middle of the road. She slammed on her brakes and just sat there wishing she had the top up so she could lock all the doors and keep out whoever those lights belonged to.

"Cara." A voice called for her above all the outside noises. She wasn't sure but she thought she recognized it. "Oh Cara you bad, bad girl." The voice taunted again and her eyes caught the movement of a dark figure just to the side of the car before her. It moved within the beams of light and further towards her. "Who's there?" She heard the fear in her own voice. "Don't be afraid, I just want what you are giving out to your brother in law."
"I don't know what you mean." Don't admit it; don't admit it, her brain shouted inside. Who was this man coming towards her? "Who are you?" She

asked as he came close enough for her to see him. "Your worst nightmare." He said and she gasped at the sight of her father-in-law's right hand man looming above the front of her car.

She didn't know what to do, she sat up in her seat and reached for her bag looking for the mace she always carried but her hands were as numb as the rest of her body. "Where do you think you are going?" He saw her movements; she was his deer caught in his headlights. He moved fast and right for her, she leaned as far as she could but she still had her seat belt on, fumbling to release it and she felt the tension loosen with the silent click it made. He managed to grab a hold of her hair and she let out a scream of pain. "No, no, no." She added to her shouts but her body was already being roughly pulled across the closed door where she had been sitting, the metal bumping each of her ribs causing pain, not as much as when her feet landed twisted on the ground the pain shooting up her legs. He was laughing at her and all she wanted was for this to be a dream and for her to open her eyes and be anywhere else.

Rain had started to fall and it soaked her to the skin fast, shivers from pain and the cold water made her body shake. He had her on the ground now, her hands above her head as one of his big hands held them both there squeezing in to her flesh as if it were only bones there; his other hand was ripping at her clothes. She felt the wet material pulled aside he was strong and she knew the moment he had made her completely naked keeping her eyes closed she never saw them flying away as he threw the scraps of fabric but they were gone and his hands were everywhere. "What, can't share some of your sweet stuff with me too?" He taunted her.

He felt his hands everywhere, her breasts as he played with them roughly, her body responding against her fear. His hand moved lower as his mouth came to her breast, he was using his knees to pin her legs down and they were open allowing him entrance to her intimate of places. "This turns you on huh?" He laughed when he felt her, his fingers moving inside her, she was so tense it felt like he had his entire fist inside her, damn her body for responding the way it was.

His hand down there left and she almost gasped her displeasure against her own protests. She felt him move and then she felt his fingers being replaced by something else and she knew he was raping her. He pumped away roughly and it was a quick release, he must have been really getting off on this. He pulled himself out and again she was filled with something this time it was smooth cold and foreign, it felt much bigger than anything she had ever felt before. "What are you doing?" She tried to move.
"You like that huh?"
"What are you doing?"
"Making sure you don't disgrace the family."

She heard the sound of a gun being fired, the shooting pain through her body and she felt the burning in her lungs as she tried to breathe in enough air to shout for help. Another shot fired and another and everything started to spin and get dark, her entire body was in so much pain and she didn't understand why.

Vince remained holding Cara by her arms as he watched the life drain from her once beautiful dark eyes, blood seeping from the side of her mouth as she died the questions and shock on her face. He knew the moment life had left her body and he let go of her wrists, getting straighter he pulled what he had put inside her out from between her legs, the long metal gleaming in the light from the headlights as the blood dripped from it. He dropped the gun and with one more look at her body he went back to his car to get the garbage bags to finish off this mess.

CHAPTER TEN

Mathew had just tucked in a very sleepy Izzy after he had let her stay up a little later than normal to let her help him get things out and ready for dinner. He had given her the task of mixing the Cajun spices for the steaks and she had been yawning heavily. By the time he had finished doing the salad and the potatoes were in the oven baking she had almost been falling down where she was half playing half laying on the cold tile floor.

Walking down the stairs he heard a car pulling up and had taken the last few stairs two at a time, sure he was going to fall but didn't care; he had been so worried since Jamie had left with Steve. Before he could open the door the door opened for him and he had been about to grab the female coming through but noticed before it had been an embarrassment that it was Mel. "What are you doing here?" He asked her. "Nice to see you too brother dear." Mel gave him a quick hug but noticed her looking around. "Okay, hi Mel what's happening?"

"Steve called me; he sounded vague, told me to meet him here."

"When?"

"About ten minutes ago. Where's my sister?"

"With Steve."

"My turn, what's going on?"

"I have no idea."

They both heard the truck pulling up in front of the house at the same time and both watched as Jamie and Steven walked towards them and stood back to allow them to get in to the house. "Well?" Matt asked his wife.

"Let's go in the kitchen I'll explain everything there; Steve has to speak to Mel." She raised her eyebrows and making sure Mel didn't see made him understand with that one look what Steve would be talking to her about. "What's going on?" Mel looked at the three of them and knew something was up as none of them; even her

82

steadfast sister would make eye contact. "Steven will explain." Jamie took Matt's hand and pulled him in to the kitchen letting the door swing closed behind them.

"I'm getting a really bad vibe here." Mel said looking at the man she had so easily fallen in love with. He was handsome and kind and mostly gentle with her, always making sure he wasn't pushing her too fast or taking their relationship to any other levels than the fun one they were currently on. "Let's sit down." He touched her back slightly as he gestured for the couch; he felt her slight flinch and felt the fear filling up inside his already nervous stomach. "Steve." She frowned watching him sit down next to her. "I don't know where to start."
"Does this have something to do with my sister? You and her, you weren't?"
"Oh, no, no she had someone she had to see and well Matt asked me to go, this is something totally separate."

He took a deep breath needing some extra oxygen in his blood stream. "Remember I had that sore knee, I had the check-up done on it?"
"Yeah, Jamie was waiting for results." She paused letting his words really hit down low. "She got the results in." He was sat there his elbows resting on his knees and he couldn't look up, he didn't want to see her response and he didn't want her to see the need in his eyes for her to be there, every small step of the way, to desperately tell him she loved

him whether he remained a SEAL or not. "It's bad isn't it?" He felt the hand on his arm, her body leaning towards his. "Yeah it is." He felt the unfamiliar sting of the tears welling up, this was all he needed and he tried to make them go away.

Mel waited; she knew this had to be hard whatever it was. "I'm having an operation tomorrow, they found a cancerous tumor in my leg, there's some fancy word for it that I can't remember but they have to go in and remove the tumor and some of the bone."
"I." Mel stammered. "I don't know what to say." She leaned back giving both of them room. "They are taking it out tomorrow?"
"Jamie has some specialist coming in."
"Wow, you must be having a hard time swallowing this. How long will you be off active duty?" Steve took the chance to look up and he saw when she understood the answer to her question. "I'll never be that SEAL Mel, the best I can hope for is a knee strong enough to jog on. I'd be a liability to my team so it looks like team seven will be getting a new member."
"You won't leave the Navy altogether?"
"No, but the only thing left for me is a teaching position and even then I might get transferred."

"Is there anything I can do for you?" She laughed nervously. "That sounds so obvious, I'm sorry I don't know what to say."
"It's okay." He stood up.
"No, it's not and I wish you wouldn't be so okay

with that."

"I don't expect anything from you; in fact, if you were to leave and not talk to me ever again I would understand and never hate you for it."

"Do you think that's who I really am? I thought we were a couple; couples help each other during rough times. You helped me."

"This is bigger than a little rough."

"And I can still help. I want to help."

"I'm not going to be able to do much walking or activities for a while and there's going to be chemo maybe radiation therapy, I'm not going to be too fun to be with."

Mel stood up, coming to stand before Steve making him look in to her eyes. "I'm going to be with you every painful, emotionally draining piece of this journey."

"If that is what you want."

"It is."

"I told your sister we would eat with them."

"Okay, maybe I can get some information from her about what to expect and how to take really good care of you."

XXX   XXX

Even with the weather still warm Jamie watched as her husband used the grill on the new stove top they had bought a few months back when they had redone the kitchen. Both of them had fallen in love with it because of the option to grill indoors on those days when the weather was too icky to do it outside had been something of convenience. She could tell her husband was tense he was unusually keeping his distance and being quieter than usual.

"How did Nick look?" Matt asked his back to her as the grill sparked to life and he opened the oven below to check how the potatoes were doing.
"Matt." She began but he turned around and the fire in his eyes was not from anger but from fear, fear of what might happen, fear of losing her like he almost did before they had been able to get to know each other. "Robert went missing."
"I see, and he thinks you should go in and rescue him, wherever he is and whether or not he may be alive."
"Hey, that's not fair."
"It wouldn't be too fair if Izzy had to grow up without her mother."
"Screw you." She snapped back. "You go off all the time with the team to places I can only imagine doing things I know you are trained for but knowing I may never see you again after you walk out that fucking door."
"Are you going to go?" He plainly asked as if he hadn't heard her biting words which he had and was trying hard not to feel the nauseous feeling the fear was bubbling up in his throat.

"I told him I couldn't." She turned back and waited for her anger to lessen. "I explained I wouldn't because of Izzy and you and because I have an important surgery tomorrow."
"And?" He threw the steaks on and could hear the

sizzling as the smell began to waft through the air. "He reminded me of how Robert wouldn't think twice to save me if I was in trouble. That he has always been there for me." She took two beers from the refrigerator and put one over the island counter towards him and opened the one for herself. "Did you fall for his guilt trip?"

"No, but Steve thought he had an idea I didn't think was a very good idea."

"What?" Matt finally gave his wife his front to look at.

"Well firstly, the reason he was coming over was because he wanted to run the idea of proposing to her with us. Then he was thinking maybe Mel could go to wherever Robbie is and check things out."

"Is he nuts? I wouldn't want either of you there alone; do you know where he was when he went missing?"

"Nick wouldn't say but I'm hoping it's nowhere near the Middle East."

"What's nowhere near the Middle East?" Mel asked walking in followed closely by Steve. "Well." Jamie began taking a long swallow of beer for courage.

"Tell her." Matt pushed, he was still angry over the entire situation.

"Nick called." She plainly said and watched her sister's forehead crease.

"Nick who?"

"He works with Robert."

"Are you going back to the Middle East? After what happened last time?" Mel was looking between her sister and brother in law she had never seen them like this ever, there was a definite center of tension between them.

"I don't know where Robert is, no one does, that's the point. Nick wants me to go and find out what has happened." Jamie explained.
"But you can't go." Mel sounded like she was begging. "We all almost lost you last time; I can't believe you would even consider this. No wonder Matt looks so pissed."
"That I am." Matt grumbled while turning the steaks.
"Hey I told Nick I couldn't do this, I know what happened last time, I was there remember, I lived it, you just got to see it on a screen. Every time they hit me it was my body that formed a scar and mentally I always see them in the mirror so why don't the two of you get off your high horse and make it seem like I don't know all this already, that I'd be stupid enough to do this with what I have now." Jamie slammed the back door as she left the three of them there to go outside and calm down, she couldn't believe their nerve to feel the need to remind her what happened with Atwa. Truth be told, she had more mental scars than they could ever understand, thankfully they weren't there the first time she had gone over there and killed the man's son, the reason he had come for her those five years later. She was responsible for the death of two men, father and son; she had a harder time trying to forget that.

CHAPTER ELEVEN

The curry had been great, the company even better, it was helping him to forget the urgentness that was his life at the moment. He couldn't stay like this forever, there were people back at his office who would begin to worry, especially 'mother' his contact. He hadn't called in the last two days and he could imagine what would be said in the office behind closed doors.

Beth was a really smart woman and had somehow managed to get him to tell her things he wasn't sure he should but with the food and good wine he had been able to relax enough, careful though to not reveal his real identity, so far she only called him John. That was good for him for now.

Once they had finished he had cleared off the table and begun the cleaning up in the kitchen only to find Beth with a dish towel in hand ready to dry the things he washed. He didn't comment on their earlier deal but passed her the items as they spoke; he was still waiting to hear more about her. "Where in Boston do you live?" He asked passing her the oversized pot the curry had cooked in. "In Cambridge between Central square and Harvard." "I know Harvard, but not the other."
"Its south of Harvard towards the Charles River, I live on the second floor of a four story building which is mainly home to half of the college population of Cambridge; well at least it feels like

it."

"I get the feeling you don't like the college population."

"Hey, I was in their position not so many years ago. When I moved in they were all working people but with the increase in rent and the increase in enrolled students it became Collegeville pretty fast."

"How did you meet Brett?" He switched it to a more personal question.

"He works in the same office building as me but in the welfare department."

"Did you know he was married before you two started dating?"

"No, I found that out a few dates later."

"It didn't bother you?"

"Yeah, but I was stupid like always and thought if he wasn't bothered by it then nor was I but he had a hard time keeping track of both me and his wife."

"Like always? You date lots of married men?" He rinsed out the dish sponge and put it back on the drainer he had taken it from. "No. This was the first married man but not the first idiot I thought was going to be the one."

"But you planned this vacation with Brett."

"It was his idea; he had been here on this island before and thought it would be a good place for us to go where we didn't have to worry someone he knew or his wife seeing us."

"I'm sorry."

"Hey, don't be. I was actually contemplating becoming a nun before I spotted you on the rocks."

"I can't see you as a nun." He laughed watching her face light up. He hoped she had been jesting because a woman as beautiful as she was would be an injustice to lose her to the order of the church.

"You're right; I'd probably make a terrible nun. I don't even go to church." She laughed loudly and hung the towel to dry on the handle of the oven. "I was planning on taking a walk down the beach; I don't suppose I can bribe you to join me?"
"I don't see why not."
"Let's go then." He was surprised that she took his hand and led him barefoot out to the back deck and on to the soft sand. The night was cooler and the lights along the coast of all the other homes lit like beacons in the darkness. He couldn't see the ocean as the moon was hidden behind clouds but it roared like an animal waiting to eat. They were quiet as they walked feeling the cool sand beneath their feet and to anyone who may be watching from any of the darkened houses he knew sat along where they walked they would look like any normal couple out for a romantic stroll after dinner, hand in hand he tried to remember they were nothing more than accidental acquaintances.

"Have you thought about how you might get out of this trouble you are in?" She asked. "I don't know. I can't risk a lot of things and one is getting you in to any danger."
"There must be someone you could call even if it's not a person where you work. Maybe a friend who could relay a message to them?"

"I was sent here to gather information about someone Beth, I must have been close or asking the right questions because you found me washed ashore after my late night bound swim. If they have any idea I'm still alive they'll have people keeping an eye out for me. There's no phone in your house and I'll have to go in to the town and find a pay phone. If anyone sees me and follows me back here, they'll come here and stop at nothing to get to me."

"I didn't realize this was so double o seven."

"There's nothing glamorous about it." He stopped and made her look at him. "I am grateful for what you have done but I can't risk getting you hurt."

"I'm tougher than I look."

"I don't doubt that." His sincerity changed to mirth. "Would you call someone if you could though?"

"Yes, why?"

"I have a cell phone back at the house."

"You do?"

"Only problem is its dead and I forgot to pack the charger."

"We could get a new one."

"Charger? Would one of the stores in town have one? I could go in tomorrow and by lunch you could call."

"That would be great." He didn't know what was going on; the sudden feelings of being a teen were racing through his blood system. Her delicate smile and strong enthusiasm to help him were enlightening.

"Whatever that smiles for I like it. When you first

came too you were so very straight looking. Now you look like a man that likes to have fun."

"I do, my job takes away a lot of my fun though."

"Are you working right this minute?"

"Um, no."

"Good, let's get some more fun in you." She let go of his hand and pulled the hem of her t-shirt above her head removing it to reveal a lot of skin and a slash of material that wrapped around her breasts. "What are you doing?" He couldn't keep his eyes off her even as she got out of her shorts. "Going for a swim." She said before heading off towards the sound of the water.

XXX   XXX

"I'm sorry." Matt said coming out of the door holding his beer in two hands. Over the last four years this was their first real argument and he didn't like the feelings it evoked in him. "Yeah?" Jamie just remained seated on the edge of the deck not looking anywhere but towards the night sky. "I'm so worried you might get hurt or worse that my mouth lashes before my brain can really think about things."

"I think you got that right." Jamie felt him come to sit next to her.

"If you have to do this I will try to understand but I don't want you to go alone. I'll go with you." Jamie turned to look at him, he was as handsome as she had thought the first time they had really talked when she could let herself admire his boyishly good looks.

"I'm not going." She took a sip of her beer. "I can't'.
"Because of the operation tomorrow?"
"Because I mentally can't Matt. You were right, the last time almost did kill me, you know I still have infrequent nightmares about it and I can't imagine being strong enough to survive something like that again even with the strength of knowing you and Izzy need me too."
"We could do this together."
"No, you might, I can't. What makes me feel worse is knowing I'm letting down the one friend that has done everything he possibly could for me but I couldn't do this for him."
"He knows you care. How about I go, I have some vacation time due, you said it would be a couple of day's right? Izzy will be with your parents and you'll be busy with Steve's surgery."

She sat there looking at her husband. "You're serious aren't you?"
"I'd rather I do it."
"So if you die you can with a clear conscience that your daughter still has her mother."
"I'm not going to die."
"But you could, just like I could if I went."
"I'll go with him." The voice came from behind them; they turned to see Mel standing in the doorway. "I can use your passport and we could be a normal couple enjoying some time alone, that's less suspicious than a person going by themselves and safer too if one gets caught there'll be another to get the word out."

"I don't know about this." Jamie looked from her sister to her husband.

"You take care of Steven and his operation tomorrow and I'll make sure nothing happens with your husband." Mel made the deal.

"Call Nick back. Tell him we'll leave as soon as he can get us out." Matt said walking back in to the kitchen to find Steve taking the would have been burnt steaks off the grill, they looked perfect from his obvious attention. "What's the plan?" His buddy asked.

"I'm going to go with Mel to wherever Robert was last seen."

"Really?"

"Yep, should be interesting wouldn't you say."

"Take care of her." Steve looked serious.

"I will, when we get back I hope to see you a bit happier as well."

"I might be missing some body parts but I should be fine."

"Are you sure? I wish I could be there for you."

"You will be by looking after Mel. I think I should thank you for leaving me with Jamie. I don't know what I would do if it had been anyone else who gave me that news."

"She'll make sure you are as good as you can be."

"I talked to Daniel about a teaching post. He says I might be able to get one here on base." Steve put each steak on a different plate and then walked around the kitchens island to put a plate at each of the settings. "Any trainee would be lucky to get you."

"Thanks. I can do that job while I recuperate and sit in a wheelchair for the next year but I plan to try my damndest to get your wife to admit I can still be a SEAL. Hell I'd go back to hell week to prove it."

"I think that's the best attitude to have." Matt put his beer down and watched as his wife closely followed by her sister walked through the kitchen to the living room. Jamie looked neither pleased nor sure about this, it was written all over her face.

Jamie took the disposable cell phone from her sweater pocket and hit redial. The line was connected with Nick after just two rings; the man's deep baritone laugh came through to her before any of his words. "I knew I could count on you Buchanan."

"I'm not doing it but I have a solution for you."

"Shoot."

"My sister and husband will go instead. They can pretend to be a married couple. I'll give her my passport."

"Sounds like it could work but isn't your sister a screw up?"

"Not anymore." She paused. "Where are they going?"

"Oh, I can't tell you that. They'll find out when they get to the airport."

"Are they going to the Middle East?"

"No, much closer to home. Tell them they won't need any language skills and to pack lots of tropical clothes."

"What time and where?"

"Ten am at Lindbergh field. I'll meet them at the Delta terminal."

"Right; and Nick."

"Yes."

"If they get hurt I'll hold you responsible." All that came back to her was his laughter before the line was cut.

"So?" Mel asked the moment she knew her sister was done talking.

"Let's do this while we eat." She walked on out to the kitchen where both men stopped talking to look at the two almost identical females come through the doors. Jamie's hair was a little longer than when she had first come to Coronado but still very blonde and that natural wave that Matt loved so much was there. Mel on the other hand had recently died her blonde hair to a medium brown with blonde highlights, its length now to her shoulders and bone straight. The only other way to tell the two apart aside from when you talked to them was by their eye color. Jamie's were vivid blue much like her husbands and Mel's were hazel.

They all watched as Jamie sat at the island in front of a plate holding only a very juicy looking steak. The others sat too, Matt to her left, Mel to her right and Steve sitting on the other side of Mel. "You both have to be at the Delta terminal at ten tomorrow." She said heaping a tong full of salad on to her plate.

"Where are they going?" Steve asked.

"I don't know but you are to pack tropical weather clothes." Jamie turned to her husband. "Are you sure about this?"

"Actually we were doing a high altitude jump tomorrow so I'm pretty glad to be getting out of it."

"Did you call Daniel yet?" Steve interjected.

"I figured I'd wait until after we knew the details, not that I can tell him too much."

"What's tropical weather clothing?" Mel asked with a mouthful of salad, the dressing trying hard to slide out.

"Probably shorts and t-shirts and some bathing suits." Matt answered.

"I only have one thing to say about all of this." Jamie put her fork down and they all looked at her. "If you fall in love with Mel while away." She pointed at her husband. "Or do anything intimate other than a peck on the cheek, I will kill you." She turned to her right where her sister looked nervous. "As for you, the same and you know I will kill you too."

"Hey, he's my annoying brother in law." Mel laughed.

"Hey." Matt imitated back. "I take offense to both of you. I'm neither likely to do anything to your sister and Mel, I'm not the annoying one." Matt smiled wickedly at her. "I really wish I wasn't missing this one." Steve laughed louder.

CHAPTER TWELVE

The water had been a lot colder than he had expected. He had kept his sweat pants on because his underwear had been left to dry back at the house, he wasn't sure she would find his naked skinny dip appropriate. They had splashed each other like kids and he had yet again forgotten where he was, by the time they had gotten out and retrieved their clothing it was getting late, almost midnight.

Excusing himself away once inside the cool air conditioned house he went to the room he had been using and stripped out of the wet pants wrapping a towel around his waist so he could look through the pile of clothes on the chair for something dry to wear. As he came out of the bathroom he saw Beth sitting on the end of the bed, wrapped in a large fluffy white robe, her back to him. "I wasn't sure if you heard me with the water running in there." She said keeping her back turned.
"Didn't hear what?"
"I figured you hadn't realized this is a one bedroom and my clothes are in here too."
"Oh, I'm sorry." He felt awkward. "You can err, turn around, I have a towel on."
"It's okay." She looked so very tiny in that robe and his heart stopped for three beats before he swallowed. "I don't want to embarrass you but I saw more of you earlier when I was cleaning you up and you were out of it, I just didn't want to

shock you."

"How much more of me did you see?"

Beth blushed as she felt her cheeks flame up and her mouth had gone dry. "When I was taking off your sweats your." She blushed and stammered.

"Underwear?" He helped.

"Yeah, they came down a little."

"Wow, now this is embarrassing." He had to laugh he had no idea what else to do, strange feeling for him, a man who could adapt to any situation or figure out any problem. "I could think of other reasons to be embarrassed but not from what I could tell." She stood and walked past him to the bathroom. "If you don't mind sharing we can each take a side of that California king bed there, much more comfortable than the bamboo couch in the other room."

"As long as you are fine with it, my back will thank you in the morning." He watched her smile and then close the door behind her, hearing the sound of the shower turning on and he picked up the pile of clothes from the chair.

Most of it was cargo shorts and plain collared short sleeve shirts, all in neutral tan and white. There was one loud shirt that he laughed at, knowing he would never in his life wear it. At the bottom he found what was inside the plastic his hand had felt. There was his saving grace, clean, unused boxer shorts, all white and his size. The last thing he had wanted to do was wear some other man's underwear. He would have gone commando before that would happen.

Changing in to a pair of the new white under shorts and using his t-shirt from before he walked over to the bed and felt the softness that called to him. He hoped that in sleep he would be able to let his always active brain just shut off. Freshly dressed he climbed in to bed after leaving the towel on the patio. He was sure to make certain the door was thoroughly locked just like he had the front and back door after they had returned. He was just getting comfortable when he heard the water shut off and the lock in the bathroom door turn.

The only light in the room were the two small lights on the headboard, no doubt there for the use of using when wanting to read instead of keeping the bright overhead light and the chance of keeping whoever was sleeping next to you awake. He was laid back under the covers and he looked asleep, it was her chance to get a good look at him without him knowing she was starring. His hair was longer than she would have figured for a man in a government job, his strong jaw line covered in ample stubble that she just wanted to touch and his eyes, wow, his eyes had been amazingly strong and showed a man who could love and be loved deep to his soul.

"What are you looking at?" One of his eyes popped open and she almost jumped out of her skin. "You." She smart mouthed back.

"See anything you like?" The words were out of his mouth before he could even think them through and he cringed internally. "Lot's." She walked around to her side of the bed and took off the fluffy robe to reveal the smallest pair of shorts and an exercise top, he laughed and hadn't realized it was out loud. "What?"

"Are you going for a jog or going to bed?"

"You are a smart ass." She pulled the covers back and sat down pulling the comforter back up to her torso.

"It was just an observation." He could feel those rarely used muscles in his cheeks strain from his smiling. "Well, I usually wear different items to bed but they aren't very appropriate for this situation."

"Hey I'm all for being comfortable. Wear whatever you brought." Beth looked at him but didn't say anything. "It's okay." She finally said not missing that killer smile he gave her all straight perfect teeth and his cheeks showed dimples. Man she was a sucker for those. "Really, it's cool."

"Do you usually sleep naked or something?"

"I err." She stammered again.

"Go ahead, take them off, I promise I won't look when you are asleep."

"Though I trust you one hundred percent I still think this will be better."

"Then may I offer a solution?" He lay there, head propped on his arm.

"Which is?"

"Take those clothes off and use the robe it's at

least softer." She just looked at him again, her mind trying to figure whether or not to take his suggestion.

She walked back to the bathroom and did as he had suggested. He was right; the robe definitely was a more comfortable option. When she came back out he had rolled over to the other side so he could see her coming out, His head still propped on his hand, his boyish smile still in place. "What?" She asked.

"You say that a lot you know." His smile was infectious and she found herself smiling too. "Well you keep staring at me."

"Sorry."

"You're forgiven." She retraced her steps and was below the sheets pulling her robe so it lay flat. He had rolled back the other way so his body although across the bed was not too far from her.

"If this were not such a weird situation for me, I mean hiding out and totally out of control I would chastise you for being so quick to believe my story and welcome me here in to your house and bed. I could be a murderer or rapist or anything like that."

"Are you any of those?" She simply asked.

"No." His smile faded. "Still you should be slower to invite strangers in."

"I found you unconscious on the rocks and looking like you were close to fish bait. I didn't find you in a bar and invite you here."

"You have a point."

"Plus only I could have a situation like this on my hands." She laughed. "I finally get a very attractive man, a man who seems more together and less detached than the ones I usually date and you are some G man whose name I don't even know. I get you in to my bed and I don't even get lucky. Yeah, this can only happen to me."

Using the knob on the side of the light on the headboard she plunged the room in to darkness unable to see the face Robert was making. He was shocked and stunned from her words.

XXX   XXX

Miguel was spending the evening with his father. It was a tradition they had done since he was young. Tuesday nights were always for their time. No other siblings, no wives and no children. Not that he had any to care for. He asked very little of his wife Cara, she was attentive to his needs and ran the house well but she was more into her life and all that could be bought than having kids. She had put her foot down the first year they had been married telling him it would wait until she lost some of her good looks and her waist.

He had shared a nice meal cooked by his fathers trusted housekeeper, an old colored woman in her fifties who said very little, she had lived on this island her entire life and had never been across the water, not even to another island. He knew she had a brother that ran a small grocery shop down in Port Elizabeth and that her only child a deaf boy of about thirteen helped at the uncles store stocking shelves, his uncle the only male role model after his father had been lost at sea in a fishing expedition.

The house his father had lived in since their arrival on this island was the grandest of the island, sitting atop the water at Shark bay, the view on either side breathtaking, it felt like the house had always been there and the island had grown around it. The inside was just as grand as the exterior and the room they sat drinking brandy in from crystal snifters was paneled in deep rich wood that held the smell of his father's Cuban cigars and he could imagine some days his mother's perfume too.

It was a little before eleven and he knew he should get going back to his own house south of the islands capital down in the lower bay but something was keeping him here tonight, inside he just didn't want to go home and have Cara piss and moan about her latest fad. The last few weeks it had been something about going to the States for another one of her hundred thousand dollar sprees. He knew as long as he lived he wouldn't understand why women needed fifteen hundred different pairs of shoes but his wife was determined to prove it to him.

With the study on the ocean side of the house neither had seen the car coming up the path from the main road. Their first clue someone was there was when Gloria the housekeeper knocked on the door waiting for her boss's gruff American voice to call her in. "Mr. Santos, there are some police men here." Her French accented English said. "Let them in." His father sat, cigar in one hand glass in the other, no intention of getting up or welcoming the men he felt were beneath him.

A tall, dark tanned white officer and a shorter rounder island officer, both in their stark white uniforms came in, their hats in their hands. "Evening gentlemen." The white, ex-American cop said, the other remained stoic and looked nervous to be before the islands most infamous resident. "What can we do for you?" Mr. Santos asked. "I'm afraid we have some bad news."
"Then spit it out." Miguel's hair stood on end all over his body at his father's sharpness. "We found a red BMW convertible an hour ago down on lower bay road." He began and Miguel unknowingly sat forward in his seat knowing the only person on the island with that car was his wife. It had been shipped in specially for their second wedding anniversary last summer.

"Is my daughter-in-law okay?" Miguel looked at his father and wondered how he could ask that so calmly. "I'm afraid she's dead sir."
"Dead?" Miguel squeaked out.
"It looks like she stopped her car for someone and they killed her."
"Damn." Mr. Santos had a smile a mile long inside;

his orders had been carried out the way he had wanted. The cheating whore was no longer a problem for his son or the reputation of the family. Hopefully poor Miguel would never find out now that she had been having an affair with his half-brother.

"We need someone to come and officially ID her and then we'll have the doc's issue you a death certificate."
"My car's outside." Miguel stood but felt his legs turn to jelly.
"Nonsense, you shouldn't have to remember her the way she may be now." Mr. Santos stood. "My other son Luis will go." He told the officers as his large gate moved to the desk where he picked up his phone to call Luis on the house intercom. Luis was yet to find his own place since dropping out of Miami State University. "Luis." He boomed down the phone. "You need to come down, there's been an accident." He hung the phone up with no other words and walked over to his cherished son. "Fix yourself a stiff drink. I'll have Vince drive you home when he's home." Miguel was ordered and like an obedient son he walked over to the cabinet and refilled his glass. This time with the strong amber liquid of his father's favorite whiskey.

He watched his father walk the officers out in to the hall and walked over to the window, the night was dark and the only light was from the moon and stars glowing off the water as it came and went along the shore for miles. He put his glass down on the window ledge and wondered why he wasn't more than shocked his wife was dead, he felt no sadness or loss and wondered if it was mere shock setting in.

Mr. Santos watched his son leave with the officers, he looked dazed at the news his sister in law was dead and sick at the thought of having to ID her corpse. Leaving his other son alone in the study he went across to the open living area where he had seen his right hand man sitting back reading the daily island paper. "Vince." He said.
"Mr. Santos, was that the police?" Vince played innocence while a smug grin sat on his lips. "Yes, poor Cara was found dead."
"Why that is outrageous. I hope they find the sick bastard that would do such a thing."
"I sent Luis to ID her; I thought Miguel should be spared the image."
"Good decision." Vince had to chuckle, his boss was just as twisted in his revenge as he was, later in privacy he would explain how the woman had gotten what she deserved. "You really think they'll find whoever did this?"
"No." Mr. Santos managed a smile. "I am certain they never will."

CHAPTER THIRTEEN

Sitting on the edge of their bed, he watched as his wife did her nightly routine in the bathroom. When he was away he would from time to time figure out what time it was in San Diego and then picture what she would be doing.

His bag was packed, sitting on the floor downstairs next to his daughters. He had called his boss and had received three days leave plus the coming weekend to help his sister in law find a man so twisted in to the fiber of the family that he wasn't sure she should be going; that any of them should. It was more than likely he was dead and he was the last person that wanted the job of telling his wife, or even having to deal with Mel and one of her breakdowns.

Jamie was wearing her favorite pajamas, a bright pink t-shirt that exposed her stomach from the cropped pink pajama bottoms. Her hair was down and looking silky and clean. After Steve and Mel had left after dinner they hadn't said too much. He knew exactly what she was thinking, he had to be stupid not to after her blatant warning in the kitchen. She was worried something was going to happen between him and her sister while they were away pretending Mel was really Jamie. He knew all the differences between them yet he knew there were some similarities that worried him. The main one being aside from certain colorings they were from the identical beginnings, they even had the same DNA.

She came out of the bathroom, turning the light off as she left. Matt sat there deep in his thoughts. She climbed up her side of the bed and came up behind him kneeling a knee either side of him and putting her arms around him. "I love you." She whispered in to his ear and felt his body shake slightly from the sensation of her breath on his skin. "I love you too." He returned holding on to her hands with his. "Are you worried about where you are going?" She asked leaning her chin on his strong shoulder. "No, I'm just thinking about this masquerade and Steve's surgery."

"I can't help you with the first one but I can alleviate some concern for your friend. I'll be there every step to make sure he is both fine and comfortable."

"I know you will, it's just it makes me wonder what I would do in his situation."

"You would be lucky enough to have a family to rely on to give you support. Speaking of which, I spoke to Patti earlier." Jamie referred to the senior chief's wife Patti Polanski. "She is putting together a schedule for visitors so that Steve can have someone with him at all times. When the team is training the wives are going to be there."

"I think he'll appreciate that."

"I also asked my father to get Izzy to call. I'll explain before she leaves in the morning what is going on, I know Steve is very fond of her and maybe a call will make him smile. He's going to need as many of those moments as we can give him."

"I will obviously have my cell so I'll call as long as I have reception. I know your sister will want to find out how he's doing."

"I hope she does." Jamie's tone changed as she let go and moved from him. Matt turned to see her applying her vanilla scented hand cream to her hands and feet. "What do you mean by that?"

"I hope she doesn't flake out on Steve it's not what he needs from her."

"She said she wanted to help him through this."

"Yeah, and then offered to go away with my extremely handsome healthy husband."

"I don't think she would have chosen differently had he not been sick."

"Let's hope so." She paused. "I thought Steve wanted to ask her to marry him."

"I asked him while you were getting Mel some of your things. He said he didn't think it was the time to do it."

"No time like the present."

"Maybe he'll do it when we get back."

"It would be weird to have them married. Actually it's not Steve getting married that is so weird anymore, it's my sister getting married and to our friend."

"I think she's changed his ways; he no longer plays around with different women. Maybe she brings out the good in him."

"As long as she doesn't hurt him." Jamie put the lotion bottle down and snuggled in against Matt who was laying down, one hand behind his head as her head rested on his chest.

XXX   XXX

111

Steve had not intended to do anything more than make sure Mel arrived home safe from her sisters. He had followed her car in his truck and had stayed on the road as she pulled in to her parking space in front of her apartment. He watched her park and get out and watched her walk towards his door window. He lowered it all the way so she could lean against the metal. "Are you coming in?" She asked wondering why he hadn't parked like he normally would. "I don't know. I kinda have to get some things together for tomorrow."
"Just for a little while?" She lowered the time from what she had wanted to be all night to maybe something a little easier for him to handle.

"Okay." He sighed knowing he had so much to do; he had yet to call his mother who undoubtedly would be on the next flight out to smother him with her vast wisdom of nothing. If he was lucky she would remain sober the entire time too. He had lived his eighteen years with her up in his home state of Illinois, she was always starting a new boyfriend every week and the house he had grown up in had been less than warm and comforting. He had promised her he would graduate high school but the minute he was through with classes he was through with the town and the whispers about how his mother had been married four times. Husband number four was happy to see him leave he was sure, but not as happy as he had been to get the hell out.

Enlisting in the Navy was his best move he

thought, he had served a few years onboard a destroyer in the Asian waters before signing up for SEAL duty. The training had been fierce and harder than anything he had ever done before but he was motivated by the knowledge if he couldn't succeed he would have to return to the middle of nowhere town and his mother.

Something he would have gone down fighting to ensure.

Since joining up their relationship had been better, she called him twice a month and he visited once a year now she lived in Ohio and mainly because she was always too busy to visit him in San Diego. He knew deep down that this operation would bring her to the California.

His own father had died of a massive heart attack at the age of thirty when he was in second grade. He had been a construction man and had loved his mother so much, treating her like a queen. After he died, she changed, trying to find someone who would treat her as well as Steven Schlome senior had. As he pulled the truck in to a parking space he tried to remember what his father had looked like and realized he didn't remember any more than the strangers light brown hair.

Mel had already gone inside, the light from her living room illuminating the darkness outside where the street lights couldn't touch. The door left slightly ajar in waiting for him to come in and close it. There was so much familiarity with the apartment, the smell of Mel and the lingering fragrance of meals cooked. Inside was spotless, and very few nick knacks adorned the beautiful yet basic furniture she owned. His own apartment was a mix up of all the things he had come across since arriving in California. His prized faux Tiffany lamp he had found on the curb waiting for the men to collect it with the garbage, he had picked it up and brought it back and after cleaning it up, a quick fix to the plug had set it above his thrift store bought desk in his living room.

He stopped his eyes wandering around the living room as they fell upon a picture taken at last year's team picnic. Mel and her sister, Matt holding a much younger Izzy and him, they all smiled for the lens, Kristen the team leader's wife had just bought a new digital camera, some big flashy Nikon that he had only ever seen overzealous reporters using. Everyone that day had been captured by the camera; all the pictures he had seen so far had been amazing. Daniel had tried really hard to get her to put the damn thing down but she had laughed, made her usual sparkling smile and he had been mush in her hands. It was nice to see the leader crumble some times.

"That was a beautiful day." Mel said coming up behind him.
"I won't be in there this summer." His voice low and somber.
"Maybe not standing but you'll still be there." He

felt her arms tighten around his waist. "No, after tomorrow I'll no longer be a member of the team."
"Sure you will." Steve, moving her hands so he could turn, slowly spun to face her.
"I'm not going to be on that team Mel, at least not for a year, and by then they'll have found someone to replace me, they have to replace me to keep the team even. If I return it's possible I'll be sent to another base."
"I'm sure Daniel would make sure you came back to team seven."
"Right now that's not so realistic." He moved away walking towards the couch but didn't want to sit and get comfortable, the fear that he would fall asleep and his last day for a long time of standing would come.

"Tell me what you're thinking about." Mel shoved her hands in her pockets because she knew she wanted to wring them, he was making her nervous; she had never seen him look so lost. "I feel worried about you leaving." He lied, not wanting to speak his feelings, his fears. Like what if he didn't wake up after the operation? How could he make this young woman he had fallen so in love with stay with a man whose future was so unclear? That losing his leg was a smaller fear compared to losing her.

"Don't be, Matt will be with me." Mel sighed before giving her best solemn smile.
"Are you going because your sister couldn't or because you still love him?"

"Love who? Matt?" She laughed.

"Robert."

"Oh, baby." She moved closer so she could touch him. "I never really loved Robert."

"But you two were together."

"For a few days that spanned almost two years, he was gone most of the time."

"I've been gone a lot too."

"Yeah, but I love you, that's the difference."

"Do you? Love me, even now?" She could have sworn she saw a tear appear in his right eye but it was gone as quickly as it had appeared. "Let me show you." She touched his cheek with her palm and he was about to move away but the devil on his shoulder told him to take advantage of this, God only knew when he'd get laid again, if ever again by Mel. He needed this more than she could know.

He took her hand and leaned closer so he could kiss her, telling her with his unspoken words everything he was wanting.

CHAPTER FOURTEEN

The sun was glaring so much on his shoulder he could feel it through the haziness of the sleep he was still very comfortable in. He wrapped his arms tighter around the pillow he had cuddled up with and his legs were bent, he straightened them and found the unfamiliar feeling of silky soft skin rubbing against his own coarsely hairy ones. Who was so close in the bed with him? Who had he gone to sleep with last night......?

'Holy shit' his mind screamed as he mustered enough energy to open the eye furthest away from his pillow.

Lying there in his arms, their limbs entwined was the female who had so unwisely opened her door to him for haven, not knowing him from Adam and believing every word out of his mouth. It was just a good thing he was what he said he was. Not knowing from where her head was leaning against his chest if she was asleep or not he was mortified to wake her. This had not meant to happen; the bed was more than big enough for the two of them.

He looked around more, his brain knowing something else was wrong but in that morning after a few more glasses of wine through the night before he couldn't exactly make his mind pin point what it was.

"Shit." He breathed out softly. Her robe, the big white comfy looking one from the night before was no longer encasing her body, the only real thing between them were the clothes he was wearing. 'Why did I have to suggest she wear it'? His mind raced, the endorphins were kicking in as he tried to remember whether or not they had, nah, they couldn't have, he put his head back down on the pillow and his movements made her stir, she rolled over and for the first time since waking John dared to move, quickly sitting up hanging his bare legs over the edge of the bed. His sudden movements must have woken her slightly because he could hear the sheets moving and a slight groan from her as she stretched out.

"Hey." He said softly when he saw her eyes open. He wondered if she were the kind of person who would be awake and comprehensive the moment their eyes opened or if it would take a few minutes. "Hey." He saw the recognition in her eyes. "What time is it?" She asked licking her lips. He couldn't help it; he was watching her pale pink tongue as it moved across her lips. "Oh." He shook his head a little getting it clear, turning slightly he saw the alarm clock on the bedside table. "A little before eight."
"Time for a jog before breakfast." She sat up and he couldn't help but watch to see if she knew what state of undress she was in.

Beth watched as John's eyes followed her movements and she realized he was a little spazed out by her missing robe. "It's okay, when I got hot during the night you told me to take it off promising you wouldn't look."
"I did?" He stood there on the cool floor looking down at her covered only by the pale blue sheet.
"Yeah, you look like you are going to be sick. Am I that hideous to look at?"
"No, it's just, well, when I woke up we were sort of tangled and I was worried I may have overstepped the mark."
"Oh." Beth smoothed down the back of her hair

praying her usual bed head was not too evident.
"I'm sorry, I should have left the other clothes on, I didn't mean to make you feel nervous."
"I'm not nervous." He sighed. "I just really didn't want to have taken advantage of your generosity by doing something."
"I appreciate that but I am a big girl and have been through much worse situations so forget about it."

She cleverly wrapped the sheet around her not once showing any more than the bare skin on her shoulders. She picked up her exercise wear from one of the chairs she had left it on the night before and went in to the bathroom without saying anything.

XXX   XXX

After a night as long as his, he was still trying to find the stomach to do much more than sit on the hood of his car looking out in to the Atlantic Ocean and watch the fishing boats coming back with their daily catch, some would go back out but most were all done. The fresh sea air and the warmth did nothing to settle his stomach.

The image of his sister in law lying on that cold slab of steel, her skin looking blue as he had viewed it through the glass window down at the islands small medical center window, the room was usually used for trauma patients waiting to be flown to Kingstown's large hospital. A white sheet had covered her until a doctor had lowered it so he could see her from her shoulders up. He had prayed it would be someone else but it had been the wife of his older brother, the one he had been screwing for a while, meeting whenever they could get together. With this such random killing happening he could think of only two people capable of what the police had described as 'the most sadistic sexual attack on any of the islands in decades'.

One would be his father the other Vince. Though he pegged Vince as the actual doer, he'd bet all the money in his bank account that it was an order from his father. Someone must have found out about the affair, seen them although they had been as careful as they could. Maybe one of his father's whores had seen something. What scared him more was, if this was what came from the family for Cara then what would be his punishment, when would it happen? Would his father really have him killed too for hurting his unsuspecting fool of an older brother?

Sure he hated the way his father adored Miguel because of some stupid idealization he had for his first wife but it was far from normal how it had transcended down to his brother. He hadn't started the affair to get even or get back at him but in a way try and rock the boat. Never in his life had he thought they would kill her because of it.

Everything was his fault, he wondered if there was a way to ever escape their father's strong hold, maybe fleeing back to America, the old man would never go back there but he would more than likely send someone to get him. Plus, all the money he had was held by his father's accountant, it would raise a flag if they saw him taking large sums out.

He shook his head and wished they hadn't thrown that American CIA agent from their boat. He would have been willing to give as much information on the old man as he knew, and he knew a damn lot. He loved his father as much as he had been raised to without ever showing weakness but the man was evil, down to the core, he wished his two-bit whore of a mother had aborted him, at least then he wouldn't be stuck in the web of this family waiting to see when and what his punishment would be.

XXX   XXX

Matt had given Izzy a big hug when his father and mother in law arrived to collect her and while Jamie was getting dressed for work he took a quick shower and dressed in his best looking cargo shorts and black t-shirt. "Do you have everything?" Jamie asked coming in to the bathroom while he was combing his hair. He put down the black plastic and turned quick enough to pick her up in his arms. "I love you in that uniform." He growled. "I thought you loved me in my bikini." She laughed, Jamie felt like a woman loved this morning, her husband had been a very attentive lover during the night and she could still feel her skin tingle everywhere he had touched it.

"I am so going to miss you."
"You'll have my sister to keep you entertained; I know how much you just love all her jokes." Jamie wrapped her legs around his waist and her white skirt had risen up to show all of her tan, long, lean thighs, his hands held her there as he turned around and rested her on the bathroom counter. "Remember what I said about having to gag her, it might just come true."
"As long as it's gagging on something other than you I don't care." She shivered as he ran his finger down the delicate curve of her neck and lower, it was like he was following one of his combat maps, coming to rest where her shirt was unbuttoned in between her two breasts. "I'd never let her close enough for that."
"Good."

Jamie instigated a hot long kiss that made him want to forget about what was going on but the sound of the door downstairs opening and closing and Mel's voice shouting. "Jamie, Matt."
"He's up here." Jamie shouted and relinquished a hold on him. "It's so odd not to have you and Izzy both here for the next few days."
"Hopefully I'll be back before our daughter and we can get some alone time in."
"You want to get me pregnant again?" She winked and he felt the heat rise again but this time in his cheeks. "I would love too, but last time was so hard on you." He bowed his head remembering how

devastated she had been when she had become pregnant about a year after having Izzy but nature hadn't wanted them to have another yet because Jamie had miscarried after just two months. There had been a lot of tears and neither had brought up that memory or the one of having more children until this moment. "It was, but I had you to help me understand it was nothing I did, it just wasn't time."

"Wasn't time for what?" Mel asked leaning against the bathroom door. Jamie turned her head away from her sister and Matt knew he had to reply something else or she would get suspicious, they had never told anyone what had happened, not even her sister. "It's nothing." He said keeping Jamie where she was. "How's Steve this morning?" "I don't know." Mel shrugged her shoulders. "He stayed at my place for a while last night but he said he had to do some stuff before the surgery, I figured he was going to spend the time walking around on his own two feet." Matt watched his sister in law when she was talking and something was off.

"That dress looks good on you." Jamie changed the impending subject of Steve's surgery to the dress she had borrowed from her sister. "I'll be down in a minute." Matt told Mel and she took the hint with a minor laugh. "She's wearing your dress?" "Yeah, she has to be me and I know a stranger wouldn't know her style but I don't think miniskirts and barely down to your belly button t-

123

shirts are mine or a happily married woman's style." She paused for air. "She should have her blue contacts in too." Jamie looked down at her hand resting on the counter and the rings he had given her for their engagement and wedding. "I didn't give her my rings though; she should have the set from my mother that Dad gave her years ago."

"I didn't notice if she did or not." He moved away.

"Worried about how she looks more like me?"

"Yes and no, if she starts acting and talking like you then I'll be freaked out."

"You should be; she's never acted like me."

"Are you sure you have time to drive us before getting to base?"

"Yeah, let me do these up and get my bag from the office and I'll be ready."

CHAPTER FIFTEEN

Jamie had dropped her husband and sister off at the Delta terminal early on her way to the base, the doctor due to do Steve's surgery was going to run through the procedure with her before getting Steve comfortable and in to the operating room. She was looking forward to seeing the doctor; he had been her first mentor once she had entered the navy to complete her medical training.

Pulling in to her designated parking space outside of the medical building she saw her old mentor getting out from his chauffeured base jeep. She hurried herself up and was pressing the lock for her car as she struggled with her own bag and running across to the sidewalk. "Dr. Harmon." She called out. He stopped and turned a smile a mile wide on his face. "Jamie Buchanan." He said watching her make it across to him. "Let me help you there." He said taking her bag and putting it over his shoulder with his own. "Thank you sir." She said, they began walking in to the building as they continued to talk.

"I've heard a great deal about you in the last few years." He held the door open for her.
"Really?" She felt a blush coming to her cheeks.
"You definitely look like you have been living for a change instead of hiding out."
"I got married."
"I know, to a SEAL no less."
"You really have been following me."
"I was a little disappointed when you didn't take me up on the orthopedics fellowship, I think emergency medicine was a good match for you but I had to keep an eye on you in case you ever looked like you might change your mind."
"I would never have met my husband if I had taken your offer."
"My loss is your gain." They walked down the long office corridor.
"The powers that be assigned you the office opposite mine." She stopped between the two doors. "Let me get settled, get a cup of coffee and we'll go over this morning's procedure. What time is our patient due in?"
"Eleven hundred."

"Good, that gives us forty minutes and then we can run through it with him." He paused. "It really is good to see you James."
"Same here."

XXX   XXX

"I feel I need to apologize again." John said sitting down next to Beth on the big wicker couch out on the deck that looked out to the ocean. "Please, don't." Beth shook her head as she read one of the magazines she had purchased in Boston's Logan airport and had yet to read. She had left the room after waking up earlier and had not said a word or been around in the last two hours and he felt so bad. "I have to."
"I get it; you were concerned something might have happened. It didn't, chill out, there's nothing for you to feel bad about."
"Look." He began. "I'm not any of those guys you date that are so flaky and use you until they break you. I'm not going to hurt you because although I think you are a very selfless, gracious, beautiful female you know nothing more about me than what I have told you, you don't even know my real name. It wouldn't matter if I was here for however long as your friend or lover, I can't do that to you, I can't play that mind game with you. I have to keep you safe; I can't afford to get you anymore tangled in this."

She watched him, not sure what to say. "I was going to go in to town in a while, is there anything other than the cell adapter you need?"

"Beth, do you understand what I just said."

"I got it loud and clear." She stood up putting the magazine where she had just been sitting. "It looks like it may get hot and I want to get back so I can get some sun, I spent all of my tax return money on this vacation and I'll be damned if your problems will keep me from getting the tan I've been dreaming of."

"Beth, please."

"John please don't apologize anymore." She walked back in to the house and it took all his will power not to chase her in and apologize yet again.

Looking out to the water, hearing the door close behind her and the crashing of the occasional waves before him he sat back and closed his eyes for a moment, he wasn't sure how long he had them closed before he heard a noise not far away past the underbrush that kept their privacy from the eastern neighbors.

With the hair on his neck standing up on edge and his hand automatically going to his hip only to find his holster and gun missing he stood to go back in to the house but whoever had been making the noise must have heard him because he suddenly heard the sound of a female voice, one laced with the local flavor of a mixture of ancestry to the island. The sight of a slender looking older woman came in to view, her skin so dark and her black hair long to her waist in a braid. The white and blue flowery sun dress she wore hung in the soft breeze that was keeping everything for the moment somewhat cool. "Hi there." She said as she came from her side down the stairs of the neighboring villa and across the dry sand in her bare feet. "Hi." John leaned against the railing of the enclosed back deck.

"How are you liking your villa?" She asked coming to stand at the bottom of the steps. "It's great, do you own them?" Although his heart was pounding he was trying to keep the conversation light. "No sir, I just get them cleaned up for the owner."
"Well he must make a fortune; I know my girlfriend and I will rave about this place when we return to the states."
"It's been a little slow, what with the weather this time of year. I'm here because we have a late booking coming in tonight."
"Really?"
"It happens a lot around here." She blocked the sun from her eyes with her hand to her forehead. "This beach is so quiet; at least you and your lady will have another couple to talk to."
"Ah, we're here to be alone, I'm sure they are great people but I brought Beth here to keep her all to myself. I hate that she's gone in to town but I'll have her back soon." He winked. "Many a man has made their woman pregnant here." She laughed.
"Today is Wednesday, I clean these houses on Fridays, I just thought I'd let you know."
"Thank you."
"You have yourself a great day." She turned and walked back just as fast as she had come and John

decided he was going to wait inside.

XXX   XXX

"Lieutenant." Captain Harmon MD said when he entered the private hospital room in the hospital. He had spent the last hour going over the entire procedure with his old student Commander Jamie Buchanan and he was looking forward to getting this operation done and being able to get back to Bethesda to his patients there.

Steven stood up, knowing every time he did it was one of the last for such a long time but the doctor was a captain and he needed to be shown the same respect he gave all higher ranking officers. "Relax." The doctor waved off and Steve almost stumbled not sure what his feet should do. "Jamie will be right along she was going to get your latest blood work results." He told Steve who just nodded. "I hear you are on the SEAL team Jamie was sent to."
"Her husband is one of my best friends and I'm dating Jamie's sister."
"Ah, the mysterious Melanie." He laughed. "I never knew she had a sister until she missed rounds one day during her third year rotation. I was rather shocked there was more than one of them."
"How come?"
"She's so different from Jamie."
"She sure is but then they are very alike."
"Will Melanie be coming by to visit you? I'd like to see her again."
"She's on vacation for the next few days."

"Even with you going in for this major surgery?"

"It was already booked; I didn't want her to lose her money."

"Well, I guess you have Jamie, she's always had a great bedside manner." His words sparked a curious thinking in Steve. Was there something about the relationship this doctor had with Jamie he didn't know? He looked at Dr. Harmon, his hair white and his skin wrinkled and looking like leather.

"Good, you are both here." Jamie came in, she was wearing her blue scrubs and white lab coat and Matt's words about what they did to him came to Steve's mind and he had to smile. "How are you this morning Steve?" She asked her friend.

"Nervous, anxious to get this all started so I can begin the recovery process."

"That's the attitude." Dr. Harmon sat down. "Jamie is going to assist me in the operation and I unfortunately have to leave soon after so I won't be here for long when you wake up but I have all the confidence in Jamie and you'll be great."

"What should I expect after today's operation, you know when I wake up?"

"We'll keep you on a high dose of pain killers so the pain should be slight, more like a funny tingle. We are going to be removing the portion of your upper tibia where the tumor is, we'll be trying our hardest to make sure we salvage all tendons and ligaments that we can. We'll use some rods and artificial pieces to rebuild what we take out. When you wake up you will see your leg elevated and in traction, that is to allow for the rods to set and take. We'll insert a few chemo wafers if the labs insist it is needed and in a few days you'll start a round of chemo. Jamie will follow how the restructured knee and leg looks like and hopefully in a week we can begin physical therapy."

"Is it true chemo will make me unable to be a father in the future?"
"Yes, are kids something you've thought about?" Dr. Harmon asked.
"Once it wasn't but lately yes." Steve looked at Jamie and she knew he was referring to Mel. "I think we could make some arrangements for you, your surgery isn't for another hour, I hope you really do perform well under pressure." The doctor joked and Jamie had to look away because Steve was blushing uncontrollably. "That would be great; I'll try not to be too nervous." Steve quipped back after he had recovered.
"Any other questions?"
"No." Steve looked away out the window where a team of navy men were running in a group around one of the fields.

"Jamie's going to help you get settled in and ready and I'll be back in a little while, relax and I guarantee you once the procedure is over we will all be here for your healing." Both Steve and Jamie watched Dr. Harmon leave the room closing the door behind himself. "He seems like a good doctor." Steve got up again and went back over to the window. "He's the best the Navy has."

"He knows a lot about you, he talks like he has a thing for you."

"He doesn't, he's been married for the last three decades to the same woman. What he is to me is a man I learnt a great deal from."

"I still think he has a thing for you."

"Were you really serious about freezing your little soldiers so you can have kids some day?" Jamie changed the subject.

"Of course, I mean, I may never but I want that option."

"With my sister maybe?"

"Have you heard from either of them yet?" It was his turn to change the line of conversation.

"They've only been gone two hours, I doubt I'll hear anything till later, we'll know after we come out of surgery, I'll let you know when I know."

"Oh, Jamie. I have a favor to ask."

"Anything, you know that."

"I called my mother last night to tell her about the surgery. She said she was going to fly in but what with last minute bookings and everything and me being the procrastinator I am she won't be in until after the surgery and I was wondering if you could arrange for someone to pick her up?"

"If it's after the surgery I can go and get her."

"I don't want you to be burdened."

"I think you don't want me talking to your mother." Jamie laughed. "Is there a reason behind that?"

"I told her about Mel."

"What did you say?"

"I had found the woman she would love to have as a daughter in law."
"Wow."

CHAPTER SIXTEEN

"Miguel." Luis called as he walked in to his older half-brother's house. Since leaving the medical building where Cara had been taken and seeing her laying there her eyes open but not seeing anything, it was an image he still couldn't shake out of his head. It had been the whispers from two of the island police about how sadistic and sexual the murder had been that was making him question what the hell was going to be coming to him.

"Miguel." He shouted again and saw him sitting out on the back porch looking out to the other end of the bay where the islands main town lay, Port Elizabeth, the name sounded like shackles rattling to his ears. "I was looking for you."
"You found me." Miguel sat there a glass of amber liquid, no doubt whiskey in his hands. "I wanted to see how you were."
"My wife was murdered; how do you think I am doing?" There was no snap to the voice as he had expected, no emotion at all. "I'm sorry." Luis chocked out. He really wanted to tell his brother what was going on, get some help because he just knew deep down he was next but just as their father favored Miguel, Miguel would never believe

anything bad about his father. He would have to explain how he knew, explain that his wife was really sleeping with him instead of whatever excuse she gave him, that she was a money hungry whore and had said time and time again that she couldn't stand to be around her useless husband.

"I'd just like to be alone." Miguel downed the last of his liquor and got up coming to stand right in front of his little brother. "I want you to leave."
"I think you need to stop drinking and maybe come with me, maybe we could go over to see Dad? You shouldn't be alone."
"Is that what you think? Since when do you care?" Miguel started walking in to the house and stopped at the side table on his way to refill his glass. "Was it you that told the details to the press?" He held up the morning's paper, the one that held all the gruesome details. "Of course not."
"Say's here, Cara was having an affair with someone, some female came forward to say she was with Cara the night of the murder with a man she won't name and doing things I didn't think Cara was in to. Seems I knew nothing about my own wife, the cops will make me for the murder because of how she was killed and with the witness accusing her of adultery."
"Dad won't let them take you to jail."
"They won't get a chance to."

"What do you mean?" Luis came closer.
"I'm going to find this female, this witness and I'll find out who the man was and then I'll have his

balls. No one gets away with making me look stupid. Then when I've taken care of that I'll go back to the states."

"Why don't you go back now, Vince and I can take care of your revenge."

"No, I need to see this through." Luis's gut twisted, this was not his older brother, the one of them that was so not really bad at all. He didn't have it in him to hurt anyone no matter whose genes he had.

"Then let me help you with this."

"Why? You didn't even like Cara."

"It's family, this is what we do."

Miguel walked back to where he had been with a full glass of whiskey, the air was heating up and the sky was turning the blue of the summer. Luis was trying to play it cool; he couldn't let his brother know the truth now. He had to find the female he and Cara had played with, the one who would tell everything for the right price. He couldn't afford to pay her off, aside from his meager allowance; their father held all the real money and would become suspicious if he withdrew too much. The only thing for him to do was find her and get rid of her, he couldn't wait around for Miguel to find out and come for him.

XXX   XXX

"I'm back." Beth shouted coming in to the villa, she was sweating and her tank top felt wet and horrible as the air conditioning hit it. The walk had done her good; she was feeling better than when she left. She knew her biggest problem was not with John but that she had come to this beautiful place so she could get as much sex as she could with the man she thought cared enough about her to leave his wife for the vacation. She knew now she would have to settle on a friend and not a lover and it was wrong of her to put her disappointment on John who wasn't even part of her previous plans.

"You look beat." John said looking up from the magazine Beth had been reading before she left. "I feel beat, the sun's blazing, I think I might go for a swim, want to come?"
"Did you get what we needed from the store?" He looked at the bag she was carrying; it was one of those canvas tote ones all eco-friendly people used. "Actually, they didn't have the adapter I needed but the store owner is getting one shipped in for me, it should be here late tomorrow."
"What's one more day?" John sighed, after putting the magazine down.
"Read anything interesting in there?" Beth smiled pointing at the latest issue of Cosmo. "I learnt fifty-seven new sex positions that will satisfy my man." He joked back. "Well, you might find this more interesting." She threw the islands newspaper on to the counter. "The man at the store his sister works for this family and it's all been scandalous, though he say's scandal is always rife with the man who controls most of this island and has interests on one not far from here. I figured if you were some big law officer, here to get info on someone,

these would be my number one family."

John looked at the front page of the newspaper laid out before him. Beth had hit the nail on the head; this had been the family he had been getting information on. He tried hard to keep his face neutral as he read how the daughter in law of Mr. Santos had been brutally murdered. The reporter had somehow gotten the gritty details of the extent of damage her body had been exposed to by the person who had brutally 'shot her in her vagina and the bullets had ravaged their way through her body damaging nearly all her vital organs, she had bled to death in minutes'. Knowing what he did about the family he knew which one of the family was capable of something this heinous. Well, not a blood relation to the family but more the man who was right hand to the man in charge.

"Did you read this?" John asked.
"I sure did. Everyone in town is talking about it. The store owner said his sister was there when the police arrived."
"This is all very interesting."
"Tell me why you say that. Was I right, was it them you were tailing?"
"Tailing?" John had to laugh. "I can't tell you either way but I have to say this is very interesting."
"Come on, just a little something."
"Beth, until today I had never heard of these people." He smiled and she smiled back.
"Liar but I won't ask anymore."
"Good, we are going to have to be extra careful, we

have some people coming to stay next door. We'll have to play the happy couple, if that's okay with you?"

"I think I could handle that; how do you know someone's coming?"

"The woman who cleans the houses on Fridays was there getting the place ready and saw me and came over to talk, that's why I'm in here and not out there getting some sun."

"I'm going out; I need to get some sun so when I go back to Boston people don't think I really went to Maine for my vacation."

"I might come in a bit."

"Good, I'll need someone to put some oil on my back."

"Let me change in to a pair of cargo shorts." He got up.

"Oh, hold on." Beth rummaged in her bag from the store. "I knew you didn't have a bathing suit after last night and no one should have to wear sweats on a day like this so here." She took out a small plastic bag and handed it to him. "Beth." He said as his hand went inside and came in to contact with some material, he pulled it out and was speechless. She had got him a bathing suit alright. One of those Speedo's only men in Europe wore to the beach.

"Okay." He said and she cracked up.

"Come on, you're meant to be hiding out, who would be looking for a macho American wearing a garment like that?"

"Sometimes I wonder where you get these bits of wisdom."

"Cosmo." She laughed harder. "Come on, wear it."
"I think I'll stick with the cargos."
"Chicken."

XXX   XXX

Nick had been waiting for them when they arrived at the Delta terminal. He was discreetly standing at the end of the drop off bay smoking and Mel had felt the heat Matt was feeling towards this man. It had been odd pretending to be her sister. Even Nick had looked thrown by the way she looked. Matt had given her the same speech her sister had. Unless it was a situation of life and death there was to be nothing more than hand holding between them. That was fine with her; she wasn't attracted to Matt and didn't see what her sister obviously did.

They had been handed tickets and nothing more aside from an address of where they had been booked to stay until they found out what happened to Robert. Taking the first Delta flight from San Diego to Philadelphia, Pennsylvania where they switched to a USAIR flight to Barbados. They sat there next to each other inside the terminal waiting for the SVG Air flight over to Bequia, their final destination neither had really said more than a few words to one another since they had left. Mel was nervous about going to where they might find Rob dead and on the other side worried about what was going on with Steve back in San Diego. All through the day she had been looking at her watch and wondering what he was doing.

"Do you think Steve would be out of surgery now?" She asked Matt, his eyes were closed but she knew he wasn't asleep; he had taken a combat nap during the flight to Philly and had been restless since. "I guess he would be."
"Think it's okay for me to call?"
"Sure, I'd call your sister first to make sure everything went good first."
"Good idea." She took out her cell phone and Matt went back to looking at the inside of his eyelids. She wondered how Jamie could live with such a none talker it would drive her nuts. Pressing the preprogrammed number, she heard the phone ring twice and then her sister's voice. "If it isn't my husband stealing sister." Jamie laughed down the line. "Very funny, are you being me now?"
"Ah, no one could be like you, you are an anomaly."
"I would tell you what you are but then I might get hit by the person next to me."

"How was your journey and where are you going?" Jamie asked.
"Can I tell her where we are going?" Mel covered the mouthpiece and asked Matt.
"I can't see why not; tell her I'll call her when you get off with her."
"Matt said he'd call you when we are done. We are on our way to the Grenadines."
"That's it? Good, I had visions of you being in a more dangerous location. Any problems with

anything you borrowed from me?"

"Of course not, why would anyone question it? I mean I know our hair color is a little different but everything else is pretty much the same."

"Aside from our eyes and the tattoo you decided to get when you were eighteen we pretty much are. How are the contacts doing?"

"Getting dry, I think from the high altitude or maybe because I just don't like them. I think they'll be out while we are there."

"Ask Matt about it. He might think you should keep them in."

"Yes Mom." Mel laughed.

"I called to ask how Steve did today." Mel's tone changed and she heard Jamie sigh.

"He did great. He got out of surgery an hour ago, it took a little longer than we expected, he's still sedated and I'm on my way to get his mother, she just flew in and she got a place over on Coronado Island and wanted to be there for when he woke up."

"His mother?" Her question even made Matt pay attention.

"Yeah, should be interesting seeing as she knows a lot about you."

"She does?"

"That's what he said."

"You said the surgery took longer, was there a problem?"

"No, Dr. Harmon just wanted to make sure the replacement to the bones was secure and strong, he's sure Steve can be strong again for active duty."

"That's great isn't it?"

"Yes, as long as he sticks to the therapy."

"Can I call him later?"

"Call the hospital switch board and they'll put you through to whatever room he has been put in."

"Thanks, I'll talk to you later and I'm sure your phone will ring the minute I hang up."

"Actually, could you put him on quickly now?"

"Sure."

Mel passed the phone over and Matt took it feeling odd using a pink cell phone but couldn't see any of the people in the terminal looking at him so he relaxed a little. "Hey." He said looking forward to hearing his wife's voice. "Hi, everything going okay?"

"It's what I thought it would be." He was vague what with Mel looking right at him.

"Look, I'm picking Steve's mom up from her hotel, I'm almost there I didn't want you to call while I was with her, I'm guessing she'll have a load of questions I'll need to focus on. Can I call you later?"

"Sure. Have you heard from Izzy?"

"She left me a voice mail saying she was wearing her favorite princess dress while having lunch with some real princesses. She's having a blast. I asked my dad to call you and let her speak to you so expect that to happen."

"I can't wait." He smiled and Mel frowned. "Steve's okay?"

"He's strong and did well in surgery. Don't tell Mel

but he went through a procedure before to save his sperm for future use."

"He did not." Matt almost choked.

"He did. Hey, I'm at the Island inn I'll speak to you later. I love you."

"Me too." He hung up and just grinned while he passed the phone back to Mel.

"What?"

"Oh, I promised not to tell."

CHAPTER SEVENTEEN

Lying out on the sand she had not expected to see him come out. She wasn't sure how long he had been there but his shadow was what made her aware he was there. Resting on her elbows and looking up, shielding her eyes from the sun she gasped as she began to laugh and gave herself instant hiccups. Standing there, hands on hips was John wearing nothing but his little black Speedo.

"It looks as bad as it feels I'm guessing." He simply said laying out the towel he had brought down with him. "If it makes you feel any better you make it work."

"I make it work?" The smile she loved had returned to his cheeks and his dimples were showing. "You have the body for it."

"I do?"

"Yeah, if you were some big muscle freak you'd look weird and if you were gangly you'd look weirder. You Mr. Doe were made to wear something like that." She rolled over on to her back and heard his intake of breath but with her eyes now facing the blistering sun she wasn't about to open them to see what was wrong so she asked.

"What? Wedgey?" She joked.
"No." His voice sounded different. "I didn't realize." He began and she sat up, again on her elbow but resting on her butt. "Didn't realize what?"
"You were so um." He stammered and she remembered she was topless. She decided to play it off. "I don't like tan lines."
"I see."
"Am I making you nervous again?" She lay back down.
"A little but it's nice to see a good set of."
"Now you sound like a normal male." She cut him off and she heard him lay down not more than a foot from her. "Need me to oil you up?" He offered looking at her for a reaction, the sun was behind him and he was able to get a longer look at everything she was displaying and he couldn't fight it, she was a well-built woman and there wasn't an ounce of fat anywhere.

"Are you getting enough of a look?" Her head turned towards him and they weren't that far away, her left eye was shut and her face squinted a little but it didn't make her face look awful like it would some women. "I think it's only fair seeing as this bathing suit leaves nothing to the imagination." He watched her sit up and look down to his crotch.

"Like I said, you make it look good." She reached up and let her hair out of the twist she had, pulling the elastic out and putting it on her wrist. "I think I need to cool down." She got up and he watched her, wondering if the word game they were playing was leading to something else, wondering if she was strong enough to handle another sexual relationship that would not go anywhere beyond this island because he knew right now he could go for that, anything to get his last girlfriend out of his head.

Knowing it was a mistake before he even pushed himself up off the towel he was off walking down as she surface dived under a wave and came up as the first wave hit his feet, she turned to see if he had come down and he was there still looking at her, to tease him she put her hands up above her head making her chest protrude more. "Can you see any lines?" She asked over the sound of the waves.

"Nope." He was still moving closer his eyes transfixed with hers and she held her breath. "I can't promise you anything, no future, no relationship outside of this situation, if you don't want this to continue say so now." He stopped with the water just above his knees she was in just below her bikini bottoms. "I don't want promises."

"I've heard that before."

"I'm not your ex and you're not mine. This situation is different, don't we want people to think you are here with me and not some washed up on the shore no named agent of the law hiding out?"

"You have a point." He came closer and she didn't move even the wave coming back and forth couldn't move her. "I just want to make sure it's clear."

"Very."

He gently pushed his fingers into her hair, keeping the eye contact until he felt her body relax a little and her eyes close for a second, moving his lips closer so that he could feel her indrawn breath on the lips he had just made sure were wet and not as dry as he had thought they were.

She leaned closer, what she had wanted for her vacation was coming true, this man; this enigma of a man was giving her the chance to have the roll in paradise. When his lips finally came in to contact with hers she slowly moved her arms up and around his neck, he was taller then she had realized and she felt his hands release her hair and she was worried for a split second that he was going to stop but as he ran his hands down her back slowly the feeling sent a shiver down her spine and her mouth opened slightly and her head tilted back, with her eyes closed she didn't know what he was doing, she was enjoying the moment too much to care until his mouth and tongue came in to contact with her sensitive neck, again a shiver chilled her and this time his mouth recaptured her mouth and his tongue found hers as it flicked around softly. She felt the moan escape his throat as did hers and she was melting, he was slow and gentle but had the touch of a strong man who knew what he wanted and how to get it.

"We have the beach to ourselves." She said as he left her mouth again to go back to her neck. "Aha." He mumbled as his tongue again ran from just behind her ear to the tip of her collar bone. "We're going to do this here?" She loved feeling his hands roaming up and down her back. "Maybe a little further in." His hands dipped back down and to her butt before spreading out to her thighs and picking her up, she could feel every inch of him, every inch and more. She instinctively wrapped her legs around his waist until she was just slightly aware of the rising water level. He let go of her legs and in her ear said. "Put your legs down." Without saying anything she moved her legs down and before her toes could reach the ocean floor she felt his fingers untying the material that had been covering her most intimate of places.

Beth had her arms around him and knew what he was doing, taking his own bathing suit bottoms off. She was hesitant; her mind was mush but not past the point of remembering protection. "We need a condom." She couldn't believe she'd said the words. "Shit." He breathed out leaning his head on her shoulder.
"I have some back at the house."
"Okay."
"Think you can make it back up there?"
"I know I can." He reached behind his head to take

her hands and in a quick move he had her over his shoulder in a fireman carry, picking up their floating bathing suits on the way in and then their towels as they reached them. At the deck he put her down and got his first real look at all of her, she was even more beautiful than he thought she would be. "Change your mind?" He asked watching her look him over.

"Not a chance."

"Good, because I have the forty-fourth Cosmo position in my head that I would really like to try." He took her mouth again with his as he lifted her back up and used his foot to push the door to the villa open.

XXX   XXX

"I'm here to pick up Mrs. White." Jamie said standing before the inn's reception desk, the male receptionist didn't blink an eye seeing her in her naval uniform, there were very few places near the base that didn't see someone in a military uniform, it was an everyday thing. "She's waiting for you over in the bar." He pointed to a woman they could see clearly from where they were. "Thank you."

Walking over to the bar, her keys and cell phone in her hand she came closer to the woman who had just turned and seen her coming closer. She finished her drink and got down from the stool as she put her glass down. "Mrs. White?" Jamie asked standing before her a woman she would never have been able to guess the looks of and if she had she would have been completely wrong. Compared to Steven's sleek six feet and broad shoulders, dark hair and smolderingly dangerous at times eyes, his smirky smile that told you he knew it all because he had seen it all and a penchant for anything raunchy this woman was no taller than five-two, a hundred pounds soaking wet, dark blonde hair and dressed like a mother should in sensible pants and blouse. Her blue eyes held no hidden tales and there was nothing but a polite smile on her face.

"You must be Jamie." She held out her hand and Jamie accepted it giving it a firm but gentle shake. "Yes Ma'am. I hope your flight was comfortable."
"I was anxious all the way here, how is Steven doing?"
"I left him in recovery to come here, his surgery went well and he should be just coming too when we get there. He was hoping to see you when he woke up."
"This has to be the first time in years he's needed me, it's almost odd."
"Everyone needs their mothers Ma'am whether they let them know or not."
"Please, stop with the Ma'am and Mrs. White stuff. Call me Linda."
"Okay, Linda." Jamie replied the other woman's smile with one of her own.
"You are just beautiful, I imagine your sister is too, you are identical correct?" She asked as they began to make their way out to where Jamie had left her year-old Escalade SUV.

"Thank you, aside from a few differences, small ones we are the same yes."

"What does your sister do?"

"She was in the Marines." Jamie wasn't going to go in to that subject any further. "She's been working for a local photographer for a while now."

"I see; she didn't want to advance in a field like medicine like you?"

"I don't know what Steve has told you about us, we are very different women who just happen to look alike and share DNA. We've lived two separate lives and with no offense you can't really grill me like this it isn't fair to my sister. You should meet her and see how she makes your son happy and then make a judgment."

"I'm sorry; I shouldn't have put you on the spot. I was just looking forward to meeting her." Linda had stopped and put a hand on Jamie's arm, her eyes conveyed how sorry she was. "I hear she's away for a few days."

"Yes."

Jamie unlocked the door with her remote clicker and opened the door for Linda closing it and walking around blowing a sigh out before she opened her own door getting in and starting the engine. She looked at the clock and it was just before six. "Did you eat?" Jamie asked.

"I had a bite on the plane." Jamie waited for the other woman to click her seat belt before she pulled out. "Are you hungry? I was going to go and get something later, eat in my office; you're more than welcome to join me."

"No one to go home to?"

"My husband and daughter are away for a long weekend, just father and daughter."

"How old is your daughter?"

"Three." Jamie pulled the SUV out in to the traffic which was flowing steadily.

"Such a sweet age."

"It is, I'm enjoying it. I have pictures of everyone in my office; I'd like to show you."

"I'd like that." For the first time she sounded happy and Jamie found herself wondering what was going on in this woman's head.

CHAPTER EIGHTEEN

"What did Miguel do today?" Mr. Santos sat behind his desk leaning back a glass of brandy in his hand. His most loyal friend and employee Vince was there letting him know all he missed while he was over in Saint Vincent for the day doing some business, that's what everyone but Vince knew it as. To the two of them it was when he went over to spend some time with his latest in the line of young whores willing to please for the money he paid them.

"He stayed home for most of the day, Luis went and visited him and left after twenty minutes. Miguel made two calls, one to the police to find out when the body will be released and the second to the islands funeral home asking them to take care of all the arrangements. The maid said he was drinking a fair bit and he ended up going out to the town for an hour, he went to a couple of the big hotels and asked around a bit for that girl who was with Cara and Luis."

"Did he find her?"

"He won't find her." Vince grinned recalling the memory of squeezing the life from that slim neck before disposing her in a place where no one would ever find her. "I made sure neither of them would."

"Good and the police where are they looking for answers on Cara's murder?"

"Where we tell them to, nowhere near Miguel, something he is concerned about."

"Keep on both of the boys. I have a feeling I will have to have a talk with Luis before the week is through. Anything else?"

"The couple in villa two are settling in and there's another couple coming in late tonight, they booked yesterday."

"Any information on them?"

"Both in the navy, one's a doctor; the other is a training instructor. Both from San Diego, married for four years, one daughter." He read from the notes he had made earlier. "Suspicious?"

"Nothing that stands out, the agent that booked their tickets with us says it was a last minute booking because the husband has just returned from Iraq and they wanted to get away."

"Do you think we should keep an eye on them?"

"Like the other couple I don't think they are worth it."

"Good. Has there been any body recovered from our swimming CIA agent yet?"

"Nothing. It's possible the tide took him out and the fish are eating him."

"There's no way he made it to shore?"

"I can't see how. He was unconscious when he went in and we were three miles out."

"Keep an eye out for anything, I can't afford to have him wash ashore and raise questions." He took a sip from his large glass. "Where is Luis right now?"

"Down at the hotel."

"Make sure he comes home tonight. Call him and tell him I want to see him at seven tomorrow, I'll have him do some errands, that should clue him in, that he's on my shit list."

"Yes boss."

XXX   XXX

"Are there bugs here?" Mel asked stepping off the small plane and on to the tarmac lit by only a few scattered flood lights near the small terminal. There had been five of them on the plane including the pilot and it had been the most uncomfortable ride she had ever had, aside from the transports used in the military. "Define bugs."

"Anything that bites, stings or is bigger than a quarter."

"Yes, yes and yes."

"Excellent." She sighed trying to take everything around them in; although it was dark she knew which way the ocean was and could smell its saltiness. "Let's get the bags and then the car and we'll get to where we're going and settle in, we have a busy day tomorrow." It was one of the biggest sentences he had said to her all day.

She did as he asked and after a quick stop in to some very nice air conditioning they were inside a rental car, a nice American made car that smelled as new as it looked. The man at the car rental had given them a map of the island and it wasn't such a hard place to navigate around, there were less roads than in her condo development and the beach their villa was on was at the other end of the road from the airport. Once they pulled in to the driveway, lights shining from the front door and through the bushes from the lights from the neighboring villa she felt a little more at ease. For the first time since they left she could ask Matt what their plan was, what they were going to do once the sun came back up.

"Go and unlock the door, I'll bring the bags in." He said turning the car off and without a reply she did as she was asked. They had been told they would find the key under a flower pot on the steps so she began the search of the six, three on either side and each one just as heavy as the other. On the fourth pot she found it and opened the door just as Matt got there with their two bags. "Damn." She said flipping on the lights bringing the open living room and kitchen in to view noticing the large glass doors at the other end from where she was she was guessing the beach lay beyond them. "This is nice." Matt put the bags down and as he closed the door she went towards the back door.

The furniture and the color in the house were all warm and neutral; everything was pine and white with soft coral colors on the fabrics. The kitchen was what she liked, a big gas stove and a fridge she couldn't wait to stock with water and cookie dough, her latest weakness since Steve had insisted she quit smoking, a habit that she had been doing for seventeen years of her life and it had been hard but she loved him and wanted him more than anything else.

After a quick turn of the brass knob on the doors she opened them up to reveal the crashing waves they hadn't heard from where the car was parked. The moon was out, the stars shone in the sky and she heard the sounds of, she felt herself blush and walked backwards from the deck to the house about to close the doors back up when her back came in to contact with something. "What's wrong?" Matt asked holding on to her elbows. "Our neighbors are having sex." She couldn't turn around; she could feel her cheeks burning. "Really?" Matt let her go and went out to where she had been on the deck. "Wow, they are and they're noisy." He smiled and Mel had to laugh. "Please don't tell me that turns you on."
"Why does it turn you on?" He turned the question around.
"No, it makes me wonder what they're doing to make her scream like that."

"Want me to go see?" He started towards the deck stairs and Mel grabbed him pulling him back in towards the door. "Don't you need to call your wife?"

"She's calling me but I do need to plug it in." He went back inside and Mel remained there for just a minute listening to the sounds of the love making flowing on the night breeze.

"There's only one bedroom with a full bath in there and the couch out here. The bedroom has a shower and a toilet en-suite and there's just a toilet out here. I'll take the couch but we have to make sure that we leave no signs of me not sleeping in there in case someone comes here."

"I guess Jay wouldn't like us sharing a bed."

"We're not sharing a bed." He didn't even look over as he plugged in his phone.

"You won't even consider it."

"With you acting and looking like my wife." He paused for effect. "No."

"Am I really acting like her?"

"Yeah, and it's a little weird."

"A little."

"Look, I came so Jamie wouldn't have to, make sure Robert was found and to keep an eye on you Mel, I know you don't particularly like me, so let's deal with what we have to do, can you do that."

Shocked Mel had to speak. "Who says I don't like you?"

"Mel, it's written all over your face every time you look at me." He frowned while standing with his hands on his hips. "And with you looking like Jamie it makes me very confused. I love my wife more than I can ever explain to you, Jamie and I, I don't want anything to break that."

"Spending a few days here with me won't hurt it."

"As long as when we're here you act like yourself and only act like her when we're out together in public then we should be fine."

"I'm sorry."

"It's not your fault you were born looking like my wife."

"Thanks." She smiled sitting down. "I'm glad you understand my unfortunate DNA crisis."

"Is it really that bad being identical to someone?"

"Only when you tell me everything will be fine if I don't act like her."

"It's just very weird Mel."

Mel's phone began to ring and she dashed for it. She had left her number with the nurse on duty at the hospital and had been waiting for Steve to call when he came too. "Hello." She said not sure she had even pressed the on button right in her haste.

"Hey." Steve's sleepy voice said softly over the line.

"Steve, oh my God, how are you?"

"Sore, tired. How was your journey? Jay was just here she said you were in the Grenadines."

"We are, some small island where our neighbors are out on their back deck having wild sex. It's turning Matt on." She laughed. "Are you in much pain?"

"Your sisters keeping me pretty doped up, how loud are they being?"

"Loud. What has the specialist and Jamie said about everything?"

"Supposedly the amount of bone they had to remove was smaller than first thought, it's in traction right now and it's covered in bandages but I can see the pins sticking out. Jamie said they'll make me stay here in this bed for a week and then start me on my physical therapy routine."

"You'll have chemo right?"

"There are some radioactive wafers in my leg and depending on the blood work in the next few days depends on what they'll do."

"I wish I could have been there for you."

"Hey, do what you need to do, there's plenty of time for you to help nurse me. There's going to be a lot of things I'll need help with for a long time."

"Still, I should have stayed." She noticed how Matt had gone back to the back door and was standing out, the soft sounds of love making filtering in on the breeze. "Forget about it, I'm just glad you aren't in some war country again. My mom gave your sister the third degree about you and she said she had to firmly tell her to wait to meet you."

"I hope I can, you don't say very much about her, I'd like to meet her and find out some stuff about you."

"Lord help me." He laughed and Mel smiled hearing the sound. "By the way, I hear you know the doctor who was cutting me apart earlier."

"Who?"

"Dr. Harmon."

"No way, Jim Harmon huh? I haven't heard about

him in years. He was a teacher of Jamie's during med school right?"

"Yep, was there ever anything between them?"

"Romantically?" Mel scoffed. "As if, he's married to some beautiful woman and they have kids and if there was anything it was one sided."

"On Jamie's side?"

"No, she was still brooding over Robert back then."

Damn, Mel thought. She hadn't thought about those times in a long while.

"Was there something that made you ask?"

"Yeah, the way he looked at her when they were in with me before and after the surgery."

"He probably finds her as attractive as most men do."

"Not all men."

"You find her attractive; you'd have to if you are attracted to me."

"No, you and she are really different."

"Right now we're the same. Me dressed in Jamie's stuff is driving Matt nuts."

"Give him a break, he needs it. Having everything on his mind he does and then going to some sunny locale with someone who looks like his wife but isn't when there should be romance and plenty of sex is hard on a man. Let him do what he needs to do and you'll both be back in no time."

"What's on his mind?" She wondered what was going on with her brother in law.

"You know, Jamie and how she's dealing with everything."

"Obviously I don't know. What's going on with my

sister?"

"Hmm, maybe I should have kept my mouth shut. Can I blame it on the drugs?"

"Please, tell me. Is it something serious, are they separating or something?"

"Nothing like that, they love each other way too much."

"Then tell me."

"I already said too much. You should ask." Mel was listening while watching Matt answer his own ringing cell.

"I don't think he'll tell me; he thinks I don't like him."

"I know, sometimes I don't think you do either."

"I don't understand; why do you think that? I mean I don't see what Jay does but he's a great guy, a good husband, a good father, he treats her like a queen."

"Sometimes you say things that I think you mean as a joke but men take it a little differently."

"Like what?"

"Remember when you made a joke two weeks ago about how he cooks a lot and it was a woman's job."

"Yeah, but he's a great cook."

"He thought you were insinuating he was gay. There's also that time when they were doing the kitchen and he had chosen a color and you had point blank asked him if he were color blind because it looked like something you found in a baby diaper."

"I'm sorry, that color did."

"Still, you do butt heads with him a lot. I think while you are down there you should really talk with him Mel."

"I think I should too."

"And when you do listen, really listen."

"Jees, should I take offense to that?"

"No, you know I love you."

"You do?"

"Shut up." He laughed. "Hey, the nurse is back to dope me up some more. I'll call you tomorrow."

"Say hi to your Mom for me."

"Night."

"Night Steve, I love you."

"Me too."

With the phone call disconnected she turned her attention back to Matt, everything Steve had said was worrying her. The fact she was coming across as mean to him and obviously hurting his feelings and something that was wrong with her sister and Matt was being strong and quiet about whatever it was. He was out on the back deck, his back leaning against the railing and his head was lowered. With the sound of the waves she couldn't hear anything he was saying.

CHAPTER NINETEEN

His daughter had called first, it was a quick call, she sounded tired but excited about everything she had been doing with her grandparents. Her voice made him smile and his heart ached, he didn't spend as much time with her as he'd like but at the same time it was her little face he thought of when away, along with her mother's that gave him the strength in hard times to find whatever it took to make it home after any away mission safe.

As he was ending the call with Izzy, his phone beeped letting him know another call was coming in. Looking quickly at the caller ID it showed the pre-programmed name, it was Jamie. "Hey you." He said.

"Hey you back." She sounded like she was in a good mood, the last few months she had been up and down with her emotions, not that he had even been in town for most of it. He had wondered if maybe the being away was causing a problem between them but when he had asked her she had said she had just been very pre-occupied with work and she was sorry. "And how is the patient? Did you leave him?"

"I did. I just dropped his mother back at her hotel and I'm on my way home to a very quiet and alone house. He's doing good; oh Matt the chance he can return to active duty is so much higher now."

"Wow, that's great."

"It is, but I can't promise he'll be SEAL material, now as long as he gets all the therapy he needs and does it when we tell him and not before and push himself too much, if the cancer doesn't come back and it goes like we plan, he'll have over an eighty percent strength in his knee."

"That's great to know. So what are you going to do

when you get home?"

"Go for a swim I think."

"I'll picture you in your bikini later when I'm asleep."

"You and that old bikini." She laughed. "How long ago did you get to your place of operations?"

"About an hour ago. The place is right on the beach, its dark so we can't see too much but what I have seen it looks nice. I'll take some pictures and email them to your office."

"I can't wait to see what it looks like."

"What are you doing tomorrow? Still working with Steve?"

"No, I have my yearly physical again."

"Already. I thought you had one only a few months ago?"

"No, that was the dentist."

"Oh. Izzy just called me."

"She left me another message. I called dad but he said she was already passed out and I didn't want them to wake her, he promised they would all first thing tomorrow. So, what's the first plan of attack for the big hunt?"

"Go in to town, look around, check out the news for the area. Generally, just get a feel for the place."

"I hope nothing bad happened to him."

"You know Robert. He always ends up landing on his feet."

"I suppose. I'm home and it's all dark." He heard the engine of the car turn off.

"I'll let you go, get some sleep and I'll call in tomorrow."

"I love you." Jamie purred and his heart beat faster.

"I love you too, Goodnight Jamie."
"Goodnight."

Closing his phone, he realized the sounds of sex over at the neighbors was all gone, all the lights were off from what he could see. Mel was over on the couch still but she was watching him and he felt tired to the bone, she was exhausting, all the way here she had been talking non-stop, at one point he had to fake a combat nap just to make her shut up. Unlike Jamie who seemed to think before she spoke, Mel did not, verbal diarrhea of the mouth is what he had laughed at Jamie calling it.

Entering the villa, closing and checking the lock on the door, he walked towards her making sure she wasn't on the phone still, seeing it sat on the coffee table. "How's Steve?"
"Sounds good, how's Jamie?"
"Just got home, I'm going to go and use the bathroom."
"Matt." She said as he was walking in to the only bedroom.
"Yes."
"Is everything okay with you and Jamie?" She watched him stop dead in his tracks but not turn.
"Why would you ask?" He stayed looking the other way.
"Something Steve said."
"What did Steve say?" Matt turned around his hands had gone back to his hips and his eyebrows were raised. "That I should give you a break because of everything on your mind, when I asked

him what he meant he said because of everything going on with Jamie and how she's dealing with it."
"Steve shouldn't have said anything."
"Anything about what, is there something wrong? Is she sick too, are you and her having problems, is it Izzy?"

"Mel, please stop." He held up his hands and she stood up.
"Matt, I'm family, I'm her sister and I should know whatever it is."
"She didn't want you to know and I only told Steve because I had to talk to someone, he had no right to say anything to you."
"What is it, tell me." She knew she was pleading and she never did that, it felt odd.
"Mel, I'm not telling you and I don't want you bringing this up ever again, especially not to your sister."
"Is she dying? Are you or Izzy?"
"Mel." He saw how she jumped from his harsh tone. "I'm sorry."
"Please." She begged again and something in her face and voice made a lump come to his throat.
"Fine, but you never heard this and you repeat it or let Jamie know you know I'll take you out on Lee's boat and leave you far, far away with nothing but a life vest."
"I believe you would too."
"Do you promise?"
"I do."

Matt waved for her to sit down and upon moving

her cell he sat opposite her on the coffee table. "You know how much having Izzy made Jamie feel good and special, like she had made something good."

"Of course."

"A year later she became pregnant again."

"She did." Mel's mind wasn't keeping up with what he was saying and he sat there quiet just looking in her eyes while it sank in. "Oh God." She covered her mouth.

"Exactly."

"When, how far?"

"The second month."

"Do you know why?"

"The doctor said it just wasn't time for another child so Jamie tried to deal with it and it was right before the team and I were overseas for a few months and when I came back she wasn't accepting it very well, she blamed herself and thought something would take Izzy too. I took her to a friend who's a psychologist and female to female they talked and Jamie began to believe she wasn't to blame, it wasn't her past coming back to bite her in the ass, you know all the bad stuff with that guy Atwa. She started taking birth control and we hadn't brought the subject up of us trying again until she made a joke about it the morning before we left which makes me wonder. We have Izzy, I'm happy, but she has it in her head we need more, I need a boy. And no I've never said that." He paused.

"Did you ask her about why she brought it up?"

"Nope, I've been too nervous to bring it up because she's been up and down again lately like there's something going on she isn't telling me, I asked her about that and she just told me it was work, a lot was going on"

"You think she might have been trying again without telling you?"

"That's been my thought and if she was I wouldn't care and I know the team's been back and forth a lot and I haven't been around but I would have hoped she would talk with me about it."

"Matt." Mel sat forward and unusually took his hands in hers. "Jamie loves you, probably more than you love her. She has her ideas, thoughts, wants and dreams and they all include you. Her world revolves around you and if she were trying again it would be to make you happy, which you just admitted it would. With what happened, and this comes from knowing her as long as I have she probably wants to save you from dealing with a lose if it happens again, she's going to make sure everything is going great and then surprise you. Jamie's not being sneaky she's caring about you because I bet although you are a tough SEAL. When you held her and told her everything would be okay after the miscarriage and she was in tears, you were in tears too, trying to hide them from her but she knew and she would have hated hurting you in that way."

"Thanks." Matt coughed out. "I don't know what just happened here but you just made a lot of sense."

"More than when you talked to Steve?"

"Almost."

XXX   XXX

"Holy shit." John rolled on to his back as Beth lay there a smile on her face, her lips red from kissing and totally naked like he was. They were laid out on the back deck on a blanket they had brought out. He had suggested going down to the sand but she hadn't been too thrilled about that and so this was their compromise. He wasn't sure how many times they had started and stopped in ecstasy or even what time it was but he was amazed he had been able to do it so many times; it was a definite record for him.

"I can't believe you could do that." She rolled on to her side and rested her head on her palm so she was sitting up a bit, not caring how her body was. "I could say the same for you." He sat up and looked back giving her his biggest dimple filled smile.

"What?"

"You are very limber." He laughed and she sat up leaning against his side and he wrapped the arm on that side around her, holding her close. "I was a ballerina when I was younger and I still practice but not as much as I'd like."

"Were you good?"

"At ballet? I was no Julliard scholar but I was good enough."

"My sister was a jazz dancer."

"Was?"

"She started suffering from MS when she was in her late teens, it got too hard for her to even walk."

"I'm sorry." Beth touched his knee but a question of whether it was a truth or a lie again hung in her mind and she knew he was thinking what she was thinking.

"Our neighbors have arrived." John changed the entire conversation to something neutral. "I wonder if they heard us?"

"The way you scream, I bet they did." He loved seeing her face flush and he passed her the robe she had come out in, the same big fluffy one she had worn to bed the night before. "Oh God."

"Hey, they're probably getting it on over there right now because we got them thinking about it." He wrapped the blanket from the floor around his waist and followed her in to the house. "Wow, it's ten, are you hungry?"

"A little, but I'd rather snack on you again."

"How about I fix some salad and sandwiches?"

"A man needs his energy." He put his hands on her hips while he walked behind her and in to the kitchen area. "I don't know if I have enough food to fill all of you up." She joked as she took things out of the fridge, the bag of lettuce, a carton of tiny tomatoes, a cucumber, a yellow pepper and the salad dressing. Next he watched her take out the things they'd use for sandwiches, the bread, deli meat, and mayo.

"Can I help with anything?"

"Why don't you read the rest of the paper I bought today, see if you can find anything interesting." Feeling let out of domestic duties, John walked over to where the newspaper sat at the breakfast bar, he returned to his stool and opened the first page to finish reading the write up on the murder of the daughter in law of the man he had been getting information on, Beth had been right. He became so engrossed in the words the reporter had written that he had no idea everything was made and ready to eat until Beth put the empty salad bowl before him and the big bowl with the salad in it next to him. A plate of neatly made triangle sandwiches also sat there looking too good to eat.

"Thank you." He said after he had finished his heaping of salad.

"You're welcome." She said finishing up what was in her mouth.

"My energy is nearly all recharged." He took a bite of one of the sandwiches.

"You'll have to let me catch up, unlike you I'm not used to these sex marathons."

"Hey, what makes you think I'm used to it?"

"Where else would you build the stamina up like you just did?"

"It's called months of hiding from my feelings about a woman and having no sex with anyone."

"Oh." Beth thought for a minute. "Well I'm glad I could help you get out of your rut, it really is selfish of me to enjoy your misfortune but I won't apologize for it."

"I'm glad."

"How long has it been?" She asked and he turned his head sideways, his ear length long hair falling down on one side. "Too long."

"A year, six months?"

"Two years, three months and sixteen days."

"Can I quote you on that?"

"I would, it's very accurate."

Finishing his third sandwich he felt her hand on his back. "I have something special for dessert so save some room."

"Tell me more about this dessert." He turned so he could see all of her as she got up to take away their empty plates and serving bowls. "It involves chocolate spread, peanut butter, whipped cream and I was going to add a banana but I think you have something I want more." She came back towards him.

"You have my attention." He winked.

"I want this." She ran her fingers gently across the material that covered the erection that was beginning to come back to life. "Do you really?" He whispered in her ear as he moved the hair back to kiss where she reacted so well. "I do."

"Then it's all yours."

CHAPTER TWENTY

Jamie entered her house, all the lights were off and there wasn't a sound to be heard. It was odd how her life had changed in just a few years, she knew things were bound to change but she didn't expect to have to go through everything that she had, if it hadn't been for Matt, with his love and support she would probably never have survived even the last two years. After they had lost the baby she had fallen apart inside and she hadn't been able to get it all together. The pain of guilt over backing away from her precious daughter for fear of losing her too cut deep every time she looked at her.

Turning on only the lights she needed, she walked in to the kitchen and opened the refrigerator door; the coolness against her skin stopped her for a second before she began looking through the Tupperware and packages for something she felt like snacking on. Deciding there was nothing there she felt like heating and eating she turned off the light in the kitchen, then the living room and then turned on the light on the stairs deciding to go up and maybe have a bath and soak for a while.

With the house still, the lamp on her bedside table on and the dim lights above the bathtub on she began to run the bath she had been thinking about. Her uniform she had been wearing with the exception of during surgery she took off and placed it with the others in the laundry basket marked for the dry cleaners and stood before the floor length mirror on the bathroom side of the door. In just her underwear she stood there looking at the woman she had become, her hair was longer than it used to be, unlike her sister who had cut hers shorter and added some brown where hers was still the same blonde it had always been. Her body wasn't as slim as she remembered it, Matt always told her she looked the same but she could see the differences. Standing next to her sister she knew them all too well.

But as she did look a feeling of being content filled her because she knew what was going on in the inside, that was more than worth what made her cringe about the outside. After the miscarriage, getting through the pain she had decided she couldn't let Matt go through that with her again. She saw how he was just as devastated by what happened. She could deal with something bad happening again if she just knew the pain would be only on her shoulders. But things were getting better, yesterday was the three-month mark to the baby growing inside her, she had only found out two weeks ago that she was even pregnant, it had been a total surprise. After the loss she had begun taking birth control but with the side effects and the feeling of being bloated all the time she had thrown them away and waited to see what their future held.

She had planned to tell Matt this weekend. With Izzy away and having time to themselves she knew if he did get mad at least no one else would feel his anger. She hoped she knew him well enough to know he'd be happy and not mad but like most women whose men were away during times of war and terrorism they didn't get to see enough of each other. Remembering the bath water was getting high she went over and shut it off, deciding to get her cell phone and calling her husband while she was awake and in need of some time to be honest with him.

Jamie lit the candles around the edge of the tub and shut off the overhead light, undressing and getting in the hot water she lay back and pressed the button that would dial her husband. "Hey." He said on the third ring, he sounded like he had been asleep. "Did I wake you?"
"Yeah, it's okay, is something wrong?"
"I hope not." She said and heard the sounds of waves get louder in the background.
"What does that mean? Are you okay?"
"I'm fine. There was something I was going to tell you this weekend while Izzy was away but you're not here so I thought." She trailed off and wasn't sure how to say it.
"Tell me what?" She heard the hesitation in his voice.
"We're pregnant again." She said aloud. There was no response on the other line aside from a slight muffled sound and she knew he was crying.

"Matt?" She felt the tears coming to her own eyes.
"Oh, Jamie, how long have you known?" His voice sounded pinched but closer to normal. "Two weeks. I found out right after you left the last time."
"How far along are you?"
"It was three months' yesterday."

"I thought you were on the pill."

"I didn't like the way it made me feel, I haven't taken it for over a year, I did tell you at the time." She felt like he was accusing her of something.

"Are you mad?"

"Not at all, this is just a shock. I wish I was there with you."

"Same here."

"Jamie."

"Yes Matt."

"I really am happy."

"Good."

"What does the doctor say? Have you seen him?" He was referring to her OBGYN.

"I saw him to confirm two weeks ago but I haven't been back, I guess I've been too nervous."

"Would you go for me tomorrow, I want to make sure you and the baby are doing well."

"Okay." He heard her sigh and wondered if she would.

"I'm hoping we'll find Robbie soon so I can get back and be with you."

"I'm sure you'll find him; I just hope Mel helps you."

"Actually I planned on leaving her here as much as I could and getting more leg work done."

"I'd feel better with her with you in case someone decides to do the same thing to you as what happened to him."

"I'll be safe, don't worry."

"I'm your wife, I love you, I'm allowed to worry."

"Fair enough" He chuckled and turned away from

the waves to see Mel stood there in her boxer
shorts and tank top.

"Mel's up, she must have heard my cell phone."
"Don't tell her just yet."
"I won't." Matt promised. "Thank you."
"For what?"
"Loving me."
"I think I should be the one to thank you for that,
I've put you through a lot."
"No you haven't, not when you count how much
I'm away and you are alone."
"You make me proud, I miss you when you're away
but I know it's what you do, it's one of the reasons
I married you." She paused. "You better go, get
some rest. I'll call you after I speak to the doctor."
"Goodnight sweetheart."
"Love you, goodnight."

Matt was very aware of Mel just standing there
looking at him, he was wearing only his boxer
shorts too and he came back inside of the villa. "I
heard the phone, is everything alright?"
"It was just Jamie, she wanted to talk."
"Oh." Mel fidgeted with her hands. "I'm sorry, I
thought."
"What?"
"It was news about either Robert or Steve."
"You know Steve is doing well, we won't be getting
any help with Robert, we're on our own for that."
He moved back over to the couch where he had set
up his bedding and she remained there. "Mel, go to
bed."

"I can't sleep." She said and he had laid out on the sheet he had spread across and was just about ready to pull the blanket over himself. "Why?" "Because this is stressing me out, Steve's surgery, Rob missing."
"Are you fidgeting because you need to drink or do some drugs to calm down?" He asked without turning and he didn't see her face but could imagine what it was. "That's not fair." She snapped. "No, but I have the right to question you seeing as something could go down and you're meant to be watching my back."
"I have been clean for twenty-six months."

Remembering the night over two years ago that Mel had arrived at their house in the middle of the night, it had been when they had found out that she and Rob had split up. Jamie had asked her where she had been because Rob had called looking for her four days before. She had been vague and insisted she just needed sleep. Setting her up in the spare bedroom he had returned to bed while her sister had stayed to talk to her. His head had just hit the pillow, full sleep calling from behind his eye lids and they had started arguing. Izzy, at just eleven months had woken to the sound and started to cry. He had gotten up again and snuggled with his daughter while the conversation in the next room continued. "Keep an eye on her and don't let her leave." Jamie had been so mad with anger when she came in to the nursery. "What's going on?" He asked while she took the baby and walked towards their bedroom. "She's high and I don't want her in the house. I'm going to change and take her over to the rehab at Harbor view."

"What if she tries to leave?"

"Use all force necessary."

Jamie had changed quickly in to sweat pants and shirt and taken Mel to the detox, she had spent thirty days there and since then everyone had gone out of their way to make sure she wasn't stressed out and in need of anything to keep her calm. So far it had worked but at the back of their minds they wondered when the next day would come. And right now Matt was hoping it wasn't this exact moment.

"And I repeat my question, are you fidgeting because you need a substance to abuse?"

"Fuck you Matt. I know I probably deserve that but a simple 'wanna talk about it' would have worked much better."

"Wanna talk about it?" He mimicked her and she was no longer in any mood to deal with him. She didn't know if he had done it on purpose but his question had made her mad and unable to think about either of the men. "No." She said walking back in to the bedroom and closing the door.

CHAPTER TWENTY-ONE

"Good morning father." Miguel said walking in to his father's study. The old man had always made a point to be in his chair going over papers and business reports well before the average man got up. He prided himself on it and expected those around him to do the same, especially his eldest son, the one who would one day take over the business.

"Miguel." He stated rather than a greeting, his face covered by the New York Times.
"I was hoping I could take the day off." He said waiting to see what his father would do. "Why?" His father lowered the paper, careful to make sure his coffee wasn't disturbed. "My wife was murdered; I have some things I need to take care of."
"They can wait."
"I'm taking the day off." For the first time he stood up to his father and turned to leave for effect. "If you walk out that door, don't think you can come back." The voice of authority simply stated and he stopped but didn't turn around. "This isn't up for negotiation." Miguel tried again.
"I know why you want this time off; you hope to look for the woman in the newspaper who knew about your wife and her lover." Turning back Miguel saw his father's grin. He hated that he was so well informed; sometimes he wondered if they were being followed and bugged or that his father just possessed powers in the sixth sense.

"Yes, I do."
"She was a whore who never loved anything more than the money you earned, you're better off

without her. I have a project for you to do later with Vince but right now I have more important things I need taken care of."

"She was my wife." Miguel felt his anger rising, no matter what Cara had been, she was still that. "If you want to call her that, go right ahead." He lifted his weight out of the antique leather desk chair that no one else would dare to sit in. "But I want to know where you and the others threw that CIA agent the other night, there's been no bodies washed up and I don't like sloppy work, that's what it was."

"We picked him up from his hotel over on Saint Thomas and took him about three miles south of Fort Recovery and tossed him overboard. He was unconscious from Luis's blow to the head; he probably sank and became fish food." His tone was sarcastic as he pointed to his fathers framed map of the islands.

"I want you and Vince on that boat and looking along our coast line for anything of this mans. I don't care what it is, a piece of clothing, a finger, hell even his bloated dead body but I want some proof that he's gone. I don't have to tell you how important this is do I?"

"No father."

"And Miguel, two things. One, you ever talk to me like that again and I'll deal with you myself. Second, you show up to my house to start work looking like you slept in the clothes you're wearing smelling of my antique scotch again and you'll be back in the states working a fast food joint to make money, you understand?"

"Clearly."

"Go find Vince and call me when you have something."

"Want us to take Luis?"

"No, I have other plans for him."

Mr. Santos watched his son walk away in the direction of the small house at the side of the property that his right hand man had lived in for the last fifteen years since he came to this island with him. Both of them running from the law but for two very different reasons. Vince, an excellent special forces ranger had been quite the killer, in and out of the battle field. There were more than twenty unsolved murders back in the eastern states of America with his signature to them. He himself had just been a leader of a gang of thugs in Miami, getting too big and too popular with the people in charge. When Miguel had been sixteen they had fled to the safety of this island because he had been accused of murder and embezzlement. For all these years he had been safe and he wasn't about to let that change.

"Gloria." He shouted to his house maid and like always she appeared in the doorway within seconds, he'd never had to shout twice and he appreciated that in a servant. "Yes Mr. Santos."

"Have you seen Luis this morning?"

"I believe he's still in bed sir."

"Thank you." He returned to his desk and prized chair and picked up the house phone that also connected every room in the house. He dialed his second son's number and was surprised to hear him awake. "I need you here in one minute."

"I was just coming down." He heard the line go dead and then the sounds of footsteps on the floor above. In less than the minute he had given him, Luis was there standing before his desk.

"Morning." Luis said looking at his father's face, he'd never see this one before and he knew whatever was to become of his affair with Cara, it was about to come now. "I know you were the man sleeping with Cara." Luis heard his father say and he knew already that the head of this house knew everything. "I was." He didn't deny.

"You have stones to admit this to me, but do you have the guts to admit it to your own brother?"

"Miguel?"

"Yes."

"Why would I do that?"

"A man always owns up to his mistakes."

"What good is it to Miguel whether he knows or not?"

"He needs to know so he can deal with this. I need his mind on his work."

"He'll kill me."

"And?" He watched his father and deep down knew this was the type of man who had sired him but it was still a shock to know his father didn't care. "I want you to tell him tonight. First though you are on market duty this morning." He was ordered and he knew he was getting the shit job, collecting rent from the hardworking islanders.

182

"Luis." His father called as he was leaving the office.

"Yes."

"If you don't tell him by midnight I will have the police arrest you for the murder of Cara."

XXX   XXX

Running was a way she usually burned stress and anger off but this morning it was a release of some of the muscles which had become tight and sore as she and her new lover made love over and over all night long. She had left him asleep in the bed that was now theirs and had so far ran half the length of the five-mile cove, slowing down for the clusters of rocks that went out to make breakers. Feeling her muscles begin to tighten again and the temperature beginning to get hotter she turned and headed back towards her villa.

Images of the things he had done to her and they had done together played in her mind, she had never had such a lover before and knew that going back to Boston would be hard, she would miss the sex for sure but she also hoped that one day she would know the real name of the man she had been letting slowly in to her heart although she knew to expect no promises.

As she crossed the set of rocks where she had found John two days before she heard the sound of a car starting and her eyes flew to the house where the new neighbors had arrived sometime during the night. A silver sedan pulled out and she couldn't make out any persons. A movement on the back deck of the house caused her eyes to move to its direction, a female holding a mug of something had come out to the back and she was walking down aimlessly towards the water just thirty feet from the bottom step.

"Morning." The female said as Beth came closer, she slowed down figuring she would see what she could find out about the new neighbors to ease anything John might ask. Her first close up impression of the woman was of awe, she was tall, her body shaped like a model and muscular in the arms, her hair a mixture of brown and blonde and looking fresh from a soft pillow somewhere, but still she was gorgeous in her boxer shorts and tank top. "Hi." Beth stopped. "I'm your neighbor."
"Oh, hi." The female seemed preoccupied. "I'm Jay."
"Beth." She accepted the extended hand and they shook.
"How long have you been here?"
"Three days, my boyfriend and I are here together, you?"
"Husband, he just left to go to the market for some food."
"My boyfriend, John, he's still asleep."
"I bet you were keeping him busy last night." The female winked and Beth knew she had heard them.
"I am so embarrassed." Beth blushed.
"Hey, don't worry about it, it turned Matt on."
"He's your husband?"

"Yep, and what a guy he is." Beth saw something that was a little off about the way the woman had said that, she thought it seemed a little suspicious.

"Are there any activities in town you could recommend?" Beth listened.

"Um, I've only been down to the port, we came here for sex only as you know."

"I should be so lucky." The female laughed. "I don't know when he'll be back, knowing him he might actually go and fish instead of just buying the stuff from the store. I guess I'll start the sunbathing while he's gone."

"That's what I was going to do too, would you like some company?" Beth had to ask because there was just something she couldn't put her finger on about this woman, she wondered if it was because she was so good looking and Beth knew she always took people at their face value, summing them up a little too early instead of letting herself get to know them. A little like how things were between her and John. "Sure."

"I'll see you a little later then." Beth picked up her jog again and in a few minutes was opening the back door to her own villa.

"John." She shouted as she came in.

"Beth." He shouted back, she could smell something, eggs, definitely eggs and she found him in the kitchen pouring out a fluffy omelet. "That smells really good."

"It's ham, mushroom and pepper with a little cheese thrown in."

"It's for me?" She asked as he handed her the plate and went back to the stove.

"Yes, I saw you heading back; I have enough for me here."

"Before you cook it, come here." She let him put his fry pan down on the stove but she kept her plate in her hand and pulled him to the back window. "I met the neighbor's wife." She said but when they got there, there was no one around. "Damn, I wanted you to see her, no big deal; I'm going to go and sunbath with her later." She watched John go back to the stove, he was wearing just his boxers but she knew what was underneath.

"What's she like?" He asked pouring the mixture in as she sat down and cut a piece of hers off. "Very pretty." She put the piece in and sighed at the taste.

"Good?" He asked coming over and leaning far enough over the counter to give her a kiss. "Very." Beth said meaning more the kiss than the food but he didn't ask her to clarify. He moved back to flip his omelet and she continued to eat. "What's her name?"

"I think she said Kay." Beth frowned, "It was some letter."

"Did she say anything else?"

"She's here with her husband who sounds like a right asshole, he left as I was coming up the beach in their rental car and she intimated that he was going to the market but might be a long time."

"So you asked her to sunbathe with you?"

"I thought you might want to know more about

them, I figured what better way than to actually get to know them."

"Good idea, but they're just here on vacation, not everyone saves a federal agent on their vacations."

"So you are a federal agent." She smiled at his slip up but knew he would be mad he had let his guard down. "Yes I am." He replied with a smile instead.

"I thought you'd be mad I knew that much."

"No." He laughed. "Do you know how many different agencies there are?"

"Probably not."

"Then you don't know any more than ten minutes ago. So what am I supposed to do while you are doing the female bonding thing?" He poured his omelet out and joined her on the other side of the counter.

"You could join us?" She smiled finishing off the last of her food

"I'll skip it; I have some sleep to catch up on so I can feast on you again later." His words warmed her but she had to keep remembering this was just like a long one-night stand and although she knew her body was okay with that she wasn't sure that her mind was. "Maybe I can exert some of your energy with you before I go out?" She winked. "I'd like that."

"Oh, and later I have to walk in to town."

"To get the charger." He remembered, all the sex had clouded his mind. "I have to admit; I did forget that."

"I don't know if that's good or bad."

"Right now that is very good."

"I have to ask something." Beth said and John nodded okay because his mouth was full, he was rushing to finish so they could get the sex started. "Why hasn't anyone come looking for you, the people you work with I mean."

"Because only one person knows where I am, that person would worry but would wait for some news, a dead body, mysterious explosion or fire and then conclude it was used to cover up my disappearance. If this happens I have to get home on my own or contact home and they will help me."

"I just thought if we waited long enough maybe someone would come looking."

"I'm afraid not." He swallowed the last piece of the food. "Ready for more?"

"Of course." She laughed. "You meant sex right?"

"Ah, yeah."

CHAPTER TWENTY-TWO

Every hour a nurse had come in and woken him to check his vitals and change IV's and give him medicine, he was so tired and filled to the eyelids with pain killers he didn't know which way was up.

Steve was laying there with his eyes closed when he smelt something that made his stomach rumble. Laying on his back so he wouldn't move his stabilized leg he turned just his head to the right and saw on the clock on the wall it was a little before seven. Turning his head to the left he saw a familiar face. "You're here early." He said using the button on his bed to make the back go up. "Good morning to you too." Jamie laughed putting the bag down on the wheeling table. "I thought I'd sneak in some food and have breakfast with you."

"Lonely at home?" He smiled looking forward to whatever she had brought it smelt so good. "Very." She was beaming and as she sat on the edge of his bed and took out a few covered plates from the local diner and he watched her and knew something was up. "Okay Buchanan, spill. What's with the goofy grin?"

"I'm pregnant."

"That's great." He accepted the plate and breathed in the smell and then shook his head. "Really, pregnant, again?"

"Yep, I told Matt last night so I thought it'd be okay to tell you, I know Matt confided in you about what happened." Steve put his hand over the hand she was using to take off the lid of her plate. "It's okay." She reassured him.

"It was a hard time for both of you, I can only try to imagine."

"We got through it, I found out two weeks ago but I was worried he'd freak out and then you and the guys were gone and I guess I just put it off." He took the small bottle of OJ she passed and opened it for a long drink.

"He must be happy; I know I would be."

"I think it was the wrong time to tell him, but I

hope he's happy."

"I'll bet my next pay he is."

"I hope you like this." She pointed her disposable fork at the food. "I've only had breakfast with you a handful of times and I'm afraid I wasn't sure."

"This is great." He looked down at his pancakes, bacon, eggs and home fries. "Where did you get it?"

"The diner between here and my house. I wanted to get in early and get some paper work done I missed yesterday, I figured instead of eating alone I'd eat with you, I hope that's okay."

"This is very okay." He cut up his pancake and dipped it in the butter on top. "Did you speak to either Matt or Mel today?"

"Matt called quickly to remind me to go visit my doctor but no news yet."

"How was my mother last night?"

"She's a very nice woman." Jamie simply put not sure how to say she was a handful and hurt his feelings; it was obvious he cared for his mother.

"Translated that means she gave you more than a third degree about Mel." He sighed.

"She was just wondering, I mean, she meets me, I look just like the person who could be her future daughter in law who happens to be MIA, she asks me about my sister but what can I say. Ma'am, she's a recovering addict who hasn't been stressed in the last two years because we're worried she may go back to her old ways, she works as a photographer's assistant because the last three jobs she had finally found out the Marines kicked her out for substance abuse, she's a great person, really she is and your son loves her madly."

"She knows some of the stuff."

"None of the bad I hope."

"Nothing to do with the addiction, mainly because I have faith she's not going to go back to it."

"Okay, I have to hear this, why?"

"Because I love her."

"Oh, Steve, that is the cutest thing I've ever heard." Jamie had to laugh and he threw a paper cup left there from when the nurses had brought him tablets during the night. "Laugh all you want but it's true."

"Then why didn't you ask her to marry you before she left?"

"I realized I didn't want you as a sister in law."

"Ha, ha. You'd be so lucky to get in to this family."

"I know I would."

They were cut off by his room phone ringing and he picked it up. "Hello."

"Uncle Steve." Izzy's little voice said and he couldn't smile anymore if her tried.

"Hey Izzy, where are you?"

"At Disney I'm having breakfast with Cinderella this morning."

"I don't believe it, the real Cinderella?"

"Yes and Sleeping beauty might be there too."

"It sounds like you are having fun."

"I am, I miss Mommy and Daddy but they wouldn't like it here."

"Why?"

"No Navy people." Izzy made a noise in the background and he thought she was passing the phone to whoever had helped her dial but her little voice came back. "Is your knee feeling better?"

"It's a little sore."

"Can I see you soon?"

"How about when you come back?"

"Sure, I want to give you a hug, when I get a boo boo, Mommy gives me a kiss where it hurts. You should get her to kiss your knee; it will make it all better."

"I'll ask her."

"I got to go, bye, love you."

"Love you."

"Izzy?" Jamie asked.

"Did you get her to call?"

"She wanted to know what was going on with you so I told her, she loves her Uncle Steve."

"And Uncle Steve loves her too."

"What's she up to?"

"Having breakfast with princesses, fitting really."

"Hey, she's a good kid."

"Who is loved by more people than I ever was at her age."

"Me too, that's why she's so lucky."

"She told me you need to kiss my knee better, seems it works for her."

"You aren't three and I did all I could to make sure your knee feels better. I could always up the pain pills and give you a hazy week and then withdraw you from them all?"

"That's just mean."

192

"Be nice to the doctor then." Jamie put her knife and fork down. "I'm done and I have to run. Your Mom should be here later and I know Patti is coming over too."

"She is?"

"Seems a lot of people care about you, weird huh? I hope you feel good when I see you later." She got up and picked up her purse.

"Thanks for breakfast and congrats on the big news."

"Your welcome and thank you. Please keep it quiet though, I don't want the rest of the team to know yet."

"My lips are sealed."

"First time for everything."

XXX   XXX

"What do you think?" Miguel asked as they brought the boat in another sweep of the immediate shoreline south of the island. Vince had been steering the craft as he stood at the bow with a pair of high resolution binoculars, he could see the hair on a fly if it was along the shore.

"That our body was probably eaten by whatever lives in these waters." Vince looked extra menacing in his tailored pants and white tank top, his shoulder holster showing because he was a man who didn't give a damn who saw and who wondered what he did with his gun. "We better find something; he was adamant we get him proof that guy's dead."

"We better keep looking then." Vince turned the boat out towards Bequia and kept on a direct course to the island when his very expensive satellite phone rang. "Yeah boss."

"How's it going?"

"Nothing yet."

"Keep on it. I have something else brewing I want you in on. I've told Luis he has to tell his brother he was the one having an affair with Cara. He has until midnight, if he doesn't do it; deal with him, whatever needs to be done."

"Are you sure boss?" Vince had never in the years he had worked for this man heard him make an order against one of his own. "As long as Miguel is level headed everything will be. Can you do this?"

"You know I've wanted to deal with him for a long time."

"Then this could be your chance, he has no back bone and I doubt he will tell Miguel."

"I'll keep an eye on it, if he doesn't know the truth by midnight I'll take care of it."

"Good, call me when you find anything."

Vince pocketed his cell and looked at Miguel, he was a fine enough man but he was the weakest of the family, not Luis. Mr. Santos has it wrong he thought, if I was going to make one of my son's heir to the family fortune he would never choose Miguel. Cara had been a hot piece of ass, she had caught him looking once or twice and she fed on it, her eyes lit up from male attention, she ran over Miguel like a speeding car and he hadn't known what to do about it. If she had been his wife she

194

would have learnt day one who was boss, just like he had shown her the night he had killed and taken a piece of her.

"Your father just called."
"Yeah?" Miguel was just scanning everything with his binoculars.
"He wants me to convey how much we need to find proof our spook is dead."
"What'll happen if we can't?"
"We better find something, anything."

CHAPTER TWENTY-THREE

"It's a little early for you." The bar owner laughed as he wiped out glass after glass and hung them above his head as Luis walked in. The stools and chairs were off the floor and it was empty because this late night dive wouldn't be open until the middle of the afternoon, but it had also been the place he had met the woman he was looking for, this place had no business connection to his father and the owner wouldn't block him like many of the others would.

"I was hoping you'd seen that woman I left with last time I was here."
"Who, Gisela? Nah, rumor is she got in to some trouble and had to leave the island."
"What kind of trouble?"
"I dunno, no one really knows, why you asking?"
"I was hoping to talk to her about something."

"Huh, hey, I hear your sister in law was the one murdered."

"Yeah."

"I'm sorry." The man didn't really sound too sympathetic but then why should he.

"Could you do me a favor?" Luis took an envelope from the back pocket of his pants. "I'm supposed to meet my brother here tonight but I have some business, if I don't make it in and you see him could you give him this?"

"Sure." He took it and walked over to the register and put it in.

"You take it easy Don." Luis said turning and leaving. The weather had picked up some extra humidity and his white linen shirt and linen slacks were getting too much but his father expected a certain standard in dressing when they were working.

Putting his sunglasses on he looked up and down the beach front of downtown Port Elizabeth, the place was bustling with the tourists who all stood out from the locals, their white skin, camera's in their hands, the maps, a man getting out of a silver sedan took his eye, he was tall, with medium brown hair but had an air about him, the same air the CIA man they had killed did but as he continued to watch he had to smile, the man took out his camera and began milling in with the other tourists, stopping in the first souvenir store, his first impression had been wrong, he was just another mainlander who probably had some high paid job as a lawyer or banker and that's why he seemed too confidant.

Turning away, Luis walked down to the corner where the local grocer, the brother of their housekeeper ran a store. It wasn't a very big store but it carried everything you could need from food to small electronics, the place was always busy but he always seemed to run in to Gloria's teenage son, the kid had a look in his eye that although he was deaf he had eye's like a hawk and saw everything. Like always, Haden was stocking cans in the first isle and Luis smiled but the boy did nothing in return and he continued to the back where George manned the counter with a smile for all the customers, and as expected, Georges smile changed when he saw Luis, no doubt he knew why he would be stepping in a store he never came to.

"Afternoon George." Luis was feeling extra polite today and figured it would throw the owner off enough to get this over with. "Luis." He almost snarled back.
"I'm here for my father."
"I figured that." He moved to the back wall and called in to the back, his wife appeared and gave Luis the same look of disdain and went back to wherever she had been in the back only to return moments later with a thick brown envelope for him. George came back and instead of putting it in the hand Luis had extended he slapped it down on the counter quick to turn away to a customer with a smile.

Shaking his head, Luis turned and saw the man from the beach with the silver sedan, he had a basket full of groceries and was asking George whether or not they had any suggestions for a restaurant in town where he could take his wife for a little romance, Luis noticed while George was talking that the man had a few newspapers and a painted shell, something a little tacky sold as souvenirs in all the island stores.

XXX   XXX

Having called Steve only to have him tell her he would call her back, his mother had just arrived, Mel went and changed in her bedroom in to a bikini she had yet to take the tags out of. Her sister had bought it for her that past Christmas, it was this wild pink and white thing with sequins and beads, putting it on she felt almost naked, it had been a very long time since she had worn something this small.

Mel shook her head thinking she had gained a few awkward pounds since quitting smoking and this bikini hid nothing.

Feeling a little unusual she went out to the living room and looked out to see if the female neighbor was out and saw no one. Remembering she had forgotten to add some sun tanning cream she went back in to her bedroom and over to the bathroom, she had a small trial size bottle she had picked up in one of the first three airports they had been in when they knew where they were going. She flipped the lid and squeezed out a quarter sized amount and spread it over her arms and legs and was just finishing up when the sound of her cell ringing stopped her.

In the living room on the coffee table is where she had left it after calling Steve and she thought it might have been him but the ID said it was her sister. "Hey big sis."
"Mel, I was calling to see how you were doing."
"Well mom." Mel joked. "I'm about to go out and lay in the sun."
"Sounds like fun, I'm jealous."
"Wanna swap?"
"I wish I could." Jamie sighed. "I thought you might like to know the latest on Steve."
"Is it good or bad?" Mel sat down and waited for her answer.
"Calm down, it's good news."
"Well?"
"He won't be needing chemo, the wafers we put in his knee will do the job better which means he'll be able to concentrate on his recovery."
"That's great right?"
"It's the best news right now. I actually just sat down to start planning a schedule for his rehab, I was thinking a lot of water time, you know how he loves being in the water."
"Makes him a great SEAL."

"Speaking of that, his mother was coming over and

I'm keeping clear."

"How come?" Mel interrupted her.

"She's a little different to her laid back son, she's been asking a dozen questions about you and looking at me like your head will pop out of my shoulder."

"I'd really like to meet her; I hope she's there when I get back."

"Oh, I think she's planning on staying until she's met you, anyway, as I was saying, his mother was coming over but so was Patti, you know Chris's wife. She saw he had company and came looking for me. She asked if you were around because she had something she wanted to talk to you about."

"God, I'm not helping with this year's end of summer party, Mary and Sarah can have that big fun."

"It had nothing to do with that, and I believe Karen and Emma have that job. No, Patti wanted to know if you'd found a job because she had a friend ask her if she knew anyone for the place where she worked."

"What is it?" Mel sighed expecting her sister to say something far from what she would ever do.

"Peer counselor at the high school Patti's boys go to."

"Are you kidding?" Mel laughed. "I'm not exactly a role model for anyone."

"You may not think so, but Patti must think highly of you because she already gave the principle your name."

"What? Does the principle know all about me?"

"That's what I asked and it seems that he's more interested because he thinks you could reach them on a deeper level some regular person who hasn't done what you have could."

"I don't know."

"Think about it, I think this would be good for you; I think you could do it."

"No you don't."

"Yeah, yeah I do. You've been clean for two years, that's a big deal."

"That means a lot to me." Mel felt herself getting a little chocked.

"Hey, I have to go, Largo's waving at me and pointing to the clock, I have rounds to do. Give my love to your husband." She laughed.

"I will."

"Bye." She heard Jamie hang up and she stood, trying to figure out what it was she was going to do.

Her eye caught movement out on the beach and she saw the female from next door getting herself settled down on the beach. She grabbed the towel she had taken out and remembered to collect a bottle of water and then opened the back door to be hit by the humid hot air. It took your breath away as it seeped down in to your lungs. She was used to the heat in San Diego but this was so much worse. Leaving her flip flops up on the deck and putting a baseball cap on to cover her head she walked down towards where her new friend was getting a start on her tan.

"I thought you'd changed your mind." Mel heard the woman say over the sound of the waves, she was lying on her stomach, her top off. Mel had always thought her body was near perfect but this female was toned in all the right places, and there were no visual scars or imperfections and she felt the pang of envy, the same one she felt when she looked at her twin. "I was on the phone with my sister; she was calling about a friend who's had surgery."

"I hope they are okay; it must be putting a damper on your vacation."

"A little." Mel got down and with her towel spread a few feet from the other she decided to lie on her stomach also untying the strings of her top and pulling it off.

"Where about in the states are you from?"

"California, you?"

"Boston, I'm a New York City transplant, I never knew weather like this existed anywhere other than the movies." She laughed and Mel wished she could remember her name. "I've lived all over the country but I've never been to Boston, my sister has." She chuckled at the memory.

"I have a younger brother, is yours older or younger?"

"Older."

"Must be nice."

"Sometimes, she can be a royal pain in my ass."

Mel smiled looking at the female who was so friendly. "I know this would sound bad but I don't remember your name."

"It's okay, I'm Beth."

"Jamie." Mel returned. "So you're here with your boyfriend?"

"Yeah." Beth lied. "We've not known each other too long but he's a nice guy."

"My husband was the best thing that happened to me." Mel thought about how Jamie was more complete and content since she had married Matt. "What do you guys do for a living?"

Mel thought for a split second, she couldn't tell the truth, or could she? "I'm a housewife and my husband is in securities."

"I work for the social services and John is a teacher." Beth lied too.

"How long are you here for?" Mel asked.

"Two weeks, you?"

"A few days." The sound of a boat not too far from the beach got both of them to turn their heads around. "Is that guy on the boat looking at us?" Beth asked squinting.

"The perv has a pair of binoculars."

"We should give them something to look at." Beth turned around completely so that her bare chest was in full view, leaning back on her hands and shaking out her long ponytail. "You are evil." Mel stayed exactly where she was and the sound of the boats engines revving up let them know the boat and its occupants had seen enough and were moving on. "Thank God they've gone." Mel said keeping her eyes to the house while Beth lay back on to her stomach.

CHAPTER TWENTY-FOUR

Having found nothing in the Port, Matt got back in to his rental car. He couldn't just flash around a picture of Robert and ask, he didn't know who the enemy was and he didn't want to make him or Mel a target.

The sun had been coming down heating everything to a burn, he didn't seem to feel it though and he figured it was because a few days before he had been in a country hotter than this, aside from the ocean there was about as much sand where he and the team had been. For the first half hour he had felt the watchful eyes of a man he had seen first when he had parked and then again in the grocery store. He must have been some one because the owner didn't seem happy to see him. To be less obvious Matt had bought a good deal of groceries he would have had to anyway and after the young man had left he had heard the whispers between the owner and the wife. Being a tourist Matt had asked who the guy had been and the man had told him. "He's the son of the worst thing that ever happened to this island." Matt didn't ask why but was sure when he got back he would do some digging on the internet.

After the store and now with groceries he didn't want to get spoiled he had taken a few pictures and then got back in the car that in a space of less than an hour had heated up to an uncomfortable temperature inside. The drive back to the beach house was under ten minutes, even with the thirty mile an hour speed limit. He carried all of his items in and then began to put them away before he realized Mel wasn't inside. Concerned he walked over to the back door and was surprised to see her out sunbathing with someone he could only reason as being the woman from next door.

Once finished getting all the groceries in to the fridge he took out a bottle of water, stripped off his shirt and went to get his bathing suit, changing quickly and coming back out he couldn't wait to hit the water and get some swimming in, a day of traveling on different airplanes and he could feel the need to get out in to the water beckoning him. With his water in hand he began the walk down to the women and was about twenty feet away when he realized they were both laughing and topless. "Hey." Matt crouched down before them, he was not worried about seeing the other female's breasts but he didn't need or want the image of Mel's forever in his head. "Hey honey." Mel smiled and he had to smile back at the absurdity of her statement.

"Matt, this is Beth, she and her boyfriend are staying next door, you remember hearing them last night." She winked and Matt saw Beth's cheeks redden like he felt his own. "Nice to meet you Beth."
"Likewise." She smiled.
"How was town?" Mel asked.

"Busy, I didn't find that fruit you wanted, I did get plenty of groceries though."

"I was hoping you would have found it." Mel knew he was referring to Robert and played along. "I'm sorry, there's stuff in there for lunch if you get hungry, I'm going to go and get some swim time in."

"Have fun." Mel watched Beth's eyes follow her brother in law; there was some interest in them.

"He has a really good body." Beth frowned.

"He works out a lot." Mel rested her head back down on her crossed arms, savoring the heat warming her back. "How long have you been married?"

"Three and a half years."

"No kids?"

"Does this body look like it's been through that?" Mel laughed and then thought she should have just said yes.

"Does John have a good body?" Mel changed the subject just slightly.

"Oh yes." Mel could see Beth was thinking about it. "He definitely knows how to use it."

"I heard." She couldn't help it she had to laugh. Seeing Matt's bottle of water stuck in the sand she reached over to get it to put with hers further in the sand to keep it cool, an old Marine trick, she was surprised even a SEAL didn't know that.

"That's some tattoo, is it real?" Beth said looking at the center of Mel's lower back.

"It sure is, I didn't want the usual type, the guy I went to made it shimmer with the different inks."

"Why a dragonfly?"

"When I see them, they look so free and able to do whatever they want; to me it symbolizes calmness and freedom. Do you have a tattoo?"

"No, but I always wanted one."

"What stopped you?"

"The needles I guess."

They talked for about twenty minutes before Matt reappeared looking all wet, his feet covered in a layer of sand, He sat down just in front of Mel and Beth looked up. "Hey, I'm going to go up and get something to drink, I'll be back in a minute."

"Okay." Mel smiled and watched as without spilling any skin she put her top back on and stood up dusting the sand from her arms. "She seems nice." Matt said.

"She is, but there's something about her, I just can't put my finger on it. Also, there was a boat here earlier, a guy on the front with a pair of binoculars checking out the beach."

"A Leo?" Matt referred to the local law enforcement officers.

"I don't think so. What did you find out?" Mel kept her eye on Beth and saw her open and close their back door disappearing. "Strange things have been going on here the last few days. A savage murder of a female that just happens to be the daughter-in- law of the islands big kahuna, rumor is she was having an affair and was killed because of it. Whoever the man is better watch his back because the female rumored to be with them too just went missing also; her face is on page three of the paper."

"You think this big Kahuna is somehow tied to Rob going missing?"

"It would make sense, and if you're right about our boat guests earlier I'd say we need to be extra cautious, make sure no one can question us."

"Does that mean we have to?" Mel waved her fingers around.

"No, we still don't do anything aside from hold hands, at least in public we have to, here on the beach is another matter, oh and please don't turn over until you have your top on."

"I've seen you shirtless more than once." She pointed to his chest.

"I'm a man and if Steve or Jay finds out I've seen yours they'll kill me and you."

"Back to the mission, what's the next step?"

"Tonight we go in to town, we do a little dinner, walk around see if we can find something to help us, if we strike out we may have to see about day trips to other islands, there's one over there." He pointed out in to the distance but she didn't dare move and show him anything. "I'll go in soon and check out the names in the paper see what I can get."

"What can I do?"

"Right now? Just get some sun; your job of being my wife will happen later when we go in to town." He lay back supporting the back of his head with his hands. "You didn't borrow any black dresses from Jamie did you?"

"No why?"

"Just making sure."

XXX XXX

"Am I interrupting anything?" Jamie poked her head around the door of Steven's room. Kevin, Ryan, Lee and Max from his team, team seven were there visiting, his mother was nowhere to be seen. "Commander." They all stood at attention for her rank and she waved them off as she closed the door behind her. "Guys, you're on my turf, stop with the formality, we're all friends."
"This is still Navy turf though." Max said seriously, it got a little on her nerves the way they were all so damn polite and stiff until you got them off base and at someone's house for a party or just hanging around shooting the shit. "Then if any of you do that again when you are visiting Steve I'll have you admitted and a course of aggressive enemas will be given." She picked up Steve's chart and felt their smiles because they all knew she would do as she had threatened without blinking an eyelid. She wasn't just a wife of Matt's, a once member by mistake of the team, she had proved she could be one of them, she had their respect.

"How's the pain?" She asked Steve coming over and with his chart in her arm checked the valve on the IV. "I don't have any."
"Not even when you laugh?" Jamie frowned. "I was sure I'd connected your funny bone to your stitches."
"You're so funny." Steve shook his head.

"Why are you in such a good mood?" Max asked
"She got rid of her husband for a few days." Lee
laughed. "Where did Mr. Serious go?"
"He, err, had some things to take care of with his
brother."
"Really?" Kevin asked not buying it.
"I have some very good news." Jamie ignored them
and spoke directly to Steve.
"I won the lottery?"
"No."
"You got Catherine Bell to agree to come and visit
me?" He referred to the actress who had played a
Marine Major on a successful military TV show.
"No." She put her stethoscope in her ears and the
BP cuff around the top of his arm and was silent
while she checked his blood pressure.

"Well?" Steve asked when the stethoscope was out
of her ears.
"Pathology got your results back."
"It wasn't cancer?"
"No, it was but the wafers we put in will be enough
treatment so the chemo I know you were looking
forward to won't be happening."
"That's good right?" Steve questioned.
"It means instead of six weeks of rest and sickness;
you can begin your PT this Monday without being
held back. I don't need to explain the sooner you
start therapy the quicker and better the outcome?"
"No, you don't."
"Good, everything looks good. I'll send Petty officer
Cole in to give you a bed bath when you're all free
from visitors." Jamie put the clip board back on the

bed. "I'll see all of you later." She left the room and they all turned to Steve a frown on his face as he watched the door closed. "Why the long face?" Ryan asked. "A nice sponge bath from a nurse sounds good."

"Petty officer Cole is a he." He watched as his four friends all broke out in stitches of laughter at his expense.

CHAPTER TWENTY-FIVE

"John." Beth shouted as she came in to the air conditioned house, the coolness made her shiver for a minute but when John came out of the kitchen in just a pair of boxers she soon heated up. "How's the bonding going?"

"Good, aside from them both being really good looking they are actually a nice couple. She's really nice and I'm glad you've been in here because she has a perfect body and looks like a model."

"I doubt she can compare to you." He said putting his arms around her waist and he saw her look away, for a minute he had forgotten the situation and that statements like that would make things so much harder. "Any other information detective?" He began kissing her neck and the stiffness he had felt her body turn to was melting away.

"They are from California, he does securities but his body is well sculpted and he looks like one of those boyishly rugged leading men. She's a housewife. Oh, I told them you were a teacher. It was the first thing that came to mind."

"Good job, respectable." He was kissing lower and his hand was pulling aside one of her bikini triangles revealing her breast for him to continue working on. "She has an older sister and they're here for a few days." She paused to sigh. "And she has this amazing tattoo on her lower back, it's a dragonfly but it looks like colored silver paint." She felt him go tense and she looked down.

"What?" She watched him move back and turn his body around.

"She has a tattoo?"

"Yeah, do they turn you off or something?"

"No, it's, hold on what are their names?" He took her shoulders in his hands.

"Jamie and Matt."

"Really?" He let go of her and with the biggest frown and look of disbelief she watched him walk over to the back door. "John, what is it?" He was freaking her out.

"Where are they?" He saw no one on the beach.

"They were there when I left."

"Look at me." He turned her back to look at him, his hands holding her shoulders again. "I'm sorry I have to ask this but I need to know who the hell you are."

"You know who I am. I'm Beth, Elisabeth DeVeuve, I live in Cambridge Massachusetts, I work for the department of social services and like always I date men who use me and treat me like crap, the latest one I slept with, well, he's freaking me the fuck out right now."

212

"I said I was sorry." He let go of her. "You just told me the neighbors are called Jamie and Matt correct."

"Yeah." She shrugged still frowning.

"Do you remember the story I told you the first night about my friends?" He watched her thinking back to sitting at the table, the curry they were eating and everything he had said. "Oh." She said. "Is it them?"

"I don't know, aside from you describing Matt perfectly you got Jamie all wrong, well, the part about the tattoo."

"Then it's not them."

"Her sister Mel has one like that."

"Your ex?" He saw her change from confusion to doubt. "How likely is it that your ex and her what, brother-in-law are staying right next door?"

"Very slim, but I have to know if it is or not?"

"What are you going to do, go over there in your boxers and get your ex-girlfriend back?"

"No." He went over to one of the stools where he had put his cargo shorts earlier that morning with all intentions on going outside. "I'm going over there to make sure it's who I think it is because if it's not you are in danger."

"How?"

"It wouldn't be too hard to do a background check on me and then plant something to make me come out of hiding, if they're imposters I want to know."

"Maybe it is them and they came to find you?"

"Why would anyone send Mel? She doesn't care for

me and anyway, it's all past history." He was walking back over to the back door and she stopped him.

"Wait, if they are your friends I want to be there to see this for my own two eyes, if they're not I might help them to kick your ass."

"Thanks for the support." She followed him out in to the heat and down the steps to the sand.

"Hey, Beth, want to join us for lunch?" A female voice called and she watched as John picked up from his stomp and in to a jog. He stopped so abruptly at the bottom of the stairs that she almost didn't stop before hitting the back of him. "Shit." She heard him say. As she heard the two on the deck say similar words. "It's good to see you guys." She watched from the sand as he went up the stairs and first shook the hand of the man and then gave the female a hug that looked uncomfortable. "Beth." He waved up, she wanted to go back to her villa, she knew it was selfish but she knew she no longer had him to herself and she had grown to like him, her heart even more.

"I don't know what these liars told you but that is not his wife." John had a smile on his face and she had only seen it when they had been laughing after one of their sessions of mind blowing sex last night. "Thank God, the charade is over." Matt laughed. "Excuse me, you are married to someone that looks just like me and you used to date me." She pointed one at a time to each of the men and then remembered Beth was there and how awkward she must feel. "It was a really long time ago and it was never serious." She said to just Beth but she could tell from looking in the woman's eyes that she had closed herself off to something, a wall was beginning to be built and Mel would bet it was around her heart.

"Where's Jamie?" John asked his friends as they all took seats around the round table, John was opposite her and she watched him, this changed person. "She couldn't come." Mel began. "You remember Steve."
"Your new boyfriend?" Beth watched his face while he said that and the minute he made eye contact with her she saw the hurt those simple words put in them. "He had to have knee surgery and being his primary physician and good friend she needed to be there."
"Plus we had no idea where you were and no offense but I wasn't about to let Jamie anywhere near something you were involved in." Matt finished.
"He almost had my sister killed four years ago."
"I know." Beth smiled. "She sounds brave; I'd like to meet her."
"She'd like you." Matt said giving her his biggest grin. "Jamie was the one contacted by a friend of yours though, it was all very cloak and dagger, we had no idea where you were until we got our tickets to here."
"Who contacted her?"

John watched Matt look at Beth and then back and

John bowed his head. "Before we go on." He stopped Matt and looked at Beth. "You have two choices, you can either go back to the villa and never know the truth about who I really am or you can stay, hear what we have to say and be in danger."

"I'd like to stay." Beth wasn't about to move.

"Then let me begin this." John rubbed the back of his neck. "My name is Robert Wakefield and I live in Virginia and work for the CIA."

"Robert." Beth nodded her head and Mel closed her eyes to hide the pity she had for the woman who was so clearly falling in love with a man she really did know nothing about.

"For the last two years I've been looking for a guy who was once the leader of a big organization in the states, he was rumored to be in money laundering, weapons dealing and a few murder cases. He disappeared fifteen years ago when we believe one of the local judges he paid off tipped him we had acquired a warrant for his arrest. His wife and fifteen-year-old son went missing along with the girlfriend he had on the side and the four-year-old son he had fathered with her. He just vanished and we thought he had returned to South America where you know we would never have gotten him; the Mexican government doesn't like to let us have one of their own."

"I tracked him down to one of the islands down here in the Caribbean Sea. A few months ago I got the go ahead to come down and get information so we could later extradite him back to the states. I had the perfect cover and I hopped from one island to the next until I got here, I was staying here on Bequia and easily came stumbling in to the hornets' nest they've built right here on the island. I must have asked the wrong thing that tipped them off because three nights ago while in my hotel room on St. Thomas they captured me and took me out on their boat where they knocked me out and threw me bound over board. I washed up here on this island and Beth found me and brought me in to her villa no questions asked."

"I think I know who the man is you're after." Matt turned the laptop he had been using towards Robert and he looked at it and nodded. "That's him."

"Then did you read today's paper? His daughter in law was murdered."

"That was in yesterday's paper."

"And today the female accusing her of being with her and another man in an affair has also gone missing."

"The old man is cleaning up."

"I don't like the sound of this." Mel spoke up. "We need to get off this island and now."

"I can't go anywhere; all my ID's were in that hotel room."

"Call Nick, get him to sort it out." Matt passed his cell over.

"Nick can't come on to this island, this man." He turned the lap top around so the women could see his picture. "His right hand man and Nick used to work together and he'll be in danger the minute he gets on the plane in the Bahamas."

"Why the Bahamas?" Beth asked.

"I don't know how they do it but they have information on everyone coming in to the island."

"I got in." Matt shrugged looking at the three of them.

"Yeah, but to anyone looking you wouldn't be listed as a SEAL and Mel, well, they'd have nothing on her."

"I came in as Jamie, that's the cover, husband and wife on a romantic vacation."

"That's how we can do it."

"Do what?" Matt looked at Robert and had a feeling in his gut he wasn't going to like the answer. "Have Jamie get ID for me. Have Mel fly back to Miami and switch places with Jamie there and have Jamie fly in."

"No." Matt sat back his arms crossed over his chest. "I won't have you drag her in, not if this guy is as bad as I think he is."

"You and Jamie can go to another island straight after, you won't need to hang around here once I have ID."

"What about Beth" Mel asked looking at how still Beth was being. "She's in danger now too."

"I'm not going anywhere, I came down here for sun and relaxation and nothing's going to make me leave it before my scheduled departure day."

"I agree with Mel; you'll have to leave too."

"I will not, who knows you were even with me?"

"Is that why the boat was here earlier with the guy

with the binoculars?"

"What guy?" Robert turned white from Mel's question.

"Some guy, I couldn't tell you anymore because they were too far away but they were here, Beth showed some breasts and they left."

"It could be them looking for you." Matt pointed out.

"Mr. Santos must want proof I was taken care of."

"I need some moisturizer." Beth lied and got up from the table and left to go back to her villa. Rob got up and Mel stood too. "You better make sure she's on board or she could be the one to get us in trouble."

Ignoring her like he had when they had been dating Mel watched Rob chase after Beth and lost sight of them behind the bushes. He caught up with her as she was reaching the top step of the deck. "Wait."

"For what? You're rescued Robert, go and get on with the rest of your life so I can."

"Can we talk about this?"

"What is there to talk about? Your life came to rescue you. Go back to the states with your friends and forget about me."

"I can't just forget about you. Please, stay with us; I have to make sure you are okay as well."

"I don't want to leave."

"Then I'll arrange for you to stay somewhere else when we leave, I'll pay all your expenses."

"I don't want that."

"I care about you Beth, God, in three days you've

become important to me, I'm not just going to let you slip through my fingers. If you knew what this man is capable of."

"I read the paper yesterday; I know what they can do."

"Please." He wasn't used to pleading. "If I, us, your own welfare means anything stop being stubborn and let us help you."

"I'm being stubborn?" She had to laugh at that one. "I just don't want my vacation ruined anymore, it might sound trivial or incomprehensible to you but I had to save up two years to pay for a holiday like this."

"I ruined your vacation?"

"If you had never washed up on this beach I wouldn't be in this situation."

"You saved my life, I owe you the same."

"Let's call it even for all the great sex we've had."

"Great sex?"

"What, that wasn't your best?"

"I never felt like I was ever that good until I met you."

"Trust me you are, surely your ex Mel told you that?" She was using fighting words now. "Forget about Mel, this is about you and me."

"There is no you and me. Remember the not promising anything after being here, you couldn't promise a future or a relationship beyond this situation and I was fine with that."

"Are you still?" He asked.

She stood there looking up in to his dark eyes, the

eyes that had held her gaze as he released his pleasure inside her, as he made her feel things for him she didn't want to allow herself to but had anyway. "I don't know."

"Good, because I can't stick to what I said, you've gotten under my skin and I like that."

"Even though I don't measure up to Mel?"

"Please." Rob shook his head. "If you knew her you'd never say that. She's got nothing on you."

"I don't want to believe you but for some reason I do, it's your eyes, there's something there."

"Please, come here." He held out his arms and stood there expecting her to turn and leave but she walked in to his arms and gave him another of the kisses that left him with his nerve endings screaming all through his body. "Stay with me." He whispered in her ear and her body swooned slightly backwards and he let his hand travel down to cup her breast as he nuzzled on her neck. "Yes." She sighed back.

CHAPTER TWENTY-SIX

Mr. Santos stood at his window in his office. He rarely left during the day unless there was urgent business he had to take care of. He had just heard from Vince, they had found a t-shirt covered in diluted blood and various insects on one of the beaches at Rocky bay. Supposedly it was the same kind of shirt the CIA man had been wearing when he had been thrown overboard. Still feeling a little concerned about the man still being alive he had told Vince that he and Miguel would return to the boat in the morning and continue looking, there had to be something more than a shirt as proof.

His son Luis had been home and had left again after dropping off the rent money from the land he owned and had showered and changed before leaving again. The sun was beginning to set and looking at the antique grandfather clock he knew his son's time was running out. He wanted Miguel to hear from Luis what had been going on because he had all faith that his oldest son would take care of the bastard son he should never have admitted as being his. It had been a time of sorrow for Charlotte, his first and only love. After Miguel she was unable to have any more children and finding out her husband had sired a bastard had near killed her.

"Charlotte." He sighed softly, her painting hung over the fireplace behind him and he had a quick look at the beautiful woman she had been, his high school sweetheart who had left her family and friends behind along with shame of her actions to be with him after everything had gone bad. The first few years on the island as he set his operations up and became known as the outsider buying up as much free space as he could, she had been content. She had personally cared for their garden and taken care of Miguel as though he were a prince but once he was away at college she changed. She became a sort of zombie going from one place to another and as he watched he could do nothing to help. He knew the absence of her family, friends and son was too much for her to deal with and she had begun to shut even him out.

One morning he came down to find her dead on her favorite couch in the living room. She had taken a bottle of her anti-depressants with a vodka chaser. Miguel had come home for her funeral and left again soon after, she had been cremated and her ashes added to the garden she had once tendered with so much love. The following spring her prized rose bush had grown enormously and bloomed the prettiest lilac flowers. He contributed the growth to Charlotte and when the new gardener had been hired he had been warned to do nothing that would kill the plant.

"Boss." Vince's voice came from the doorway. "Luis went out."

"I know; I have Joe on his tail. He really has until midnight?"

"No, I moved it up. Find him after dark and make it look like an accident. We can release it to the press that he was guilty over the lie he was keeping about his affair."

"Are you sure?" Vince didn't care either way, the kid was going to be dead, the question was, was it early tonight or later. "Are you questioning me?" Mr. Santos shot out. "No boss, just making sure I understand."

"Make sure it hurts; don't make it easy on him. I want to ensure he goes to hell guilty."

XXX   XXX

Jamie was with Steve and his Mother when her cell phone rang; she excused herself and went in to the hall. "Hey, is it good news?" She asked hearing her husband's voice. "Yeah, you're never going to believe this."

"Try me." She laughed.

"We found Rob; he was in the villa next door the last few days."

"You're right, I don't believe it."

"He was having wild sex with this incredibly cute brunette while we were all worrying about him."

"So you'll all be home soon."

"Well, we have a little snag."

"Which is?"

"He has no ID."

"That's a snag; I'm guessing you need me to do something."

"Can you contact Nick and get ID ASAP."

"I still have the cell, it's at home. I was about to leave after I say goodbye to Steve."

"How's he doing?"

"Missing Mel I think; I know weird to imagine but she must make him feel something."

"I know what she makes me feel." Matt's deep laugh made her smile wider.

"Now, now. So we get ID and then Rob can come back with all of you."

"Back to the ID." Matt paused. "We need it fast and it seems Nick can't come anywhere south of Miami with it."

"Then how will you." Jamie stopped. "Are we going to pull a fast one with Mel and I switching?"

"Very good, I knew you'd figure it out."

"I can get two days leave, I'll just tell the captain that I need a few days' personal time."

"We won't be staying long. I think Beth wants to meet you but I don't want you on this island any longer than we have to be here."

"Situation that bad?"

"It could be. Did you go to the doctors today?"

"I did."

"And?"

"They did an ultra sound; I didn't want to know the results until you were there but I did hear the heartbeat. That's a great sign Matt; it's a small percentage of women who have miscarriages once the heart beat is heard." She had another surprise but wanted to do that in person. "That's excellent news."

"I'll tell you more when I see you. Let me get home and call Nick and I'll call you back."

"We'll be here, I was going to go in to town with Mel for dinner and a look around but now we know where Rob is we're going to stay here, should be interesting, what with old lover new lover and everything. I'm just glad I get to watch."

"Sometimes you can be so twisted and I love it." Jamie had her turn to laugh.

"Give Steve my best for me." Matt said.

"I will, love you."

"Love you too."

Having been pacing up and down the hall Jamie turned back and went in to Steve's room only to see his mother wasn't there again. "Where's your Mom?"

"She needed a cigarette."

"She'll have to go quite a way; I hope she doesn't get lost."

"Oh well." Steve shrugged with a smile.

"That was Matt."

"What's going on?"

"They found Rob; I don't know the specifics but Rob was in the villa next door to where they are staying or something. Plan is now he needs ID so I'm off to get that cell Nick left and pray it is still good."

"So they'll be home in a few days."

"That's the plan."

"You look really happy Jamie, what's going on, it's more than Rob being okay and Matt coming home, you've been like this since you came in when the guys were here."

"I had a doctor's exam today."

"More good news?"

"Can you keep a secret?"

"Sure."

"I have four more weeks before we can tell the gender but I already know we're having two babies."

"Holy shit."

"My thoughts exactly, I think if I haven't made Matt old and grey with worry this should send him over the edge."

"He'll be so excited he won't have time to worry."
"He will, I'll call you later and let you know what's
going on." She leaned over and kissed him on the
cheek. "Mel will be home soon."
"Good."

XXX   XXX

In bed, the sun having gone down a while ago, Rob
held the woman he knew he had fallen for but
wasn't ready to admit. After coming back to the
villa when she had stormed off they had made the
best most passionate love he had ever experienced
and after as she had fallen asleep, her head resting
on his chest he had started smoothing her hair
down as he let himself wonder what it would be
like to have her around when they weren't in a
place as wonderful as this.

A knock on the back door startled him back to the
harsh reality they were in, he wouldn't be happy
until all of them were off the island. Careful not to
disturb Beth he moved her over to the pillow and
pulled the covers over her before he went in
search of his clothes. Finding his pair of sweats, he
went out of the bedroom and in to the darkened
living room, snapping a light on as he went. "Who
is it?" He called.
"Very funny." Matt stood there a hand holding up
the door frame. "Jamie's going to web conference
with us and she said she won't believe you're alive
until she sees you so you better come over."
"Let me get a shirt."

"Don't dress on my account." Matt pushed himself away and walked back to their villa.

"Was that Matt?" Beth came to stand behind Rob putting her hands around him so that they rested just above the waist of his sweats. He took it as a good sign that she was doing something so intimate in its nature. "He wants me over to their place to talk with Jamie."
"She's calling?"
"Better, she's video conferencing; would you like to meet her?"
"Try keeping me away." Beth let go and before he could see what she was doing she was back in the bedroom returning in her BU sweater and shorts. "Ready?" She asked.
"Let's go." He said grabbing a t-shirt as they left closing the door behind them.

In the other villa the smell of food was mouthwatering. "Who's cooking?" Rob called letting Beth walk in before him. "Me." Matt shouted coming in to view. "Worried Mel was?" Beth watched a dish towel fly from behind the wall and hit him square in the head. "No fair." Mel's voice said though they couldn't see her. "Is Beth with you?" She asked. "I'm here." Beth answered thinking it odd this female was asking for her and wondered if maybe she was going to be talked about if they had said she wasn't. "Hey good." Mel appeared and pushed past Matt and Beth smiled at how sibling like they behaved. "Did you eat anything yet?"

"No, we were err." She was blushing and she knew it.

"Having sex?" Mel bluntly offered.

"Yeah." Rob answered.

"Lucky for some, I get a husband for a few days and none of the benefits."

"Let's stop that talk right there." Matt interrupted. "If Mel can look after the food without burning it we can speak with Jamie, she had to call Izzy but we were all connected."

They followed him over to the dining table and Beth got a view of the screen as Matt sat down at the seat and they stood behind him. Before them on the screen was a wall covered in framed pictures and Beth wondered where the view was from. "Hey." A voice said as the screen blurred a moment with something white and when everything settled Beth could see that the white had been the shirt of a naval uniform as the woman on the screen took a seat before her camera. The image wasn't perfect but it was the best she had ever seen and she had to look back in the kitchen and laughed when Mel waved back, obviously she had been expecting that reaction. The two women really did look alike but the closer she looked the more differences she saw, she thought maybe the hair was a different color but with the woman on the screen wearing it pulled back she couldn't really tell.

"Hey Babe." Matt said. "Hear me okay?"

"Sure can, how am I on your end?"

"A sight for sore eyes." Matt replied without missing a beat.

"Oh, I figured with my sister there you'd miss me less." Beth loved seeing the jovialness this husband and wife were having. "For some reason I just have this urge to strangle." Matt continued the joke and Mel came over putting her head close down by his. "Hey sis, how's Steve?"

"Doing good, he misses you for some reason."

"I feel so loved sometimes." Mel stood straight and winked at Beth and she knew these females must do this routine a lot. "Go keep an eye on my food." Matt told her lovingly and she left willingly.

CHAPTER TWENTY-SEVEN

"So, where is he?" Jamie asked and Matt got out of the seat and let Rob take his place. "Ah, Mr. Wakefield, I believe." She had a drink from a bottle of water before it disappeared from the camera's view. "That's me, how's it in San Diego?"

"Hot, but you know me, I stick to my office or the medical building."

"Smart girl, how's Izzy? Is she there?"

"No, didn't Matt tell you? She's with my parents up at Disney for a long weekend; this was supposed to be a special weekend alone together."

"I'm sorry; remind me to make it up to you."

"Izz' would love that, she misses her uncle Rob. Where's this gorgeous woman I heard about earlier?"

Rob extended his arm and gently pulled Beth to sit on his lap. "Beth, this is Jamie, Jamie meet Beth."

"Hi." Beth said softly.

"Wow." She heard Jamie say and hoped that was a good one. "Beth, are you suffering from heat or something? What is a girl like you doing with a man like Rob? You know I know a drug that."

"Hey." Rob butted in and Jamie started to laugh. "She hasn't known me that long; let her find out for herself what I'm really like."

"Okay, Beth, I hope we can meet in person soon, I'd like to hear all about everything."

"I hope we can meet too." Beth got up from the lap she was finding comfortable and went back to standing next to him. "So what's the plan?"

"Nick called me back, he's in DC. I'm on a transport to Andrews in three hours. He'll meet me there, and take me to Dulles; he has ID for you that he'll give me along with money and credit cards. I'll get a flight from Dulles to Miami where my sister and I will switch back Nick thinks your bad guy has a few men in Barbados so they don't need to see there's two of us. There should be a ticket waiting for Mel at your airport for the morning, I'll e-mail the details after. I'll be in Bequia by early afternoon tomorrow. I'm still working on the rest of the plans but you know I can get some tickets that are open so if you two want to take some time you know."

"Jay, quit it."

"Okay, so is there anything else anyone needs?"

"I think Matt needs some time with his wife.

Thanks Jay."

"You know me Rob, anytime." She winked and Beth was taken aback by the similarity between the two sisters doing that.

Rob stood up again and Matt took his place. Beth went over to see what Mel was cooking while Rob seemed thoughtful stood over at the back door watching the ocean. "What are you making?"

"I have no idea." Mel chuckled. "But it serves Matt right if it gets ruined."

"It smells great."

"Doesn't it, it's not fair, both Jamie and Matt are good cooks and I can't boil water without burning it."

"I love to cook."

"Then Rob will never let you go. His idea of gourmet is a pizza with more than three toppings." Mel turned and saw the look on Beth's face. "Beth, I know it must be awkward with me here, I'll be gone in the morning but you don't have to feel threatened or weird around me. Rob and I started out the way we ended, not really knowing each other and more like strangers. We never really loved each other." She made quotation signals with her fingers when she said 'love'. "I was in a bad place mentally, it's still a work in progress and I needed more than he could give of himself. He's a good man and you seem like a great woman, hey, you saved him he won't ever forget that. If you love him let him know because the way, he looks at you I've only ever seen once before on him."

"When?"

"A long time ago after he broke my sisters heart and he wanted her, he settled for being her friend but you could see he wanted more, he wears his heart on his sleeve and once he realized he had made a mistake for the way he had treated Jamie he settled for second best, I'm an example of that. He deserves the best and I think that's you."

"I don't know; this has been playing out like a James Patterson attempt at a cheesy vacation romance novel."

"Look, take Matt and my sister for example." Mel stopped; she was turning the heat off from under different pots and pans and putting them on the butcher block island. "I just realized Rob wouldn't have told you anything about them."

"Actually he did, seems it was the only true thing he told me."

"I'd like to hear what he said about me."

"Nothing bad."

"You said that too fast girlfriend." Mel shrugged off. "Did he tell you how they met?"

"Jamie was sent to his team."

"A woman SEAL." Mel looked lost in thought and Beth waited.

"There was this mission where Jamie was captured."

"Because she killed some guy's son."

"He did tell you."

"Keep going anyway."

"So they were neighbors right, there was an attraction, they'd been hanging out outside of the

233

team and getting pretty close, he even invited her to go to their team leaders wedding dinner that weekend. She looked killer like always and he made every man in there jealous. After the party, it's reported that they went to their separate houses but she called and invited him to come over and use the pool where she was. Things got hot and heavy and before the good stuff could finish she got the call about me."

"Sounds like you know a lot without being there."
"I've been tortured by guilt trips, all in good humor." Mel waved off. "You know about her being captured?"
"Yeah, that must have been hard on Matt."
"He said it was. He'll tell you point blank he didn't think he could continue for fear they'd find her dead or not find her at all. Then there were the videos the captor sent, they were gnarly, I never saw them but the second one gave our father a minor heart attack. Matt sat through them and saw what was happening and then he was the one who carried her out after they found her. For weeks he wondered whether she would come home from being debriefed at Langley and when she did he proposed. He had a ring ready and everything but even though it was so quick and they didn't really know too much about each other they had gone through this intense emotion filled experience together. I know a lot of couples but none as solid as those two, it's like they understand each other on a different level you know. Matt gives Jamie the look Rob gives you."

"Beth." Matt's voice shouted from the other room and she had been leaning on the counter talking with Mel who wasn't as bad as she first thought, the past history between her and Rob really wasn't what was getting under her skin, if she was honest it was the thought that after tomorrow she may never see him again. "Beth." Matt's voice came closer and he stood leaning around the corner. "Jamie wants to talk to you."

"Oooh." Mel laughed as she followed Matt to where Jamie was still on the screen this time on a phone. "Give me a second." Jamie smiled and Beth watched Matt go out to the back deck and speak with Rob.

"Sorry about that." Jamie's voice came back and Beth noticed the female had changed in to a thin strap black tank top and her hair was down, even with the dark lighting Beth could see it was much blonder than her sisters. "It's okay; I was just talking to your sister."

"Don't worry; I'm not going to give you the third degree about you and Rob." Jamie said and she felt the corners of her mouth turn up in a smile. "I'd appreciate you not."

"He is though adamant I make plans for you to leave when we do, he knows there's a bit of contention over it. I have his bank details here and he wants you to decide a place you'd like to go to for the remainder of your vacation time and he'll take care of you."

"I don't know."

"Matt and I are going to spend until Saturday night in Miami, you're more than welcome to join us, there's also Costa Rica, Cancun?"

"Pick something, nothing expensive."

"Sure. Are you dealing with everything okay? This must be out of this world for you."

"It's a little over whelming."

"It sounds like you're dealing with it well; I'm looking forward to meeting you in person tomorrow."

"Likewise, everyone has such good things to say about you and after being told about how you and your husband met, I have questions and awe." She heard Jamie laugh and smiled back. "I'm no one special Beth, anyone can save themselves or someone else, in a bad situation you find the strength to go on."

"I don't know if I could."

"You already found the strength to pull Rob to safety, we all owe you that, he's a really great guy, enjoy him."

"I'll try."

"I'm signing off now; I'll be seeing you tomorrow."

"Do you want to speak to Matt again?"

"Nah, I already did. Just click out of this screen and we'll disconnect."

"Bye Jamie."

"Later."

Beth watched the screen go black and then did as she had said and clicked out of the program and on the main screen below the icons was a picture of Jamie, Matt and a little girl she thought must be

236

their daughter. "That's Izzy." Rob's voice came from behind and she felt him lean on the back of the chair. "She's adorable."

"Thank you." Matt said walking by and back to the kitchen.

"I think she looks like Jamie."

"She has Matt's darker colorings." Rob added. "Did you speak to Jamie about the plans?"

"Yep, but I'll only agree to them if you'll come too."

"I." He stopped and looked down before looking back in to her eyes. "I don't know if I'll be allowed to, I'm going to have to return to Langley first."

"How about after?"

"Just remember I want to and I'll do everything in my power to be there."

CHAPTER TWENTY-EIGHT

He had received a text message from his brother, he wanted them to meet at the place they would go to when they were younger and smoke weed and drink beers before going home and trying to play off that they were fine. He sat on the trunk of his car holding the burning joint between his thumb and pointer finger, there was only the light from the inside of his car as the doors were ajar to allow the heavy beat of the music to filter out from the speakers.

It was after ten and he had found some interesting things out today while he was in town. He knew Miguel and Vince had been out all day looking for the CIA man their father had ordered them to kill. He wasn't sure if they'd found anything but he knew the man wasn't dead, somehow he had made it ashore and was staying with someone, possibly his accomplice, partner, colleague.

Waiting for Miguel was killing him, he knew his brother would be mad when he found out it was he who had been sleeping with his wife and more than likely there would be fists thrown but he just hoped he would listen long enough for him to explain what had been going on, who had killed Cara to keep her quiet and who made sure Gisele couldn't be found. Late in the afternoon a fishing boat had come in, the crew shaken by what had gotten caught on one of their nets, the head of a female yet to be identified but he didn't need any dental or medical test to know who it was just like he didn't need a clue to know who had ordered her demise and who had executed it.

The faint sound of a car coming up behind him didn't make him turn, the headlights turning out before the car came to a stop didn't either but the familiar click of a gun loading made his blood freeze and the breath escape his lungs. The shot that fired burned through his shoulder the same time he heard the loud gun blast and the joint he had been enjoying fell to the floor.

Clutching his shoulder, he slid from the hood of his car and turned, he knew there was no way his brother had just shot him and the face of the man

he feared more than his father was there, a shotgun over one of his shoulders as he came closer, a wound up length of thin rope in his other hand. "Ready." Vince's voice was calm and even.
"For what?"
"Death."
"You wouldn't kill me; my father wouldn't allow it."
"Don't kid yourself Luis. Your father told me to take care of you."
"For what?"
"Ruining the family name, for hurting Miguel. If you ask me he should have had you aborted, you are a waste of space on this planet and a big disappointment to the man who gave you more than your heritage."
"I don't believe he would tell you to kill me."
"Believe it." Vince was coming closer and Luis stood his ground. "Hey, you do have a pair." The man with the permission to kill him moved fast and Luis let him take him by his injured arm and do whatever he was planning to do.

Vince shoved him in to the driver's seat of his own car, his hands bound to the steering wheel and his feet tied together, everything went in a supped up speed of time, a little distorted and out of focus. When he was tied and the music was still playing, the engine still turned off Vince leaned over and put the gear stick in to neutral and Luis thought he was going to be pushed off the cliff and in to the ocean but the moments that passed were too long for a man who could push the little sporty car off a cliff without breaking a sweat.

He was splashed by something wet, his senses told him what it was and he closed his eyes knowing what would come next, there was only one reason someone would pour gasoline over you and it didn't end well. He turned his head just as Vince was lighting the long match the type they used to light fire places. "Now you can join your two whores in hell."
"And you'll be with us soon." Luis made one last boyish grin while he watched the match flying through the air before it came in to contact with his shirt and the intense heat that came after, the feeling of standing next to a big bonfire, the pain was intense as everything changed around him, he couldn't see and there was nothing but the smell of his flesh cooking and he could do nothing but sit there. It wasn't long before he could no longer feel the intense pain and he knew death was just a few deep inhales away.

Vince with little problem pushed the fire engulfed car to the edge and with a little extra push had it falling the sixty feet over the edge of Mount Pleasant Bay and in to the rocks and waves below. Satisfied that Luis would never tell anything he knew Vince turned, collected his red container of gas and replaced it in the trunk of his car. He lit a cigarette and walked over to the cliffs edge just in time to see the car explode even with the water having dulled the top half where Luis had been sitting.

He took out his cell and pushed one button connecting him with his boss. "It's done, call the authorities."

"Good job." The line went dead and Vince pocketed the phone. Feeling the call of nature, he went closer to the edge and unzipped his pants, he relieved himself over the edge and had to laugh to himself of the irony of pissing on Luis.

XXX   XXX

"That was the best pasta I've ever had." Beth said for the tenth time as Rob carried her on his back, her flip flops in her hand. "Matt is a good cook."

"I have to get that recipe from him."

"That, he might not give away." He put her down on the floor of the living room and he went back to make sure the door was securely locked. "Jamie should have left by now." Beth had her hands on her hips and an amazing look on her face. "I want to have you someplace where we can do and go wherever we want." She stated.

"That will happen."

"I hope so." Rob wrapped her in his arms and brushed her hair away from her face.

"Beth, if when I get out of here I go straight to Langley and don't make it to wherever Jamie books a place for you, will you forgive me?"

"Is it likely to happen?"

"It's a big possibility."

"I understand." Beth looked away. "I keep

forgetting we never promised each other forever or even after this was over. I know I was mad earlier but this has been the best few days I've ever spent with a man, sad huh?"

"No, it's not. You've had a chance to see my ex first hand; do you see why I can't be with her?"

"She is a little weird but she's nice too."

"She's better than she was three years ago. Her new boyfriend must be helping."

"Isn't he having surgery?"

"That's what Mel mentioned."

"Do you know her boyfriend?"

"I met him, he's a really close friend of Matt's but I couldn't tell you what he looks like or his name."

"Steve, his name is Steve." Beth tucked her head in to his chest and his heart was aching, all through dinner he wondered if when they left the island they would remain in contact. He hoped so but with his job and the distance between them he knew it was a pipe dream unless one of them was willing to leave what they did and move to another part of the country.

XXX   XXX

Miguel didn't like this part of the town, the locals who wanted to escape the tourists went here and no tourist had lasted more than ten minutes before leaving the drunken loud heckling they would get if they stepped foot inside the building's interior.

He parked his car in a space on the street and

242

when he got out he took a look around and saw the invisible barrier the tourists wouldn't cross. The moon was full in the sky and the other bars and restaurants had their little twinkle lights shining giving the soft ambience they all advertised.

Inside the bar was packed, people playing pool, couples sitting together shouting over the sounds from the old jukebox and most of the stools at the bar were taken. Looking around he couldn't see his younger brother anywhere and decided to have a cold beer and wait at the bar, it was like Luis to be late so it didn't surprise him. He had said on the voice mail he left earlier while he and Vince were out looking for that guy on the boat that it was important they meet, he had something to tell him, something to do with Cara.

"Don, give me a cold one." Miguel held out a twenty and waited for the owner and barman to get him his drink. They had gone to high school on the island together and Don had inherited the bar from his old man while he was away at college. His friend had never had the chance to go anywhere outside of the neighboring islands and Miguel felt bad for him, having to work hard just to keep the bar afloat. It was also one of the few places his father couldn't control because the land had never been in jeopardy and up for sale.

"Your brother not with you?" Don asked giving Miguel the beer and waving off his money so Miguel just put it on the counter. "I'm supposed to be meeting him here."

"Huh." He watched Don go over to the register and open it, taking out something that looked like an envelope. "Luis was here earlier in the day before I opened. He wanted me to give you this if you got here and he didn't."

"Strange." Miguel took the envelope and pulled open the gummed side as Don went back to serving customers. In all the years Luis had never so much as written a birthday or Christmas card and now he's leaving letters behind.

With one hand he unfolded the paper folded inside and in the other took another long swallow of the cold beer. His eyes read the words but his mind wasn't paying the attention to it that the severity of the letter held.

Miguel,
If you're reading this then what I had feared has come true, the clean-up of the scandal has finally reached to me. I must come true to you, I know I was never the man you and father wanted but then a lot has changed if I'm not sat next to you right now.

I was the one having an affair with Cara, it's been going on since not long after your wedding. Father found out and had Vince kill her. Do you know anyone else who could do something so violent? The female who went to the papers, the one that was with us. Her name was Gisele she came to this bar a lot, she went missing too and I fear she was killed as well.

*Father has always made you the important son and
I don't have a grudge against you. I made the
mistake in starting this and bringing you a bad
name. I'm sorry. I always looked up to you, I was
glad to have a brother like you.*
*Keep yourself safe; don't ever piss off the wrong
people or you might end up like me.*

Luis
*P.S. I found the man you were looking for today, he's
alive and staying in the place you lost your virginity
to Chelsea Myers at. He can help you.*

Miguel read it a third time and then a forth. The
words were floating around in his head and he had
finished his beer. "Are you alright?" Don came over
and leaned on the counter. "Do you know someone
named Gisele?"
"Yeah, she was fooling around with your brother,
though he didn't know her name until today. Hey,
think they found her body yet?"
"Her body?"
"Well her head got caught in a fishing net or
something." Don shook his head. "Whoever the
twisted fuck is he cut out her tongue."
"To keep her from talking." His head was
swimming more. "Do you have a piece of paper
and a pen?"
"Sure." Don passed him a large post it pad and a
pen like he wanted.
"If my brother comes in, give him this." Don looked
at the piece of paper the words made no sense to

him. "Is everything okay?"

"No."

CHAPTER TWENTY-NINE

Jamie, dressed in plain clothes exited the transport after a bumpy ride through plenty of storms, the east coast of the country was being ravished by humidity and then storms almost every day and as she stepped outside she felt the mugginess that had returned even with the ground wet from a recent shower.

Over to the side of the runway was a plain sedan and the driver sat inside and she knew it was who she was expected to see. Carrying her light shoulder bag, the same as the one Mel would be using of Matt's to return and meet in Miami in case they were being watched that closely. She packed her personal items that neither sister would share and Mel had been asked to leave those things that she had borrowed from Jamie behind so she could use them when she got there.

Inside the car she put the bag at her feet and looked at Nick, as usual a grin and a cigarette hung from his mouth. "Do you have everything?" She asked as he put the car in drive and drove swiftly from the Andrews airstrip. "It's all in here." He said reaching inside his jacket and taking out the thick brown envelope. "Tell Rob the boss wants him to come straight back."

"I think he was hoping to be able to be with Beth."
"He will, I think the director just wants to chew his ass out."
"When is my sister leaving?"
"She'll be in Miami an hour before you. She's going to call you and let you know where she is."
"Good."

"I heard some good news about you." Nick let his cigarette butt free to fly behind them and hit the road they had already driven on. "Like what?"
"Congratulations on your pregnancy Buchanan."
"How did you." She stopped herself from asking the question. "You shouldn't be snooping in my files."
"Sorry, habit. I remember when Rob told me you had lost the last one." Nick turned his focus on her and she saw in his face the care and feelings he rarely showed. "I was going to call and see how you were but what do you say? I figured our paths would cross again and I'd tell you."
"I appreciate it, thanks." She felt the beginnings of her voice breaking and she coughed to clear the lump.

"Did you get the information on the man Rob was there to get information on?"
"I did, lucky for you, you still have clearance so I was able to get it for you." He reached behind the seat and pulled out a file, not too thick but holding everything they would need. "It's a copy, don't tell anyone or I'll get my ass chewed too. Oh, interesting news on the searching I did. The

daughter in law of this Mr. Santos was killed two days ago and the MO looks like his right hand man's work. He's an ex special forces man by the name of Vince Guidarelli."

"Do you know him?" Jamie knew that before the agency Nick had done some military time. "I was on the same team as him, he's a real head case and he'd make Jack the Ripper look like a pussy."

"Nice."

"Anyway, the daughter in law was killed and yesterday afternoon another female body was found, first the head was caught in a net and later the body washed ashore. The head had been mutilated, the tongue crudely cut out."

"Again, nice."

"Seems he has the local cops eating out of his hand because neither murder is being investigated and it's actually being added to the mysterious tourists that have gone missing over the last decade. Seventy-six in total."

"Is that why Rob went down?"

"No, Santos was a leader of a gang of thugs who were in to almost anything illegal. Oh, and the best part of everything that's happened in the last few days it's all due to the second oldest son having an affair with his sister in law and another female, the female who talked to a reporter and ended up with her tongue cut out."

"The father cleaning up his son's messes?"

"We've been keeping an eye on the radio transmissions on the island back at Langley and four hours ago the burnt out car of the son having the affair turned up with him in it."

"He's dead?"

"From what I saw in the file and thinking about why they would have done away with the son, the oldest was the product of his first marriage to the woman who went with him when he fled the states. He had sired the second son in an affair but took them with them when they ran. The wife killed herself with an overdose and he married the woman he had been having the affair with but it looks like he has always favored the oldest."

"He had his own son killed?"

"And I'd bet Vince did it."

Nick let Jamie read the file as he continued the forty-three miles from Andrews AFB to Dulles. The traffic was light and they made good time getting there, the sun was just starting to come up. "Your flight to Miami should be leaving in thirty minutes. There's a guy in there at the desk waiting for you, his names Ted and he'll let you skip through security and here, you'll need this to carry this." He passed her a 9 mm Sig Sauer. And a black flip wallet with her picture in it and a card that labeled her as CIA, she hadn't seen this in years. "Why will I need this? I thought I was just going in and then coming out."

"Just in case, I'd rather you had it than get in to trouble without it. Let Rob know his ID's are his real ones so he can get through easy on his way back in."

"I will."

"Make sure you're all careful, I mean it when I say

these guys are dangerous, they'll not let anyone get in their way, they fled for freedom and they like it."

Heeding his warning Jamie entered the terminal and at the US airways desk met the man Nick had told her. She showed her badge and ticket and he took her straight through to the gate she would be leaving from telling the woman at the desk to let her on the minute the plane was in and ready. Jamie stood there, the thunder coming back in bursts as the lightning lit up everything in the airport. She took her cell out and dialed her husband; she needed to make sure everything was set on their end.

XXX   XXX

"Are you ready?" Matt asked Mel who was laying out the clothes she would leave for her sister and made sure that everything she had to take back was in the bag Matt had given her, the same one Jamie would be using to come in. "I am." She was wearing sweats and they figured it didn't matter what Mel and Jamie wore, people can change. "Jamie just called, she's in DC. She'll land in Miami after you so don't forget to call her."
"I won't." Mel put her cell in her pocket.
"Are you going to go straight to see Steve?"
"How did you guess?"
"Wasn't so hard." Matt looked down. "Tell him I hope he feels better and I'll see him soon."
"I will, when will you and Jamie be back?"

"I want to be back Saturday night at the latest."
"So you have one day of fun before Izzy gets back?"
"How did you guess?" He used her earlier joking.

"Hello." A male voice came from the back door and
Matt turned to see a rumpled looking Rob closing
the door. "What are you doing up?" Matt checked
the clock it was a little before four in the morning.
"I wanted to come over and see Mel before she
left."
"Let me get out of your way then." Matt moved.
"We need to talk before I go so don't leave too fast
after."
"What's wrong?"
"Jamie got an update."
"Gotcha." Rob walked in to the bedroom and Mel
just looked up at him and he saw it then, he had
looked for it during dinner and during the
afternoon and it wasn't there. The pain and hatred
she still had for him burned in the back of her eyes.

"I wanted to thank you for coming out to look for
me, you didn't have to."
"No, no I didn't but I didn't want my sister
involved."
"Nick would never have sent her somewhere he
knew she would get hurt."
"Really, how considerate of him."
"I see you still hold some hostility towards me
Mel."
"Some? Try a lot."
"Why? What did I do that was so bad?"
"How about dating me because you wanted to be

251

with Jamie?"

"I never."

"Don't." She stopped him. "I figured we're even. You helped me get on with my life after the Marines, good or bad and I came down here for you. Have a nice life Robert."

She zipped up her bag and began to move past him to go out to the car.

"Mel." He said taking her arm. "I did love you."

"Sure you did."

"It took me a long time to get over you."

"Funny, a month in detox and I was completely over you."

"That's not fair."

"Neither is making promises you can't keep."

"What promises?"

"That you'd be there for me."

"I was, and I tried. You were never happy with me because you thought I saw you as Jamie all the time when I didn't. You have the problem with your sister not me."

"I have a problem?"

"Yeah, it's time you did something not connected to her, live your own life and do something to make you feel as equal as her. If that's possible I think a lot of your problems will go away."

"Thank you doctor."

"Just think about it." Rob watched her walk out saying something to Matt.

"Tell me what Jamie said."

"Langley's keeping an eye on this island. This

Santos guy had his son killed during the night."

"Miguel?"

"No Luis."

"Shit."

"You've got that right. Nick gave her a gun too so we'll have one weapon in case we need it but I want us all off this island sooner than we had planned. If you need to stay here you can but I want the women off, after I drop Mel off I'm meeting an old friend who has some things for the new plan Jamie and I came up with."

"Fair enough, I'll make sure Beth and I are ready to go when Jamie gets here."

"Thank you."

CHAPTER THIRTY

Miguel watched the scene before him, it was surreal and unimaginable that this would have happened; he had a hard time believing what the cops and the tow truck man were saying. His brother had run off the road sometime during the night and a local fisherman out at night to get the best crabs had seen the fire burning in the bay and radioed it in. He had just left the bar when one of the cops stopped him and told him what had happened.

One of the cops had asked if he wanted them to call his father, he had told them to go ahead but to wait until a better hour, if Luis was right and their father and Vince were behind all of the people getting 'cleaned away' then he wanted some time to himself before he had to deal with them. He also reckoned that if Luis was right then they already knew he was dead. A few hours wouldn't change a damn thing.

The once red sports cars front end came over the side first and he felt sick seeing how damaged it was, it looked like just a burnt old shell of a car, nothing red remained and as the car was leveled out and the early sun rise captured his attention through the windows he saw the figure of a person sat in the seat but looking like a burnt imperfect shard of wood.

His feet took him closer even when one of the men tried to hold him back. It was futile on their part he was going to get there with or without them pulling him back. Once close enough he was able to see the burnt remains better, there was nothing left of clothing, its face or even hair to identify it but as the sun moved slower and slower to its place in the sky something on the remains glinted in the sun, woven around burnt tissue and partially hidden was a gold cross around the neck of the poor bastard who had been killed and when Miguel saw it his heart stopped beating. His brother had a cross he wore everyday just like that one.

Backing away he didn't stop to say anything to anyone of the men watching him, his mind was thinking about how Luis must have been so scared just like the little boy he remembered when they first came to the island. At sixteen Miguel had gone to spy on the woman and child that he had heard their parents arguing over, the woman was beautiful and the boy had been sat outside unsure of what was going on and Miguel had seen that look before on his own face when their father would take him on one of his jobs. He had gone over to the little boy and sat with him, not that his expression had changed but he had felt better about the small boy.

As Luis had grown up and Miguel had been away at college they had remained distant but after his mother died and their father eventually married his mistress they had become closer. He knew his brother was the man who had been involved with Cara but at the same time he felt anger about it he also didn't believe that this and what had happened to Cara and Gisele fitted the crime, they didn't commit a crime against anyone. His father may have thought he was protecting some reputation he had as the future heir of the family businesses but he never asked for it, he was sick and tired of living a life he never wanted and was forced to live.

He was disgusted; there was no other way to put it. He wasn't sure what he should do mainly because there was no one he felt like he could trust, nearly everyone on the island felt hostility towards their father but if he was to say something to one of them it would get back to his father. Luis had mentioned in his letter he knew where the CIA agent was they had meant to kill, father would be pissed but Luis deserved to live his life and not being burned alive like a piece of trash, half the DNA in his body was connected to Luis, or what was left of him anyway.

Getting in to his BMW he put his sunglasses on to hide his emotions. His plan was to go home, get at least an hour of sleep and then make it over to his father's where he would pretend he had no idea what was going on. Later he would make sure no one knew what he was doing and he would go and find the man his brother had so much trust in helping him. He wanted justice for what happened to his brother and if he had to take down a psycho and his father to do it, he had no problem with it.

XXX   XXX

After seeing Mel before she left, Rob had to take a few minutes and get himself calm; he knew there would be words between them at some point because that's how bad relationships always made things. She had said a few things as did he and he didn't regret any of them. In those few sentences they had spoken he had realized she was right about one thing, he never had really loved her the way she had wanted him too, what she was wrong about was him seeing her as Jamie. Sure, he had loved Jamie for so many years and probably always would, she's a great woman and a great friend but he hadn't seen the similarities in the twins for years.

Beth had remained fast asleep and he had crawled back in to bed and nestled her against him, her smooth soft skin turning him on like no one before ever had. He stayed awake running a hand up and down her arm as she slept but as the dawn light came in to the bedroom she had stirred and with her brown eyes full of play didn't have to try too hard to get him to be aroused for her again, when she touched him, and in the right places it was like a shock ran through his body and made things turn themselves on.

In the afterglow with the sun fully coming through their sheer curtains they woke to the sound of someone in their villa. Rob felt Beth completely scoot back towards the headboard the look of fear in her eyes. "Stay right here." He said reaching over to get his boxers off the floor and put them on faster than he had ever done before. As quietly as possible he crept across to the door that wasn't closed all the way between the bedroom and the main living area of the villa. A figure moved past when he was close to looking through the crack and he held his breath and looked back at Beth, the color had drained from her entire body.

Slowly opening the door, he saw the back of a man wearing cargo shorts and a black t-shirt in the kitchen and knew immediately that they were fine. "I would ask how you got in here but I think I know, so I'll ask, what the hell are you doing scaring the shit out of us?" He felt Beth come up behind him, a hand on his lower back.

"I thought I'd bring over some food and make everyone breakfast." Matt said turning around a smile on his face. "I got rid of Mel and I feel the need to celebrate."

"That's cruel." Beth came out to see what Matt had brought over, she was wrapped in a pale blue sheet from the bed made in to a dress and Matt raised his eyes and cocked his head to the side at Rob who just grinned. "You're just happy because your wife will be here in a few hours."

"Do you blame me? Did I tell you we're all leaving not much later than when she gets here?"

"Yes you did." Rob answered.

"What are you going to make?" Beth interrupted the conversation as she saw the cantaloupe, honeydew, strawberries and blueberries on the counter. "I had the melons but you had the others, I'm going to make smoothies and pancakes."

"I have some bacon in the fridge." Beth walked over and took it out of the fridge drawer.

"Excellent, I'll use some of your eggs and make extra, do you have any tomatoes?"

"I do, are you making a feast or breakfast."

"I see nothing's changed." Rob sat down at the counter and watched as they began working together; Beth had somehow tied the sheet so it stayed up securely. "Did you tell Beth about the latest updates?" Matt stood there chopping fruit.

"Do I want to know anymore?" She stopped laying bacon on a paper towel on the plate they were going to stick in the microwave.

"The guy the one from the paper whose daughter in law was killed, his son was found dead during the night." Rob reluctantly explained.

"How?" She asked and Matt looked at Rob to see how he was going to answer this one. "He was in a car accident."

"That's it?" Matt had to laugh at Beth's face; she wasn't buying what she was getting told. "No." Rob said.

"Then what else? Is it so bad you're both worried I might freak out?"

"You know knowledge is good if anything were to happen." Matt added and Rob sighed. "It sounds like the son was killed and then his car pushed over a cliff." Beth was buying it, Rob could see until Matt coughed and he could have thrown something at the man.

"I get the feeling there's more."

"About seven hundred degrees of heat." Matt said from the sink.

"What?"

"He burned alive." Matt coming back from the sink finished.

"He did?" She looked at Rob for confirmation.

"There's no proof that he did but it's a good speculation that he had someone kill his son and make it look like an accident."

"That's just evil."

"Now you know why Matt and Jamie want us off this island together before night fall."

"No argument from me anymore." Beth said and

her words pleased Rob, he didn't want to have to worry about her staying here after they left.

XXX   XXX

"Good morning Steven." His mother came in to the room, he had just finished up the hospital breakfast and he had thought the menu they served during Hell Week had been bad, the stuff they gave the patients was supposed to be good for you and if it was then good meant all the flavors were taken out. After this stay in the hospital he never wanted to see cream of wheat or oatmeal ever again.

"Mom." He said lowering the back of the bed down a little and pushing the wheeled table to the side near the window. "How are you feeling?" She asked putting her purse down and her blazer over the back of the chair. "Pretty good, a little sorer today than yesterday but at least I don't need chemo, which makes me forget about the pain."
"Where is Jamie this morning?"
"She's on her way to be with her husband and daughter, remember they went to Disney for the weekend."
"That's right; I hope I can see her before I go back to Illinois."
"I can do you one better than that."
"What's that?"
"You'll get to meet Mel either later today or tomorrow." He watched the look of an interested woman appear before him. "I'm glad." She simply

260

said.

"That's it? You've been grilling me and Jamie since you got here and that's all you have to say."

"I was thinking about it last night." She paused. "You've grown in to the man your father had hoped you would, not only do you remind me of him in the way you look but you've changed since the last time you came home. It has to be because of Mel and if she has that kind of effect on you then I'm happy you want to be with her."

"You are?" To say her words shocked him was an understatement.

"I just don't want you to make the same mistakes I have. I should never have remarried after your father died but I thought you needed a man around. I know they were what drove you away and I'm sorry." She went for her purse and sat on the seat next to his bed while he watched her searching for something inside the black leather purse.

"I brought this for you." She handed him a green velvet box, it looked a little worn but not too noticeable. "I thought it might come in handy." She passed it to him and he took it, wondering what was inside. "These are." He started but he felt choked and had to stop. "Yes, the rings your father gave me and the one I gave him when we were engaged and married. When I was at home I brought them out of my closet while I was packing and I think I knew I would give them to you now."

"This means so much to me."

"You don't have to use them. I know men and women these days like those big showy diamonds they see the famous people wear." He looked down at the diamond he remembered his mother wore on the plain gold band and to say the stone was small was impossible, the diamond was bigger than some he had seen over the years. "I think Mel will love it, thank you."

"I rented a car today too, I was invited by your team leader to visit where you work and I thought Jamie would be here but too busy, if you want I could get Mel, is she flying in?"

"Yes, she gets in later but you don't have to." He wasn't sure if her visit to the base and his team or the thought of her being alone with Mel worried him more. "I don't mind."

"She's going to call me later and let me know her plans, I'll see what she has arranged and let you know."

"Sounds fair."

"What time are you going to the base?"

"Whenever I want, should I take something, flowers, wine?" He laughed at her question.

"Flowers are a little feminine and I don't think they'd fit Daniel's décor and wine isn't allowed."

CHAPTER THIRTY-ONE

After calling Steve, Mel settled in at the gate Jamie was due to arrive at and sat there looking around at all the travelers coming and going inside the

Miami terminal she wondered if anyone was watching and she knew she was being paranoid. She had arrived at concourse A and had to meet Jamie at concourse E, between the two she had found a Starbucks and stopped in to get a tall, whole milk, double sugar, extra foam caramel macchiato and a piece of their marble cake. She knew the calories and fat would kill her but the stress of Rob and his attitude, what had been going on and the lack of nicotine she told herself she needed it.

"That stuff will kill you." A female voice said from right next to her ear, the voice she would never forget however long she lived, Jamie's. "Better than the things I used to do." Mel gave her a wide mouth grin full of cake.
"You might have something there." Jamie took the generic plastic seat next to her sister and put the identical bag next to the other. "You're on the next flight to LA from D forty-five." Jamie said passing over the ticket and her sisters own ID. "There'll be a connecting flight there to San Diego."
"When's your flight?" Mel juggled her coffee with her cake on her lap as she took out everything Jamie would need of her own, her driver's license and passport, the things she had borrowed. "In twenty minutes from A twenty-six."
"Let's get going then." Mel put what she'd been given as Jamie kept hers in her hand watching her sister still juggling her hand full.

"I just spoke to Steve. He said his mother offered to

pick me up when I get in."

"She did?" Jamie tried to hide her smile but Mel caught it.

"Is she completely horrid?"

"No, just curious. She loves her son and after everything she went through with her marriages she doesn't want him to get hurt."

"I can't wait to meet her." They began walking through the people towards the eastern end of the airport. "She's nice, just be yourself and tell the truth, all that matters is Steve loves you."

"He does doesn't he." She felt her cheeks redden.

"Now you know what it feels like."

"Yeah, there's no doubt who Matt loves."

"You'll have that one day."

"I hope so." They came to the concourse Mel would need, D.

"Take care." Mel gave her sister a hug.

"Don't I always." She raised her eyebrows quickly. "And before you go I have some news to tell you."

"What?"

"I'm pregnant."

"That's great." Mel hugged her again. One day she would ask about the miscarriage but for now she would wait. "Does Matt know?"

"I told him the first night you were in Bequia."

"I'm going to have to work fast to catch up."

"Good luck with that." Jamie joked sticking her tongue out as she began mingling in with everyone else walking her way.

XXX   XXX

"Where is Miguel?"

"Home in bed." Vince watched his boss looking over his glasses at the papers before him, to anyone outside they would never know the police had just left after giving the older man the terrible news that one of his sons was dead, believed to have been murdered. "Maybe you should go down and wake him, let him know the bad news."

"He was in the town last night from what Dave said. The funeral for Cara is later. You sure you want to do it now?"

"Of course, just because Cara's funeral happens to be today doesn't stop everything else."

"What do you want me to do?"

"Have you found that body yet for me?" Mr. Santos looked up for just a few seconds.

"I thought it was decided we would give up."

"No." Mr. Santos dropped his paper in anger. "I can't take the risk he's still alive. There's something that tells me he's close and I want it all cleaned up."

"Yes Boss, I'm sorry."

"If you'd done your damn job properly the first time we would never be in this mess."

"Like I said, I'm sorry; I thought getting the other situation sorted was a priority."

"That's why I'm in charge." He picked his papers up again.

Vince left the office knowing he was in the shit house. He rarely got in there but the last time was because he had taken one of the boss' whores out on the company boat and after he had done what he wanted to do he had disposed of her like he did to anyone he didn't need anymore. Before that it was because he had argued with one of the best cops they had bought off, the fight had ended in Vince having to snap the guys neck, which had pissed the boss off more than he had ever seen until today.

XXX   XXX

"Do you want to come with me?" Matt asked Beth as they sat around the table stuffed from all the food they had eaten over breakfast. They were just talking about how Jamie would be arriving soon and that Matt would have to go and shower if he wanted to smell as well as look good for seeing his wife. "I'd love to, is that okay?" Beth answered. "I have a feeling she'd be pissed if I didn't bring you." "Then count me in, I'd like to take a shower and dress first though." She was still wearing the sheet and neither man had really paid much attention to it in the last hour or so.

"I'm going to go and shower and pack up whatever is left for us to leave." He got up and started for the plates to begin cleaning up. "I'll get those." Robert said. "I'm going to be staying so I can do them." "No argument for me, I'll honk the horn when I'm outside." He was gone and Beth herself got up. "Why don't you leave the dishes for a few minutes and come take a shower with me." She put her hand up his shirt and kissed him ever so gently on the lips, teasingly she pulled back when he wanted more. "You have to follow me if you want that." She whispered in his ear. She got up from his lap and as she got closer to the bedroom more of the sheet slid from her body, he watched her until she was inside and away from his line of sight and then he was up and out of the chair and inside the bathroom before she could even get the water turned on.

Reaching for the faucet himself, Rob kissed her while making sure they would get plenty of warm water, her hands were all over driving him nuts, she had a tendency when they started to kiss to twirl small sections of hair on his chest in her fingers until things heated up and her hands would travel lower as did his.

While his mouth was dancing with hers and his hands were sliding all over the wet skin under the heavy spray from the tap he began to let his mind wander to what could be, could he have this all the time with her? Would she move and leave her family and friends to live with him? Would she even want to? It wasn't like they had talked about any of this, the agreement that this went no further after they left was still at the front of his mind, he knew he had said those words out in the ocean as she stood half naked before him but he never knew it could feel like this.

"What are you thinking?" She looked up in to his

eyes.

"You."

"Really? Care to tell me what exactly you are thinking?"

"That I'm glad fate brought us together and that I don't know what I'll do once we return back to where we come from."

"You'll see me; think you'll be able to get rid of me after what you've given me the last few days?"

"What have I given you?"

"You're kidding right?" She smirked. "How about I refresh your memory." She stood on her tip toes and wrapped her wet arms around his neck, she softly brushed her nose against the tip of his and he let her take his lips, his hands moved down to her firm bottom and gently massaged the flesh, he felt her melt as the kiss deepened.

He felt her right leg wrap around his leg and her body intimately moved against his erection making him momentarily stop breathing. Beth pulled back and the look on her face alone made him groan from the sparkle of her knowledge that she had caused that effect in him and she alone. The water was still cascading down their bodies and he wanted to feel more, he wanted to be inside her more than he wanted to take another breath. He moved her backwards so she was against the tiled wall and he knew it was cold against her skin as she arched her back and further in to him.

He lifted her butt up and he felt her silky legs wrap around his middle and before he knew it she was pulling him in to her warmth without him really having to do anything, he got his footing and pushed back as she came down making a rhythm that was just their own.

XXX   XXX

Knowing his father had them watched and followed everywhere they went, getting updates and calls about who they saw and spent time with he knew he had to have a way to go out without the men paid to be their spies.

After a few hours of sleep, Miguel had showered and changed in to his shorts and t-shirt he had just got back from the cleaners. Today was Cara's funeral but he knew his father would not expect him to go to his own wife's funeral, the affair was already turning in to a no show anyway, Cara's friends all lived in the states and she had no family he had ever had the opportunity to meet. He felt sad on one side because she had been his wife but he also knew on the other that she had married him just for the money and what came with it. She had been cold in bed and he hoped she was cold wherever her soul was now.

He called his father and said he would be going out on the boat again for some more searching. He lied and said a man in town had mentioned seeing something over the other side of the Island while they were out fishing and that he wanted to go and check it out. He wasn't sure how much he would be followed out on the water, he suspected they used the GPS system and if they did and they saw the boat stopped for too long they would know something was going on so his plan was to drop anchor up in West Cay and then use the small inflatable power boat he had never used but stored in his garage. That way he could make it to where Luis had said the man he was looking for was and not alert anyone to where he was going

In the harbor he had got the small power boat and the engine to his father's boat by putting the motor in a cooler and the deflated boat in his scuba bag, to anyone looking and watching it would seem as if he was getting ready to do some summer under water searching. He fired up the main boat engine and started off towards the West Cay, he set the boat at a slower speed once he was out and set the wheel as he went back and took out the inflatable boat attaching it to the automatic pump and letting it work as he took out the motor from the cooler and then back to the wheel. A couple of fishing boats were busy pulling in their catches but they were too busy to take any notice of him and after he was clear and the wheel set again he was back to the boat in time to stop the boat from over inflating. Once satisfied everything was ready, he went back to the wheel and put it in a higher gear and made it to the cove in record time.

CHAPTER THIRTY-TWO

Rob stood at the sink when he heard a noise behind him, he had thought it was Beth back already but when he had turned, bubbles of dish water falling from his hands he had known from the man stood behind him that he was glad Beth wasn't there. Danger had come and it had walked right in to the villa.

"Who are you?" Rob played dumb. Since they had thrown him over board he had shaved and although his hair was still a little shabby he still felt he looked different enough to play dumb. "You know who I am." The young man looked exhausted and about ready to drop. "I'm sorry we tried to kill you."
"That's comforting."
"Look, I know you think I'm as bad as my father but I'm not. I only came here because I need your help."
"That's funny." Rob wiped his hands dry and threw the towel on the counter. "Where's your sidekicks?"
"I came alone; actually I took the long way here so I could ensure no one would follow me and find you."
"Why?"
"My father ordered his sidekick to kill my wife, a woman she knew and last night Vince murdered my brother, his own flesh and blood. If he can kill Luis, he would probably kill me too."

Pausing for a second Rob couldn't tell if the man was sincere or lying through his perfect teeth.

"Why should I believe you came to me for help?"
"You have no reason to aside from I know you were here to get information on my father and possibly extradite him back to America. I'll tell you everything you need to know to help you do that."
"Again, why would I believe you want to throw your father to the authorities?"
"How about this?" Rob stood ready to jump out of the way when the kid moved behind the wall to get something, as far as he knew there was a gun or worse behind the wall.

Miguel took the suitcase he had earlier retrieved from where his father had Vince put it. It had been down in the boats cabin waiting for a night when his father would throw it in to a fire pit and ensure nothing remained. "That's my suitcase."
"It is, everything, including your gun is still in here, we packed all your stuff up to make it look like you had just up and left. My father even had your bill taken care of so no one would ask any questions. Your bosses if they looked in to where you were would have thought you'd left too."
"But they didn't, they have sent me back up and they're on their way here." He was lying but he didn't care, he still didn't trust the kid.

Taking his suitcase and putting it on the dining table he unzipped it and went straight for his gun. "If you're telling the truth you won't mind me doing this." He was aiming his gun right at Miguel's chest and the kid even threw his hands in the air. "Do whatever you need but right now I'm supposed to be looking for your remains and I left the boat at West Cay, the boat you saw us on that day in Petit Nevis has a GPS system on it and if it stays in one place too long Vince and my father will get suspicious."

"How did you get here from the boat?"

"Power dingy, don't worry I made sure no one saw me setting it up on the boat."

"Why did your father kill your wife and brother?"

"They were having an affair and he found out. He didn't like Luis doing that, he has always seen me as his favorite, the heir to his life in a few years and he doesn't want to see it marred by anything."

"The things you've been doing for him all your adult life has marred your future."

"True."

"How do you know he killed them?"

"Luis knew he was going to be dealt with, he was smart enough to leave me a note with someone my father has no ties to on this island and told me to meet him there, when he didn't show last night Don gave me this." Miguel lowered an arm and Rob took the safety off the gun. "I'm just getting you the letter." Miguel reached in to his shorts and took out the crumpled piece of paper. "Here." Miguel held it out.

"Put it on the table and then lay on the floor with your hands behind your head."

He watched while Miguel did as he had been ordered to and when he was satisfied the kid wouldn't try anything he took the paper off the table, with one hand keeping the gun on him he shook out the paper and read the note. "Chelsea Myers?" Rob asked after he read the letter. "She was the hottest island girl in my high school; I brought her here to sleep with her." He stopped and a cough came out. "We were both drunk from a party we had gone to and she was as nervous as I was. Needless to say we never had sex and neither of us denied rumors that we did. I did sleep with her a few months later but in the back of her father's car."

"You'll have to tell me everything I need to know before I can decide what the course of action will be."

"I'll tell you everything. My brother, Cara, they didn't deserve to die."

XXX   XXX

"You are a sight for sore eyes." Matt said picking up his wife and spinning her around, her bag falling to the floor and his lips making sure she couldn't respond with anything but a kiss until he was satisfied. "I'll get that." A faint voice said and Jamie broke off the kiss to see Beth bending down to get her bag. "No you won't." Jamie gave Beth a smile and then a friendly hug before holding her shoulders and giving her the once over. "You have the look of someone just recently made very relaxed by a man who must know what he's doing."

"He does." Beth blushed.

"Hey, I wasn't even there." Matt joked.

"I think she meant Rob." Beth laughed.

"Yeah I definitely did." Jamie picked her bag up and took her glasses off a moment giving her husband one of those looks where he would know she was not wanting the joke to go any further with his name in it.

"So what's the plan?" Matt asked once they were inside the car, Beth was sat in back and was sitting forward so she could hear everything that was going on. "First we're going to be flying to Miami and then there we are going to be sailing a boat around for one day and one night."

"Us, sailing?" Matt looked at his wife and laughed. Beth frowned.

"Why's that so funny? Aren't you both in the navy, you do boats all the time."

"Jay hates anything smaller than an aircraft carrier."

"He's right, I do. I love being State side so I don't have to deal with the water."

"Then why'd you arrange for a boat?"

"I thought it would be fun for Matt." Jamie put her hand on her husband's knee and Beth missed Rob like crazy and felt for the first time in the last few days a sample of what it would be like when they all left here and back to their lives.

"Speaking of a few days, I arranged for Daniel to let you have Monday off so we have an extra day."

"What about Izzy?"

"You really think my father; Margaret or Izzy want to leave Disney?"

275

"I don't suppose they would." Matt turned in to the driveway of the villa he had been sharing with his wife's sister. The three of them got out, the two women on the same side and Jamie turned to Beth. "Are you and Rob almost ready to go?"
"Actually, I need to get all my stuff together; we err, got a little side tracked earlier."
"Come find us when you are, I'm going to go and enjoy my husband for a while."

Beth waved and Jamie turned back to Matt who was looking down at her from the front steps. "Is your lap top on?" She called up to him as she made her way closer.
"Yes, why?" He waited for her to get to the top of the fourth step before he took her bag from her and picked her up, carrying her in to the villa as if they had just been married. "I have something I brought to show you." She said as he put her down on the floor. "Wow, this is beautiful." She forgot what she was saying and had walked like her sister did to the back door. "Not as beautiful as you." He came behind her and wrapped his arms around her, kissing the top of her head, she turned her head to the side and she kissed his strong jaw line. "I really want to show you something."
"As long as it's you naked and in that bed soon I don't care what you show me."
"You'll want to see this."

Jamie went over to her bag where Matt had put it next to the table and pulled out the disc she had been dying to show him since her doctor's visit.

276

"What is it?" He asked taking it and sitting down at the chair before his laptop and pulling his wife in to sit on his lap. "Just play it." Jamie put her arm around his shoulders as he inserted the blue CD and waited for the computer to read it.

In just a few moments a picture came on the screen Matt never expected, a moving ultrasound. It was like watching his own personal image of inside Jamie and he loved it. "You got this from your doctors?"
"Yep, I said I wanted you to see this too so he made this copy."
"That's our baby?"
"Look closely."
"Why, is it really an alien or something?" He squinted and sat forward and tried to make out the shapes and movement. "No alien, do you see it?"
"What am I looking for?"
"This." Jamie outlined first one section moving and then another.
"Huh? I see it but what does it mean?"
"I don't know how to tell you this Lieutenant Commander but." She paused, a wicked smile on her face. "There's two heart beats there."
"Two?" He was frowning until his brow raised as he figured it out. "Twins?"
"Yep, we're having twins."

Matt was speechless, totally unsure how to express his shock and happiness. "I knew you'd be like this." Jamie smirked. "I like making you stunned."

"Is this for real or are you just pulling some joke on me?" He was frowning again but there was a smile hiding just under the surface. "You are part maker of a serious set of twins." She kissed his lips softly.

"I never." He paused. "I mean you being a twin and all, I never thought, expected, dreamed it would happen." She felt his hands moving below her t-shirt to sit atop her smooth stomach. "It has, you know what I think?"

"What?"

"The last time we weren't supposed to have the baby we lost so mother nature is making up for it now by giving us these. Think you can handle it?"

"Now that depends on whether we have girls or boys, I'm already outnumbered in the house."

"I'm hoping for boys; we'll know in a few weeks."

"And everything's okay with them and you?"

Matt looked down and Jamie turned his face back up by putting a finger under his chin. "I heard their heartbeats, the chance of a miscarriage after that is so small. I'm healthier than I ever remember being and I have faith everything will be okay."

"I just." He stopped himself and Jamie caught a tear falling out of his right eye with her fingers. "Don't cry baby, you'll start me off."

"I'm just so worried."

"You don't have to be I promise."

"I want us to get off this island now; I don't want us to wait. I know it's selfish but I want to make sure you are in absolutely no harm."

"I never am when you are with me." Jamie got up from his lap and took his hand. "I think we have enough time to enjoy some alone time together." She pulled him up, he wasn't fighting and she led him to the room that he hadn't used yet.

XXX   XXX

To say she was shocked when she walked in the back door to the villa would have been an understatement, the gum Jamie had given her had almost been swallowed and then it almost fell on the floor as her mouth gaped open.

At the dining table was a man, his back to her tied with what looked like ripped sheets, Rob a gun in his hand was keeping the deadly looking weapon aimed straight for the man. "What the fuck?" It slipped out and she put her hand over her mouth. "Beth, meet Miguel Santos, you might remember reading about his wife in the newspaper."
"The dead one?" She squeaked out.
"Yeah, but I'm only guilty of trying to kill him." Miguel said and she couldn't get her feet to move. "Are they both next door?" Rob asked her and she nodded. "Go get them. Our plans have changed."

Not waiting for any more directions Beth willed her legs to move back in the direction she had come from. Once her bare feet touched the hot sand she ran to the other wooden staircase and making as much noise as she could because she knew what they had been planning to do behind closed doors she didn't want to see anything like lots of naked skin. "Matt, Jamie." She called when her feet touched the top step and she saw a figure come out of the bedroom, Jamie, her hair disheveled and her lips red came out first followed by Matt, the only excess of skin being revealed was his chest. "What's wrong?" Jamie came closer, worry frowning her forehead. "Rob." She rushed out, she hadn't gone too far but her heart was beating faster than she had ever known it to.

"What is it?" Jamie took her by the upper arms and looked at her. "Breath, take it easy and tell us." "One of the people that tried to kill him is over there, Rob has him tied to a chair and a gun pointed on him but he wants you two there." "Right now?" Matt sighed looking at both of the women. "I thought Mel was the only one with bad timing around here." He went back in the bedroom and came out pulling the shirt over his head, Jamie let go when she was sure Beth was calm and she too went in to the bedroom coming back out and making Beth's jaw drop for a second time.

In her hands Jamie held a gun that looked the same as the one Rob had next door. She took something and pushed it into the grip and then pulled another piece back with a weird click sound Beth recognized from hearing in movies. "Ready?" Jamie watched Matt take out his own gun, he had picked it up from a man he had met in town, a man once a member of the SEAL family who now lived on one of the islands in the area. He hadn't been sure what was going to be waiting for them and he didn't want to be unprepared. "Beth, stay here." Matt ordered.

"No, I'll stay behind you but I'm not being left out in case there's others around. Strangely I feel safer with you guys."

Following the two of them out she kept up as they ran over to the other villa and in to the room, both with their guns ready to shoot if need be. Their moves were so fluid that she wondered how many times they had done it; it was so choreographed and natural. "You can put the safeties on those." Rob told them and they all walked over and it was Beth's first time to see the man who was tied to the chair. He was young and handsome, the feeling of a well scripted Hollywood movie flashed in her head, it was surreal.

CHAPTER THIRTY-THREE

"Agent Buchanan, CIA." Jamie flipped her ID wallet in his face and the tied man looked like he knew already. "This is agent Taylor and agent DeVeuve." Jamie introduced both Matt and Beth and Beth was trying hard not to laugh out loud. Like this guy wouldn't know something was odd when everyone but her had a gun. "Meet Miguel Santos." Rob filled them in. "He's here looking for our help."

"Because his father killed his brother?" Jamie took one of the seats, turned it around and sat backwards on it. "You knew?" Miguel was shocked now.

"Our agency has been keeping an eye on everything including your wife's murder and that of a female connected to Luis and Carla by a sexual tryst."

"I don't see how you'd need help?" Matt stated. "Didn't you just have the people screwing behind your back and hurting you taken care of? People should be as lucky as you asshole."

"I need to get back to the boat. What can I do, anything, to help you to help me? I want my father taken down."

"We're going to be gone from here soon so if you are screwing us it will be your bad luck, we'll give you a number you can call." Rob looked at Matt and he knew what he wanted and Matt took one of the napkins from the table and wrote a number on it. "We'll discuss some plans and when you call we'll let you know." Rob stood up and again turned to Matt. "He supposedly used some small power boat to get here from his bigger boat. Can you take him down to the shore and just make sure he's telling the truth?"

"Sure thing."

Matt untied Miguel as Rob walked in to the kitchen putting his gun down on the countertop with a thud and rattle as it swirled a little. Jamie watched her husband take Miguel out and off towards the shoreline. She turned to Beth whose color was still a little peaked and put her arm around her. "Are you okay?"

"I've never played cop before, all these guns scare me."

"Have you ever held a gun?" Jamie let her go and stood before her. Beth had thought this female seemed so normal, she was wearing a short pair of cargo shorts similar to her husbands but the length was much more feminine and a black tank top that hugged her curves and showed what a great figure she had, throw in the gun and she looked so much less female and more like a deadly weapon. She knew Jamie had killed at least two people and she wondered if maybe there was more.

"I've never needed to." Beth felt herself shaking because she knew what was coming.

"Here." She watched Jamie remove the bottom of the gun. "These are the bullets in the clip." She showed Beth. "You push it up until it clicks."

"Okay."

"Here." She held it out and Beth just looked at it like it would burn her if she took it.

"It's okay, the safety is on." Jamie's words seemed to soothe her and she did take it.

"Is it meant to feel heavy or is it just me?"

"It is a little heavy, now, you see this piece here." Jamie pointed to the top section. "Pull it back until it clicks and then let go, that's the safety." Beth followed the instructions and felt her adrenaline beginning to pulse through her own veins. "Now all you would have to do is squeeze the trigger and it would fire." Jamie put her hand over the top of the gun and Beth let it go. "I wanted you to know in case something ever happened."

"You think it will?"

"Nah, not with the three of us around, but it's something to know, you never know down the road what could happen, when you might need to know."

Matt came back in the villa and Rob was still leaning over the counter with his head down. "Let me see that ID." Matt said to his wife and she removed it from her thigh pocket and passed it to him, he leaned half his butt on the table and opened up the wallet. "Huh." He smirked. "How old is this?"

"It's from when I worked with Rob on the mission." She stopped and looked at Beth.

"When you went undercover for him with the son before you almost got killed by the guy who took you and tortured you when you had just moved to the SEAL team, you know where you both met each other." Beth said and Matt was frowning while Jamie's brow rose. "Yeah." Jamie simply replied. "Did Mel or Rob tell you about that?"

"Rob, don't be mad at him, I asked him why he was single and he explained his last girlfriend and it led to you and how he knew you and well, once he started the story I wanted to know more."

"I'm surprised he talked about me."

"Don't be, he holds you up on a pedestal. I think he never expected to have us meet. I think you have a lot of guts to just be in the Navy these days but to survive events like you did." Matt put his arm around his wife's shoulder.

"I still have nightmares." Jamie confessed smoothing her hand along the gun before Matt took it from her and put it on the table he was sitting on. "I can only imagine." Beth said softly. "We've been through a lot but together we made it through." Matt kissed Jamie's head and Beth felt touched. "It must be great to have that connection with someone. Did you always have one?"

"At first we were on the same team and aside from being neighbors we didn't have much to do with each other." Jamie began and Matt took over where she stopped.

"We were partnered on a once around the 'O' course on base. My CO and the few of the team participating all expected to prove a point that she wasn't right for the team but she kept up with me all the way around and gained all of our respect."

"I wanted to collapse so bad." Jamie smiled. "But Matt and the others were cool. We hung out a few times outside of the team and a week or so later he asked me to drive with him to the team leaders wedding dinner, we both had no dates and seeing as we lived next door it seemed like the obvious choice."

"There were other tests she passed too before that she's forgetting, each one she aced. She looked amazing the night of the dinner; the dress she bought was breath taking. I had been thinking about her more and more over the week together and it was that night that made me want her completely."

"When we got home I was disappointed over the lack of goodnight when he dropped me off and while in my pool figured a way to get him over and when he did one thing led to another and well, before it could get to the good stuff again I got the news about Mel. While I was away on the mission it was mainly Matt I thought about, I never got to tell him how I liked him and that I would have continued getting to know him better if I hadn't left."

"And I worried my ass off that the woman I had fallen for was never going to come back and that I may have to be there when we do find the worst case scenario."

"The night I got back, we made up for everything." Jamie chuckled. "And then he made me get up really early for a surprise, he drove me out to the desert and wrapped me up in a blanket, his arms around me to watch the sun rise and he proposed."

"I thought for sure she'd laugh and say no."

"But I didn't because I knew there was nothing more I wanted in life than to be this man's wife."

"And the rest is history we can finish in the safety of whatever Jamie has planned for us." Rob butted in.

"You aren't going to help the kid?" Matt asked standing up.

"Nope, not with just the four of us, we'll go back to the states and do this the right way."

"I hope Miguel's father doesn't find out he was here then." Jamie came right up in to Rob's face.

"The guy'll kill his own son; I'm sure Miguel isn't immune to it no matter how much Mr. Santos dotes on him."

"I'm with Jay, let's at least give Miguel the choice to come back with us, get the info state side sworn by a judge and then come back, but keep the kid safe." Matt said.

"I'm with them." Beth hooked her thumb at her two new friends.

"Then what are your suggestions?"

XXX   XXX

After nine hours of traveling Mel was ready to just go home and shower and sleep for a few days but when she had called Steve from LAX on her ten-minute stop over before her connecting flight to San Diego he had told her how his mother was insisting on picking her up and he was looking forward to seeing her. In her heart she wanted to see him before anything else too but the thought of having to spend alone time with the mother of her boyfriend before she'd even really met her was daunting, especially after Jamie had told her the woman was so interested in everything about her.

With just her small bag she had switched with her brother in law to ensure she and her sister were constant in the bag they carried she exited the plane with the other thirty or so passengers and made it out to the curb without the hassle of having to go and pick up any luggage she had booked in. Steve had said he would give his mother directions to just go and pick her up from the arrival gate in the car and so she walked out of the automatic door and looked around. There were various cabs and a base vehicle and down the end was a white sedan she pegged as a rental before she saw the blonde haired lady get out and wave to her.

"You must be Mel." The short woman with the blonde hair said coming up to the curb as Mel got closer. "You must be Steve's Mom." Mel faltered for a minute until Linda took her and gave her a motherly hug. Mel tried to be enthusiastic about it but she was too tired and hoped that this woman didn't notice. "Please, call me Linda."
"Linda, it sure is nice to finally meet you."
"Please, I know my son doesn't talk about me much, he did talk about you though."
"I can only imagine what he would say." Mel frowned to herself as Linda walked around to get in the driver's door while Mel after putting her bag on the back seat joined her in the car sitting next to her.

"My son is very fond of you."
"I'm very fond of him too."
"He was so excited when he knew you were coming back early, when your sister left last night he was a little down but when he knew you were returning he picked up. There's something about you sisters, people just seem to love you. I was at the base this morning; all the men had such nice things to say about you both."

"They love Jamie, everyone does."

"Sure, but I'm more interested in you because my son loves you."

"I'm a pretty boring book; you wouldn't want to read it."

"I would, not because I'm prying but because you make Steve happy, I haven't heard him ever talk about a girlfriend like he talks about you."

"He's been good for me too." Mel looked out the window on her side. "I was in a bad place when we first met and then later he kept me going."

"What kind of bad place?"

"I was addicted to drugs and a recovering alcoholic." She admitted and Linda smiled to her. "I'm a recovery alcoholic too, it's been ten years. After Steve's father died I had a really hard time, I missed a lot and Steve left because of the mistakes I made because of the drink. It took him leaving for me to get my act together."

"I would never have figured you."

"As a drunk? I was."

"I had a hard time dealing with my mother and brother dying and my absent father. I also had my sister's image to live up to; it's a lot of pressure."

"I like your sister but I admire your honesty, not many people would admit to her boyfriend's mother she was once a drug addict."

"Maybe not but although I don't use I'll always consider myself an addict."

"I hear you're working as a photographer. I'd love to see some of your work." Linda changed the

subject. "I would love to show you but Steve forgot to explain I'm a photographer's assistant, very unglamorous. I actually just got a new job offer I am thinking about taking but I wanted to see what Steve's schedule will be like first with his therapy'.
"What's the job?"
"A counselor at the local high school. Seems I might be able to get them to listen about addiction and other subjects."
"Sounds like a good job."
"I don't know; I've never really known what I wanted to do. I think with Jamie being a doctor I feel I need to make a mark too; I just don't know what it should be."
"You'll figure it out."
"I hope so."

The conversation stayed light and flowed with the car as they made their way over to the hospital. By the time they pulled in to a parking space, Mel was bursting to see Steve and wanted to run as fast as she could but she knew she would have to wait for his mother, it wouldn't be right to be so rude when the woman had been so nice to her.

"I'm not coming in right now." Linda said turning to Mel as the car stayed running in the spot.
"You're not?" Mel was surprised.
"I think I'll let the two of you have some time alone. Tell Steve I'll be back in the morning."
"Okay." Mel looked down at her short manicured nails. "Thank you for picking me up and it was really nice to meet you."

"You're welcome and the same here."

Getting her bag from the back seat of the car she closed both the doors and watched as Linda pulled out of her parking space and drove off in the direction of the hospital gate. Carrying her bag, she quickly made her way in and after stopping at the reception to get Steve's room number she made it up to the fourth floor and stopped at the door to his room, he was asleep and she let herself look at him, knee or no knee, a SEAL or not he was hers, she liked that, the feeling of knowing someone cared about her as much as she did for them, family was different but with a man who was so beautiful as he was she felt so lucky.

Quietly she entered the room and took in all the things around, there were cards and balloons and a few vases of flowers, not very manly but from what Jamie had said many of the wives had been coming to spend time with him in case he was bored or lonely. There were a few Tupperware containers on his bedside cabinet and it looked like they were filled with cookies. She knew who they were from, the senior chief's wife, Patti was always baking something.

He didn't look like she had expected, his legs were both covered by a blanket and although one was raised with what she knew would be pins coming out of the bandages it wasn't as gnarly as she had first presumed. She put her bags quietly on the floor and took the only seat in the room. His hands felt warm and soft with the recognizable calloused spots from the different things he did with his hands. His hair was sticking out in various directions and looked like it needed more than a comb run through it.

She was careful to not pull out his IV as she stroked his hand, his long fingers that she loved touching her, hands that were strong and brave. Mel knew the risks of being involved with someone in the military; in these times of war it was more prominent than ever. After they had first started dating he had been gone for a month and a half, not all the team had gone just a few of them, Mathew had gone too. She had spent a lot of time with her sister and Izzy and whenever a phone had rung or a car had slowed outside of where they lived she had feared it was someone about to tell them the news she never wanted to hear. As they dated more and he was home and away the stress of his absence lessened a little, not because she didn't care but because she knew he would fight like hell to come back to her. She had never thought something unrelated to his job could be more dangerous. If this tumor had been left any longer he would have been far worse off.

The feeling of her warm tears rolling down her cheeks gave her comfort, it reminded her she was sober and clear headed. She loved this man and she knew he loved her. "Hey." She heard his soft voice and she looked up, his eyes were half open. "When did you get here?" He asked.

"A few minutes ago, did I wake you?"

"Yeah, but I'm glad you did. I've missed you."

"I'm sorry I went; I should have stayed here."

"You did the right thing. I'm proud you cared enough about Rob and your sister's safety to go, it shows you are getting stronger."

"I am." She felt good knowing someone noticed, someone cared enough to tell her all her hard work at keeping clean meant something. His hand wiped away the tears sitting on her cheeks.

"Everything go okay?" He inched up a little and she lifted up a little out of her seat to kiss him. "I was dying for nicotine but everything was fine. I saw Jamie in Miami; they should all be off the island in a few hours if they aren't already."

"Good, did you hear I'm doing better than the doc's thought I would?" His eyes were fluttering shut and they would fly open again. "I did, that's great news."

"I want to take you skiing."

"You do?"

"Make love to you in the snow." He fell asleep and she watched him for a few minutes before a male nurse came in.

"You must be Melanie." The man said checking Steve's IV and monitors and writing in the chart on the end of the bed. "I am. Did my sister say I was coming?" She stood up but kept his hand in hers. "No, Steve's been talking about nothing but you since he found out you were coming." He paused. "Who is your sister?"

"Jamie." Mel frowned thinking the nurse must be swiping some of the pills if he didn't see it. "I don't think I've met her."

"Dr. Buchanan."

"The Commander? She's your sister?"

"Get out of here, you can't see the resemblance?"

"No."

"She's my twin."

"Sorry, I would never have known." He apologized and Mel was speechless. "He's on sleeping meds. He'll be out until around O seven hundred if you want to go home."

"I think I will. I need to get some sleep and freshen up."

CHAPTER THIRTY-FOUR

"Miguel." He heard the voice behind him as he pulled the rope to fasten his father's boat to the dock. The voice sent the hair on the back of his neck to stand at attention. "I had no luck, that tip was a bust." Miguel said turning to look Vince in the face.

"Your father wanted to know what was taking you so long, the boat was off West Cay for a while."

"I was diving for a while, did Dad need something?" Miguel took the bag with his gear in off the boat, he had dumped the dingy and motor over board and let it sink in case a situation like this happened. "He wondered if you were going to the funeral."

"Why would I go to that whore's funeral?" He said

looking up as he got the bag over his shoulder. He was playing it cool and he hoped Vince was buying it.

"Then what are your plans?"
"Why? Dad need something?" He started for the car he had left parked not far away.
"He's worried about you, you've been off since Cara's death and there's something he needs to tell you."
"What?"
"It's about Luis."
"I know about it; I was driving home last night when I saw the rescue crews."
"You didn't call your father."
"Come on, we both know he knew, he didn't need me calling about it."
"Luis was always so weak; I guess the guilt over screwing Cara behind your back was too much."
Miguel didn't know whether he was meant to get mad that his brother was dead or if he was meant to act surprised.

"I figured out he was a while ago." Miguel threw his bag in to the trunk of his car as he took off his sunglasses and looked Vince straight in the eye. "I followed Cara one of her evenings out. When I saw Luis's car at the hotel I knew what was going on."
"Why didn't you ever say anything?"
"I was ashamed. Do you understand what it's like to not be able to give your wife the satisfaction she needs but your little brother can? That she would take all she could from me but hated me that

much."

"No I don't, but we could have helped stop her."

"I'm better off she's dead. I just wish I was strong enough to have been the one who killed her."

"She definitely got what she was deserving." Miguel felt his stomach clench as Vince got that gleam in his eyes, a smirk on the corner of his mouth. It was taking all his strength to not lash out and smack the son of a bitch. He may have told Vince he was cool but he was hoping in a few hours that he would make this asshole pay for what he had done.

"I was going to go home and clean up. Let Dad know I'll be over after. If he's not too busy maybe, we can have dinner together. Toast the people no longer with us." He jiggled his keys and watched Vince shrug. "Sure, I'll let him know."

"Cool, I'll see you both later then." Miguel got in to his car and without a glance back in his rear view mirror he didn't need to look to know Vince was probably walking down the slip to the boat, giving it his once over looking for any signs Miguel was hiding something.

Driving towards his house he made sure his cell was in his pocket and on. He wouldn't use it to call the four people down at the beach because he knew his father had traces on all the lines. He did have a disposable cell he had bought the last time he had been on the mainland, he had checked to ensure it still had minutes on it and he was still carrying fifteen dollars of time on it. He couldn't get back to the house fast enough. He wanted everything over, over soon.

XXX   XXX

"It's set." Jamie walked back in to the main room of the villa her husband had been in, after the departure of their visitor, Rob and Matt had agreed they needed to leave as soon as they could. Leaving that villa had been the first step. Beth had packed fast and Rob didn't have too much so he went into the kitchen and packed up all the food they could take with them. Matt, leaving his wife reluctantly had called his SEAL brother and had gone to meet him. The plan had changed from getting a boat further away on their departure, to now they would borrow a boat from the ex-SEAL from his small fleet.

"Where are we going to meet him?" Rob asked putting the bags in a pile at the back door. "He'll anchor up out there as close as he can. I hope you are a good swimmer." Jamie asked Beth. "I can get by why?"
"We have to swim out."
"What about our stuff?"
"It'll be fine; Matt knows what he's doing. We need to get our suits on and get ready for when he docks."
"Can you give us a moment?" Rob asked looking at Jamie, she got the message and with a smile left to use the bedroom to get in to her bathing suit.

"What?" Beth asked seeing the look on his face.

"I'm sorry we are ruining your vacation."

"Don't be, right now I'd just like to get to safety." Since meeting Miguel and seeing the urgency in the three faces she just wanted to be off this island. Her vacation was ending like it had begun but because of a different man, a man this time that she was beginning to feel strong emotions for.

"While you were packing we decided we would help Miguel."

"Good, I wouldn't want to leave knowing he could die at the hands of those men."

"I want you to see something." He took out a small file from one of the bags; she had seen Jamie holding the same file earlier. "These are the two men we need to be on the lookout for." He passed two eight by ten prints to look at. Beth took them and looked at the two men; their faces were scary alone without the knowledge of what they were capable of. "Do you think we'll see them before we go?"

"I hope not, the plan is for us to get on that boat and get Miguel and head straight for Miami. I'm going to be coming back at a later time for the father and his men. I want everyone safe first. I apologize if I was stressed out earlier but having Miguel here was a little too close, I had images of the others coming in and killing you and me."

Beth put her hands up on the top of his chest. "I appreciate the concern but I'm stronger than I look and if fate says this is my time to go then who am I to argue? I feel lucky to have been able to enjoy the island and you for the last few days and I understand it's time for us to get the hell out of here now."

"I don't know what I ever did to get here, to be able to meet you but I thank God I did. I'm going to be really busy when I get back to DC but I want to see you again, in fact if there was a way we could be nearer to each other permanently then that would be even better."

"Like having me around?" She smiled as his hands wrapped around her.

"I like how you make me feel; you look at me like I'm all you need."

"You are."

"I don't know what I did to warrant that but I am grateful for it."

"I hate to break this up." Jamie came out from the room wearing her black bikini and sunglasses and nothing else. She had tied her hair up and was holding her cell still. "But Matt has anchored down." She pointed with her cell towards the beach and sure enough about forty feet away was the white, expensive looking fifty-foot yacht. "Go and change." Rob said to Beth who left and he waited for the bathroom door to close before he said anything to his oldest friend. He took in how she looked, leaner and more toned than before and if he hadn't known she had a three-year-old he would never have believed it. "You look good."

"Thank you. I'm guessing you and Beth are going to see each other outside of this?" He watched her eyes change color as she spoke. "I'm going to try and have that."

"Good, it's about time you got a good woman in your life."

"I once did; I was too stupid to see it when it happened."

"I would never have called Mel that."

"I meant you." He looked down and then back up. "I regret being too bull headed about you, I wished things were so different."

"Don't Rob." Jamie took a step back. "We went over this a decade ago, there's too much history between us."

"Good history."

"Some, but at the same time when I see you I feel all the hurt and experiences all over again. It's been a hard few years since leaving the USS Abe Lincoln. I have to admit when Nick called me about you being lost I was more hesitant to help you because of what usually happens when we are together rather than you being in danger."

"I'm grateful you came then."

"Good, I hope you are."

"I heard you are pregnant again. Congratulations."

"Thank you." She looked away seeing her husband swimming with ease through the waves. "Do yourself a favor." Jamie looked back. "And take this the right way. Get on with your life with Beth, she seems like a great woman and you couldn't do any better but you need to get far away from the past and cut it completely from your life."

"You are my past, the closest thing I have to family." He moved closer towards her as she took another step back. "Exactly, this back and forth we do, this need to bring the other in to the others life. I'm no CIA agent, I'm a doctor, a mother and a wife, I shouldn't be anywhere near here."

"You make a good agent."

"That doesn't matter." Jamie leaned over and took her ID from her bag. "Destroy this and next time you need back up take Nick." She pleaded. "I can't do this anymore."

"Jamie please." He took it unwillingly as she walked to the back door, her arms folded over her chest. "Don't, you've dragged me in to things I never should have been involved in. I think you took my childhood problems and used them to try and get closer to me after you hurt me Rob. That's not fair and then you have to drag my sister in to it? She's more fragile than anyone with her problems and you almost killed her."

"I'm sorry."

"You always are."

"Do you really mean you no longer want a friendship with me? I was hoping to see Izzy soon."

The mention of her daughter's name spurred more anger in to Jamie she spun around. "Don't bring my daughter in to this." She bit out. "If you cared even a small bit about her then you wouldn't put me in the position to get killed all the time. I'm sick of all this Rob."

"I didn't know you would be contacted about this."

"Come on, of course Nick would call me. You know when he did Matt got that look in his eyes the one that rips my heart out. You are not only screwing with my life now but his too, I married him, I hoped for a nice quiet life where the only danger is whether or not he'll come back after a mission. That I can deal with but my heart belongs to him and our children."

"How old would our son be now?" He asked softly and she turned with eyes of fire, never in the last nine years had Rob brought it up. "The one you didn't want?" Jamie was on fire now, she wanted to hit him so bad but her husband was just twenty feet away. "I regret all of it." Rob said quickly. "Good, because there isn't a single moment I look at my daughter and not feel a stab of guilt over what I let you talk me in to but it was the best thing for both of us wasn't it. We would have never made it together and you were just so far in to your work with the agency."

Beth stood inside the door of the bedroom and wide mouthed listened to what they were saying. She couldn't believe her ears. There was something a lot deeper between the two of them and it involved a boy, had Jamie been pregnant at some point with Rob's baby? Their voices quietened down as Matt's voice sounded in the room, she was about to go out when she heard the discussion continue, Matt joining in.

"What's going on?" Matt could see from the look on his wife's face that she was mad about something, he had seen that look only once before and it made the hair stand on the back of his neck. "I was just explaining to Rob the reasons he should get some distance between us once we return."

"I tend to agree with her." Matt crossed his arms. "I know the two of you go way back but if you had to live with Jamie as she wakes up in a nightmare or with guilt over the miscarriage because she blames herself for what she did for you, that she's a bad person then you wouldn't put her through this ever again."

"I understand, don't worry, I'll follow your wishes when we get state side."

"Before we let this drop." Jamie joined in. "You ever mention our son again and I will not be responsible for my actions." Rob looked at Matt and was shocked he wasn't saying anything. "I told Matt everything Rob; I don't have any secrets from him."

CHAPTER THIRTY-FIVE

"Hey, good morning." Mel said walking in to Steve's room early to find Lee and his wife Mary sitting there. "Morning." They all said back as she put her bag down on the floor next to the bed. She leaned down to give Steve a kiss and then standing back up caught the two friends looking at her. "What?" She asked smiling as they smiled back. "Nothing." Mary said quickly and first. "How was your journey back yesterday?" She changed the subject. Mel looked at Steve not knowing what he had told them.

"They know where you were." Steve told her.

"Oh."

"And I'm shocked your sister went." Lee said. "If I was her I would steer clear of that guy."

"Yeah, well, one day she'll set him straight."

"We should get going." Mary put her hand on her husband's arm. "Mel, give me a call later, we should have lunch again soon."

"I'd like that."

"Me too." Mary stood slowly, she was eight months pregnant with her third child and Lee's second. "I hate getting up and down." She laughed.

"Jamie said the same thing when she was pregnant with Izzy." Mel said not knowing from personal experience. "I'm sure you'll understand yourself soon enough." Lee said laughing. "I'll see both of you later." Steve said wishing he could stand up and see them both out himself.

"Bye." Mary waved as they left and Mel sat on the seat next to the bed.

"What was that all about?" Mel asked, taking his hand.

"You know, the usual someone has a relationship and it's presumed they're more serious than they are."

"Oh."

"I didn't mean us." Steve closed his eyes. "We're good, they just want to see us hitched and with kids you know."

"I guess."

"Any news from your sister?"

"Nothing."

"You look worried, was it that bad down there?"

"I'm not worried; I just don't like her being anywhere dangerous."

"Matt will keep her safe."

"I know. Anyway, how are you feeling this morning?"

"Better, the pain is still there but it's getting bearable."

"Your Mom's really nice."

"She said the same thing about you this morning when she called. She wanted to get some stuff done but asked if you would be here at lunchtime, she's bringing something over."

"Cool."

"What are your plans today?"

"Staying here with you."

"I like those plans, my new doctor says I'll be out of here by Monday, then it'll be back and forth from the rehab center every day."

"Have you decided where you'll stay? Your house is a little awkward to get around, all those stairs."

"I was hoping you'd take pity on me, be my personal slave."

"Now I like the sound of that." Mel laughed and Steve loved how she looked when she did. "Do you remember me coming to see you last night?"

"Vaguely."

"You were pretty doped up." She smoothed his hair back from his forehead making it spike up, she loved his dark hair and dark eyes, they used to hold such mysterious secrets but no more. "Said you wanted to take me skiing."

"I remember that." He laughed. "I had a dream of

making love to you in the snow."

"Wouldn't that be too cold?"

"Nah, I'd keep you warm."

"Then I look forward to it."

"So." Mel began. "You'll never believe what your nurse said to me last night."

"Did he hit on you? I can still take him out from here."

"No." Mel laughed again. "He didn't see me as Jamie's sister, said he didn't see the resemblance."

"That's because there isn't much of one anymore, your hair color, your strong attitude, you are your own person now."

"I like to think so but it's the first time really that anyone's ever told me out loud."

"Makes you feel special doesn't it?"

"Sure does. I think I need to move on with my life, make some changes, stop living in her shadow."

"Good for you." He took her hand. "Just tell me your plans include me."

"They do." She kissed where his IV was inserted. "I love my sister to death, she's helped me so much over the years and I can't see my life not including her instead of being more like her I want to just make her and you proud."

"You make me proud all the time." Mel felt her heart tighten from his words.

"I talked to Matt like you said. I had no idea what he and Jay were going through. He promised me to never say anything to my sister, she doesn't want anyone to know but this may sound really bad but knowing she's not so perfect and that life troubles her makes me feel like I shouldn't be so hard on myself."

"I've been telling you that all along."

"I know, but I guess I needed to see it with my own eyes."

XXX   XXX

Beth swam to the boat with Rob beside her giving her encouragement over the waves trying to push them both back. By the time she got to the steps on the back of the boat she was so worn out her arm muscles almost didn't want to do any more like pull her from the water, Rob behind her helped by pushing her up and when they both got in she had her first look at how Matt was going to be bringing their stuff to the boat. Halfway between the shore and where she was she could see both Jamie and Matt swimming like pros through the waves behind them two small inflatable rafts with bulky black garbage bags in them.

"Is Jamie pulling one too?" Beth asked breathless.

"Of course." Beth noticed how Rob wasn't looking in the direction of his friend and his tone of voice was pissy. "I hope you can understand why Jamie's mad at you."

"What?" Rob could have chocked on his tongue right there and then.

"I heard what you two were arguing about back at the villa, she's right you know but there's too much history between you and you are like family to each other so what you have to ask yourself is what can you do to make her feel safer when you two are together."

"I don't think Jamie and I will be friends after we get back to the states. She was right you know, I have put her in danger a lot, all because I wanted something from her. I don't blame her or Matt for thinking that way but I also don't think there's a way to make any of it go away and go back to how it once was."

"No, maybe you can't, but how will you feel knowing you can't just pick up the phone and call her, visit Izzy, be there in bad times. You need to fix it Rob."

"We'll see." He kept his back from her and it infuriated Beth, sure he was torn from losing a friend but he didn't seem to be fighting for what he cherished so much, it was like he was accepting it and trying to deal with it.

"Some help over here." Jamie's voice called over the side of the boat. Rob was at the other end of the boat so she walked to the side to see Jamie looking like she wasn't fazed by the long swim and just treading water for fun. "Can you take these bags and then I'll get up and we can help Matt get up."

"Sure." Beth started taking the three black garbage bag wrapped items pulling them aboard, they were heavy or her arms were still tired but she found the strength and as she pulled Jamie up she realized though small, you do find strength when you need to. She helped Jamie get the other bags up from the more loaded raft Matt was pulling and once everyone was up Matt went straight to the controls of the boat and feeling something happen a few seconds later they were moving slowly through the water.

"Want to help me get these down below?" Jamie smiled at Beth and like Jamie she took one bag in each hand. She saw Rob still standing on the front of the yacht and wished he would do more than slot everything away like an efficient computer in to neat sections of his head. It took three trips below before they had everything out of sight and Beth was shocked at what was down there. Three bedrooms, a sitting area, kitchen and two bathrooms and enough room for Rob to ignore his friends until they got wherever they were headed. "We should be stopping again soon. Miguel is coming with us to Miami."
"Good." Beth said. "I was worried what might happen to him if he stayed."
"So were Matt and I."
"Look, Jamie, I know we don't know each other at all but I have to say something."
"If this is about what you heard Rob and I say then I really don't want to talk about it." Jamie was ripping open the bags and Beth started helping her, there were two layers of the black plastic and her arms were still sore from the swim.

"I understand but." She stopped when she saw Jamie stand up and put her hands on her hips, her eyebrows raised and there was something there that terrified Beth to her core. "Rob and I have too much history to just throw away I know but Beth, I'm not this strong invincible woman you've been led to believe." Jamie walked over to one of the benches and sat down, her head fell to her hands and Beth knew she was crying. "Everything has been so screwed up, everyone depends on me for everything, I'm just so tired of being that rock, that strong woman I've played for so long."

"You need to let people be strong too, not put everything on your shoulders. Like with your sister, I bet you feel like you have to play mother to her, protect her and make sure she's okay all the time. She seems like a pretty strong person thanks to your love and support. Take a break; let her be the strong one for a change. There's nothing wrong with that."

"Except then I feel like I let everyone down." Jamie took the tissue Beth passed her. "I think it's more the hormones than anything else but it's also the thought of losing what I have that's come to bite me on the ass again."

"You felt like this before?"

"When my mother and brother died yeah."

"How did you deal with it then?"

"Ran away, drank, got pissed at a lot of people."

"That's destructive, you were what, a teen, what do you think you could do now as an adult?"

"I don't know, every part of my life someone depends on me."

"Maybe you need to give some of it up, take a long vacation." Beth suggested and they both heard the sound of footsteps coming down the stairs from the deck, Beth watched as Jamie stood and tried to get herself straightened up and not looking like she had been having a personal moment. Matt stopped dead at the bottom of the stairs and looked at his wife and then to Beth. Without saying anything to her husband she picked up their two bags and went inside one of the bedrooms closing the door behind her.

"What's going on?" Matt asked and Beth really didn't want to get involved or in the middle of anything but something wasn't right with Jamie and she knew if left untreated the woman would break and then both Rob and Matt would be without a friend, wife and mother. "I know this isn't any of my business but I think Jamie needs a break."

"A break?" Matt frowned instead of snapping at her and it wasn't what she had been bracing for. "I heard the argument at the villa, I understand where Jamie is coming from, all she wants is a safe, quiet life. I asked her about whether she meant she didn't want to see Rob again and she broke down a little. She needs a break mentally Matt, she has the weight of the world on her shoulders and it's starting to cause problems."

"What did she say?"

"That everything in her life asks her to play this strong role and that she was tired of being that person."

"I knew she was getting run down." Matt sat down.

"This has been a long time coming." Beth sat down opposite him waiting to let him talk about it. "Jamie's always put everything on her shoulders, she does everything for her patients because they are mostly all her friends. She's supported her sister through years of problems and I admit being married to me isn't easy."

"She loves you Matt."

"Oh, I don't doubt that, every day I wake up grateful she wanted me as much as I wanted her but my job is stressful, I can be gone from a day to months without a word of where I'm going or where I've been. She went through a rough time a few years ago, she miscarried and she blamed the bad things she had done in her life to the loss, again taking all the pain on herself. I tried hard to help, I gave her the support but I was gone and since I've seen the change in her."

"She needs a rest."

"She won't take one."

"Either she does or she'll start resenting everything she loves." Beth got up. "Is Rob upstairs?"

"Yeah, he's in charge of the controls; tell him I'll be up in a while."

CHAPTER THIRTY-SIX

Matt found Jamie sat on the end of the queen sized bed, she had put on some shorts and a t-shirt and her hair was down and drying wavy. "I think it's time we talked about everything." Matt sat down beside his wife and took one of her hands. Her face looked up to him and he saw worry and sadness. "I think we should get ready for Miguel coming aboard and getting them all to Miami." Jamie looked away.

"Not until you talk to me, tell me what's going on."

"I'm just tired."

"No, there's more, I've known for a while you weren't happy. You've been so up and down."

"I am happy." She looked like she was about to cry and Matt turned and took her face softly between his hands.

"Then why do you look like it isn't?" He paused. "Is it me, Izzy; are you tired of being married?"

"No." Jamie moved fast. "I wouldn't want you or Izzy gone ever, it's the two of you that keep me from going completely crazy, you have to believe me when I say I love you so much."

"I believe you but there's something making you so sad."

"I think it's the stress just coming to a peak, Mel, the miscarriage, work, Rob's need to drag us in to crazy stuff with the usual amount of bullshit."

"Then maybe you need to make some changes. Why don't you get a leave of absence for a while, take some time off, relax?"

"But I love my job."

"And that's why you blew up at Rob earlier; you feel he's the only thing in that group you can give up."

He rubbed his thumb on her cheek. "We both

know he's too close to this family for him to ever be cast out."

"And that leaves my sister."

"Then maybe you need a break from her. You never got this stressed out when the two of you lived in different places."

"How can I cut my sister off?" A tear fell and he caught it with a kiss.

"You don't cut her off but you let her live her life, if she makes mistakes let her deal with them, she has Steve now and I get the feeling he's going to make it permanent. You know he'll take great care of her."

"I know." She stood up. "Maybe I should take some time off."

"Want me to take some off too?"

"Would you?"

"For you? Are you nuts? Of course." He stood up to hold her in his arms. "I would do anything for you James, you know that. Let me be the strong one for a while and worry about everything. You just take care of making sure these two are healthy." He rubbed her stomach. "I like the sound of that."

"Me too." He kissed her, a soft promise kiss.

XXX   XXX

Miguel packed only a few changes of clothes from his swim shorts he had on and his passport. He couldn't take the chance something he had was bugged by his father, he put about six hundred dollars in one hundred dollar bills inside his wallet along with three credit cards his father had no control over. There was nothing of importance in his house that he needed but as he went to walk out to the beach carrying the garbage bag with his stuff in he noticed a few things he did want to take. On one of the tables near the back door were three picture frames. One of he and Louis when Louis had come back from the states a few years before, one of his mother and the last of he and Cara from their honeymoon. He took them out of the cumbersome wooden frames and slipped them inside to join the rest of his things.

Not bothering to close his door, he wanted whoever came in to think he just left, no clue where he had gone. He was glad the four agents agreed to help him and a few minutes before he had received a call from one of the men as the boat came in to view not far from the shore behind his house. Without a second thought he waded down to the water until he could no longer walk comfortably and swam to the boat about thirty something feet away, he felt exhausted when he got there but the man he hadn't tried to kill helped pull him aboard and before he could relax the same man took the bag from him and ripped open the plastic as he checked everything he now owned.

"There's a room downstairs for you, go down there and dry off, we'll be getting underway, should take us almost two days to get to Miami. I hope you are hungry; the women are getting some food ready." The man smiled slightly as Miguel watched the sun just start to hide behind the horizon as he stood with his back to the Island he had lived in for so long.

He caught sight of the man steering the boat as he went down to the lower level of the modest sized boat. He heard the laughter of the two women he had seen earlier and he coughed once closer to them so as not to scare them, the blonde had been carrying a gun earlier and had looked beautiful yet dangerous. "Ah, Miguel." The blonde said. "I'm Jamie, this is Beth." He shook hands in order of the introduction and felt odd wearing just his dripping shorts. "Let me show you to your room." Jamie led him down the small hall and to the room on the left, she opened the door and he saw what had to have been the smallest room ever, a twin bunk and a small closet were all that was in there. "Sorry it's so small, the couch in the living area pulls out, you could always sleep there, might be longer."
"Nah, this is great, thank you." Miguel walked in and waited for the female to go and closing the door behind him threw his few possessions on the bed. He stripped out of his wet shorts and using the towel he had packed wiped himself down feeling the salty grit rubbing in to his skin. He dressed quickly and then sat down for a minute wondering what the hell he was going to do with his life, that's if he had one to start, he did try to kill the CIA agent upstairs, no doubt that would cause some problems.

XXX   XXX

316

"Where is he?" Vince listened to his boss yelling again. Miguel was supposed to come for dinner and when he didn't answer any of their calls Vince had personally called the man on duty to follow the son to find out he was inside his house and had not left since he returned home earlier. He had instructed the man to go inside and check; maybe Miguel was a weak bastard like Luis after all, done something to end his misery. But the man had called and said there was no one inside, the back doors wide open and nothing aside from three pictures from frames near the back door had been missing.

Knowing this Vince had gone to the basement room used for viewing surveillance on all the homes and properties his boss owned including the boats, that was over twenty places each recording information on to a hard drive stored in the room. Vince logged in his codes and then typed in the request for the day's activities in Miguel's house, what he saw stunned him, the son of a bitch had played them all, he knew exactly what was going on. He watched from when Miguel had come home late a piece of paper in his hand as he threw a vase across the room, the clock let him know it was around the time he would have driven past Luis's wreckage and then he watched the different views of the different rooms as firstly he took a nap, a few hours later got up, showered and then collected items from around the house he put inside other items. A motor and a deflated small boat.

Not having to figure out what those were being used for he visually scanned the recording as it fast forwarded to when he returned, ten minutes after they had spoken on the dock. Vince watched as his boss's favored son standing in his shorts with a garbage bag took the three pictures from next to the back living room door and stuffed them inside the plastic before retying it, Miguel walked down the back deck and disappeared from view and again, Vince knew exactly what had happened. He punched in the codes for the cameras on the boat Miguel had taken out and saw what he had suspected, once satisfied he then checked the GPS record for the boat, it had been anchored near West Cay Point which was where he had said he had been but somewhere between where the boat was and the time he had been anchored he had been somewhere.

"I think he's handed himself over to the CIA guy." Vince waited for the explosion his boss would have. "The one you assured me was dead?" His voice boomed.
"Yes boss, Miguel must have figured out where he was, the guy must have offered him something or scared him to give himself up; Miguel wasn't forced to go anywhere."
"He knows it was you that killed Cara and Luis; he's running on guilt and stupidity. He takes after his mother and not me after all." He watched Mr. Santos sit down and bang his fist loudly on the

table. "If he was at the airport someone would have called us, especially as we have a picture of the CIA agent there too. That leaves them to get off this island by sea. Do you know where he found the agent?"

"I have a feeling looking at where the boat was anchored and from where we threw him in the ocean he may have washed up near one of your rental properties in friendship bay."

"Aren't there only two villas' in use?"

"Yeah, one was a couple from Boston, only the female arrived and the other was a couple in from California two days ago, both in the navy and the female made a return trip to Miami and back today."

"Why?"

"Don't know." Vince shrugged. "One of the custom guys presumed it was to get her hair done because she came down a brunette but returned a blonde."

"I think that's our connection, they are in the military, what did it say they did?"

"She's a doctor and he's just a lieutenant commander, didn't say what he did."

"Based in San Diego it's a good bet he's a SEAL if he is connected to this."

The boss got up from his seat and went over to pour himself three fingers of scotch from his crystal decanter. "I want you to clean up this mess, go to the villa, make sure it was one of them, we can have boats out looking for them, check any boats out without a reason and if you find my son with them then deal with him. If he can turn that easily he's of no blood relation to me, he is a disgrace."

Vince didn't hang around to hear any other orders; he was shocked enough with the ones he had been given. He called one of the men out on the island and told him to go over to the two villa's check them out see what was going on as he called another man to meet him down at the docks.

XXX   XXX

With the sun down and the boat anchored about a hundred feet from the shore of the Roseau Island north of where they had started the five of them sat at the table finishing up a batch of pasta and sauce and a side of salad. Miguel had remained mainly quiet taking in the four of them. There was something going on between one of the men and one of the women and he was curious enough to wonder what it could be. The conversations had been started mainly by the other two and the blonde woman and the dark haired man he had tried to kill hadn't said anything if it involved them talking to each other.

"I think I should get back up to the controls and get us at least as far as Puerto Rico before we can relax, did you make that call?" Matt asked looking at his wife.
"I wasn't able to get a signal; I'll try the radio after I finish cleaning up." Jamie stood up and began removing dishes; Beth stood up and looked at

Matt. "Could you show me how this boat works, you know, in case I would need to know."

"Sure." Matt stood up and led her towards the stairs, Jamie looked at her husband quickly knowing exactly what the two of them were trying to do, leaving her down there with Rob, they didn't think it through too well because they had left Miguel there and Rob would certainly talk to the younger man before her, she had felt his attitude and felt a small piece of guilt, she should talk to him but at the same time she wasn't sure what the hell to say.

"I think I'll get some air." Miguel stood to leave too and Rob sighed. That left him to help clean away all the dishes with Jamie, earlier he had been so mad, upset and confused about what she had told him and now he was just tired. She was right, things between them were too stressful and he had put her in the way of danger way too many times, she had responsibilities now, a daughter he knew she had always wanted, and two more on the way, he should do her a favor and never speak to her again but he wanted her in his life. She knew him better than anyone, his father had long ago passed away and his sister had been living in a nursing home because of her MS for a while and the last time he had visited her she hadn't even recognized him. His mother having left when he was small when she couldn't handle the life she had. Jamie was his oldest and closest friend, he knew he had taken advantage of that and her willingness to help, her love for him but he had just abused it and now he had lost it all.

"Get the feeling even Miguel knows there's something going on and we need to be stuck down here together?" Jamie broke in to his thoughts and he looked up at her with his puppy eyes, the ones that cut right through her. Jamie had to look away. "I know I was tough on you back there Rob and I'm sorry." Jamie apologized.
"You don't need to be sorry." She felt him come up behind her, reaching around her as she stopped dead at the sink to put dishes in he had carried over. "You are right, I have taken advantage of what we have and our past for my own selfish needs but I've never wanted you hurt Jay." He waited for her to stop rinsing the dishes, he had seen her body tense and knew she was having flash backs of everything they had been through, he had the same flashes whenever he saw her.

"I'm sure you read the evaluation from the last mission you had me on, they didn't want me to finish after only a few weeks, they wanted me to do the full six months but I couldn't do it, I had to get back to my life, being cooped up and looked at like you're crazy would have killed me."
"Maybe you should have."
"And if I had I wouldn't have anything I have now. No Matt, no Izzy. I knew what I was doing."
"Still get the nightmares?"
"A little more than I admit to."
"I get them too; they play out just like the videos Atwa sent."

"Don't say his name." Jamie bit out.

"I'm sorry." He went back to collect more dishes.

"I'll respect any decision you make but Jay, you are all I have left, you are my oldest friend. You and my father were friends. You've always been my family."

"And you've been more of mine than Mel or my father has." She dried her hands on a towel. "I need to take a break from everything Rob. I didn't mean earlier I never wanted to ever speak to you again. I need to let myself enjoy what I have, I also need to let Mel grow in to her own person. She has Steve now and he seems good for her."

"I'm glad."

"Good." Jamie made a weak smile. "I hope you keep Beth around after you get back I like her and you seem to like her a lot too."

"I do."

"Then do everything you can to make her yours, you deserve that." She rubbed the top of his arm and left to go to the room she was sharing with her husband.

CHAPTER THIRTY-SEVEN

"I'm going to leave the two of you alone for a while." Linda smiled at her son and the woman who had stolen his heart. The more she spent time with Mel the more she liked her, Steve had made the right move getting involved with her and she was hoping he would pluck the courage to ask her to marry him before she returned to Illinois. She hoped Mel would say yes. She wanted some grandchildren soon and after seeing the pictures in Mel's sister's office she had been imagining what they would look like.

"Where are you going?" Steve asked his mother. "I'm having dinner with someone from the base; I was going to see if I could find something to wear at the mall."
"Who are you having dinner with?" Steve frowned trying to figure out in his head fast who on base was around his mother's age and single. "Donald Fuller."
"Captain Donald Fuller?" Steve almost choked. The man had been a member of the SEAL training team for years, many a man had weakened at the mere sight of the man. He was at least in his fifties but was as strong as any recruit with a mass of body and muscles to make even him jealous and aspire to be like that when he was the man's age.

"Yes, you know him?" Linda asked.
"Mom, he trained me, everyone knows him."
"I don't." Mel laughed.
"Yeah you do." Steve's eyebrows were raised and Mel thought the shock sticking on his face was priceless. "You met him the other month at Coop's birthday party, he's in his mid-fifties, has a bald head, muscles in his arms bigger than a tree trunk."
"Oh." Mel felt her own forehead mimicking Steve's. "He seems like a nice man."

"He's very sweet; we've had drinks a few times since I've been here, nothing alcoholic for me. I met him when I did the tour of your base with you friend Daniel."

"He's my CO mom."

"Of course he is." She laughed. "Is me having dinner with Donald a problem?"

"No, have a good time." Steve shook off but his face was still saying the same thing even if his mouth was telling something else. Linda picked up her jacket and bag and gave her son and Mel both a kiss on the cheek and left them closing the door behind them.

"Oh dear God." Steve said once she was gone. "I think my mother has gone mad."

"It's nice."

"Her dating my old teacher." He closed his eyes and scrunched up his face, a hand came to his face. "I really hope this is just something while she's here. Damn I have an image in my head I don't need." He opened his eyes. "Quick kiss me." He put his hand on her arm and Mel was still laughing at his entire response. She kissed him like he asked and every time it was like the first; he gave her butterflies in her belly. "That's better." He smiled keeping a hold of her hand. "How long are you staying for?"

"How long do you want?"

"I was hoping they had a bigger bed, let you sleep up here with me but they don't so how about until you get really tired?"

"I think I could stay that long."

"Speaking of which, I don't suppose I could get you to go to my place sometime before Monday and get some of my stuff, I appreciate you letting me stay with you."

"Don't be silly, of course you can. Hopefully you'll enjoy it so much you'll stay forever."

Steve let the words play out in her head like it was in his. He knew every time he saw her he wanted her for the rest of his life and he was dreading that maybe she didn't feel the same way about him but at some point he was going to have to face that possibility. "Sit here a minute." He patted the side of the bed.

"Why?" She laughed and did what he had asked, it wasn't so comfortable but she was as close to him as she would get. "This isn't how I had pictured doing this but I've been dying to do it for a while and I figured even though I'm laid up and it's not the most romantic of way's it kinda adds to the moment." He rambled as he fumbled with his free hand on the side of the bed Mel wasn't sitting on.

"What are you talking about?" She asked watching his hand and his face as he kept looking at her.

"Mel." He started and he knew when she saw what he had been searching for, her breath sucked in and her eyes were fixed on the green velvet ring box his mother had left with him. He had taken out the wedding bands and asked Jamie to hold on to them until he was out of the hospital and probably until they were needed.

With one hand he opened the box still feeling her

hand inside his on the other side. "Mel, will you marry me?" He asked and her hand was covering her mouth.

"Yes." Her voice filled with emotion as he let go of her hand and took the ring from its soft protection to place it on her engagement finger. The band fit perfectly and the diamond was shining. "It was the ring my mother was given by my father; I hope that's okay?"

"Are you kidding?" Mel wiped her tears from her eyes. "It's more than okay. Oh man, are you sure about this?"

"Totally." He knew his face had a grin a mile wide and he didn't care because she had said yes. "I was going to ask you, I spoke to Matt and Lee about it and then this came up and I figured, hey I'll wait but laying here I decided I didn't want to wait anymore, I wanted to ask you and make it official."

"Thank you." Mel leaned down and kissed him.

"I think I should be the one thanking you." His cell phone began to vibrate cutting in to their moment.

"Schlome." He said not recognizing the number.

"Uncle Steve?" Izzy's small voice asked.

"Hey Izzy, how are you doing?" His second favorite girl had timing as good as Mel did. "Good, I'm having dinner with Minnie and Donald later. How is your boo, boo?"

"Feeling much better." He laughed. "Thank you for asking."

"Mommy just called and Daddy and her are going to be home in a few days, Grandpa is going to bring me to see you Sunday." He heard her talk to someone in the background and then return. "Will you still be in the hospital?"

"I will, can you come and visit me?"

"Sure, I bought you and Aunt Mel presents." He knew Izzy was going to continue but someone cut her off. "I love you Uncle Steve." Her little voice said and then the sound of a kiss. "I love you too." He told her and waited to see if she would say anything else. "Steve." Mel's father's voice suddenly boomed in his ear. When he had first met the man he didn't care much for him over the way he had been about Jamie but in the last few years and the fact he and Jamie had reconciled Steve's admiration for the man and fellow SEAL had grown.

"Sir." Steve felt his body stiffen even though he couldn't physically stand at attention.

"Please, call me Richard." His hearty laugh filled Steve's ear. "How are you doing son?"

"Better, they didn't need to remove as much as they had thought." He began telling him his prognosis the entire time holding Mel's hand as she smiled. "Sir, there was something I wanted to ask you, I was hoping to do it in person but this is okay I presume, I've never done this before."

"Go ahead."

"I wanted to ask your daughter to marry me and I was hoping to get your blessing."

"You want to marry Mel?" He heard the senator softly. "Of course I'll give you my blessing. She couldn't ask for a finer man to ask her."

"Thank you sir."

"At least call me Dad if not Richard, the sir thing is nice but you're family."

"Okay Richard." Mel was waving for his attention. "I think your daughter would like to talk to you, do you have a minute?"

"Certainly."

"Hey Dad." Mel said excitedly and Steve watched her look at the ring on her finger, her eyes were wide and he knew she liked it. "Sweetheart, is there something you want to tell me?"

"There sure is."

"Hold on, Margaret will want to hear this." Mel heard her father call over her step mother and niece and after a beeping noise he said. "Okay, we're ready."

"Dad, Margaret, Izzy, Steve asked me to marry him."

"I hope you said yes." She heard Margaret say.

"Of course I did."

"That's wonderful honey, I'm so happy for you." Her father told her. "Izzy is jumping around the hotel room." He laughed. "Margaret and I are bringing Izzy back Sunday morning and staying over until your sister gets back, maybe we can bring something nice in and eat with you and Steve to celebrate seeing as he's in there and we're probably going to be leaving for Georgia before he's good to get out."

"That sounds like a plan." Mel told him.

"Good, we better go; we'll call you when we get to Jamie's then."

"Give the ladies a hug from me Dad. I love you."

"I love you too and I am so happy for you."

"You just made my father so happy." Mel told Steven passing him back the cell.
"No you did, you said yes to me."
"Splitting hairs now."
"No, just telling it like it is." Her phone began to ring and she laughed as she reached in to her bag, she saw it was her sister's cell number. "Big sis calling in."
"Izzy said she had spoken to her and Matt. Are you going to tell her the news?" He was still beaming.
"Yeah, but I'm going to have some fun with it." Mel laughed and pressed the button to connect the call.
"Yo Jay." Mel said.
"Hey." The connection wasn't so good and it sounded like she was shouting in to the phone.
"Can you hear me okay?"
"Barely." Mel's face frowned again. "Where are you?"
"Halfway between where we were and Puerto Rica. We had a change of plans; we're going to fly from Rica to Miami. We had a call from Nick; they've realized Rob was still alive and that we have his son."
"Wow, hold on, you have the bad guy's son?" Mel was now freaking and Steve had sat up hearing the one side of the conversation.

"Long story, the father not only had the wife killed, he also had killed his second oldest son too, the oldest is coming back to the states with us to swear out a statement about everything that has been going on etcetera."

"Holy shit."

"I wanted to see how you and Steve were doing."

"He proposed."

"What, say that again." Jamie was definitely shouting.

"Steve asked me to marry him."

"What did you say?"

"I said yes of course." Her plans to tease her sister had flown out of the window.

"That's.......we........celebr'.......get.........."

"You're breaking up." Mel got down from the bed moving herself in case it was her end.

"I said.......wonderful.....can.....when we.......back."

"Jay, I'll call you back."

"Oh shit...........speak.........followed.........Love you."

The line went dead. Mel had been next to the window and when she turned back to Steve he knew something was up. "What?"

"She was breaking up, I think something bad happened, she swore and then said something about being followed and then love you."

"It could be innocent, just a bad connection."

"Let me try calling her back." Mel dialed as Steve picked his cell up and dialed Matt, both phones went straight to voicemail and both left them a message. "I don't suppose you have Rob's number still?"

"He didn't have a cell with him but hold on." She pressed through the buttons on her phone. "I do have one better."

"Okay?" He kept an eye on her as she waited with

the phone to her ear.

"Hey, it's Mel, Jamie's sister, I was just talking to her and the line went dead, I think they are in trouble."

CHAPTER THIRTY-EIGHT

Matt had switched with Rob at the controls so he could speak to his daughter after his wife did, when she had been calling his sister he went down to check on Miguel and Beth, Miguel was asleep on the couch while Beth was reading a magazine in her room with the door wide open.

"How's Jamie?" Beth asked looking up as Matt came to stand at her door.

"Still a little stressed but we talked, she knows she needs to relieve some of her stress. She's promised me she would take a break, I'll get some too and maybe we can take Izzy somewhere for a few weeks or just hang out at home."

"Good, I like Jamie, last thing I want to see is her getting too deep in to misery."

"Know someone who went through it?"

"My brother, he had a mental breakdown in graduate school, it devastated him, he's never been the same. Last I heard he lives in a halfway house in New York City, I grew up on Long Island and my mother still lives there. My mother goes in to look for him and when she does she gives him some clothes and a meal and then some money and he goes back in to the crowd to be found again."

"I'm sorry."

"Don't be, if we'd all paid attention we could have seen it coming, all the signs were there. I don't think Jamie is that far along, I think with you and everyone she wouldn't be able to but it happened to my brother and well, it's a possibility."

"So Rob and Jay are talking."

"I saw that; I guess us leaving them alone did work. I told you it would."

"I thank you for that, Jamie would have been upset when the realization Rob was gone caught up with her. If Rob is too stupid to keep you around just know you are always welcome to visit us, San Diego can be fun."

"I'll keep that in."

Beth wasn't able to finish the sentence, the boat felt like it had been hit by something as it rocked from side to side. They heard Jamie scream and a gun shot and Miguel was awake and had fallen off the couch from the motion. Matt was in SEAL mode Beth presumed as he ran knocking Miguel out of his way to get to the deck, Beth was on his heels not thinking about what they had heard.

The first thing they saw when they got up there was a big flood of light moving around haphazardly, Rob was crouched down over Jamie who was on the deck. Matt went straight over to her and when Beth saw her she knew something was terribly wrong. There was blood and she felt her stomach plummet to the floor. "She banged her head." Rob shouted over the noise of some sort of engine, and we have company somewhere." He pointed to where the light was coming from. "Who do you think it is?" Matt shouted over the noise. "I'm guessing Miguel's father or his men, we were hit by something and then I heard a shot." Jamie's eyes opened and Matt sighed a relief loud enough for them all to hear. "Did you hurt anything?" He said before another shot rang out and Matt covered his wife while Beth felt Rob shield her body with his own. "Can you get up?" Matt asked Jamie. "Yeah." She began by turning over to her stomach and crawling over to the cover of the boat where the controls were. "I fell." She touched her head and saw the blood on her hands. "I need to see to this." She looked at her husband. "You and Rob be careful." She held out her hand to Beth and the two of them crawled towards the stairs and went down.

Miguel stayed down near where the women had gone down. "What can I do to help?" He shouted. "Steer this boat." Matt shouted back as Miguel watched the two of them take their guns from the back of their shorts taking the safety's off. "Okay." Miguel made his way to the controls and seeing the GPS locater saw the obvious direction they had been heading and that the boat had been knocked slightly off course and he corrected it. With the rudder sending them at a faster speed towards where they had been headed Miguel turned just in time to see Matt take out the spot light sending everything aside from the other ships helm and their own, Miguel could just make out one of his father's men about thirty feet from them and he knew they had come to stop them.

Robert made it to the controls near Miguel as another shot rang out and he pushed the kid to the side flipping the switch and sending their boat in to utter darkness, the only thing the other boat could do to find them was to get their spotlight working or follow the sounds of their engine. Miguel smelt something and turned to see Rob clutching his lower arm. "Were you hit?" He asked. "Yeah." Rob was ripping the bottom of his shirt off and wrapping it around where he was clutching, He heard the sounds of his curses as the pain must have been shooting through his arm. "You can't run." They heard a voice shout over some sort of speaker system. "That's Vince." Miguel cringed, he had hoped them being so far from the island they were clear but obviously his father knew what was going on. They wouldn't let him get away; they were all going to die.

XXX   XXX

With the aid of a flash light because of the lights being out, Jamie looked in the mirror at her head laceration, it was just above her right eye and about an inch long but it didn't seem too deep. She knew better than anyone that head wounds seriously gush but the fear had been drilled in to her anyway. Beth was holding the light steady and after adding a little Neosporin and a band aid Jamie looked at Beth just in time to hear another gunshot.

"I want you to stay down here." Jamie told her.
"No way, we both stay down or we both go up."
"This isn't up for debate Beth."
"Matt doesn't want you up there and I need someone to stay down here with me."
"You'll be fine."
"Let me help." Beth using the light helped Jamie find her way to her room so she could get something out of her bag. Beth almost dropped the light when she saw what she had been looking for, the gun she had earlier held being shown how to use it. "Fine but stay near the stairs, I'm not going out far, just enough to give cover to Matt if we need it. Actually, there's a radio inside the cab near the helm, think you can call in to the coast guard?"
"Sure."

The two of them made it to the stairs as Rob came and sat on the top step, they both saw the wound on his arm. "Are you alright?" Jamie asked.
"I think it was a through and through but I'm not sure."
"Pass me the flash light." Jamie took it and leading Rob down deeper away from the door to the deck turned it on to see what had happened. He cursed more when she removed the makeshift bandage. "It looks like the bullet went right through; I can't see any more, can you move your fingers?" She watched his fingers move though it looked painful nothing was pumping blood out and that was a good sign. "Stay here I have a first aid kit." Jamie

was gone and back in seconds, he had no idea where she had gone but she was fast. She took out some four by four gauze and a roll of crisp white bandage, it took her a few seconds to get it all wrapped and then as she was about to go back with him he stopped her.

"I can't have you up there."
"Try stopping me."
"Your husband will kill me if anything happens to you, we don't know what's out there, I need you and Beth down here."
"I can provide cover; I'll stay near the hatch."
"Fine, but one sign it's getting worse and you drag Beth with you and get downstairs and lock one of the rooms with you both in it."
"Aye, aye captain." Jamie wasn't liking the direction of his orders, true she should stay safe but being below not knowing what was happening would drive her nuts and choosing between helping her husband stay alive and leaving him there with Rob she knew where she wanted to be.

Matt saw Jamie at the hatch of the boat. He didn't like her being up there while they had no idea what was going on but he needed her skills as a sharp shooter. He did have a good idea where the boat was but he hadn't been able to tell how many men they were dealing with and what size boat. The moment they knocked out the light everything had gone dark and it was like they were now being followed just as fast as they were going. He opened one of the deck trunks; his friend had given him a few extra weapons in case they ran in to any trouble. Opening it carefully he pulled out the shotgun and the box of ammo. He slid them over to his wife who instantly loaded two rounds in to the chamber; he could hear it better than he could see it. He heard the sound of the engine in their boat and the one following but he could also hear something new, a smaller higher powered engine. "They are going to try and get aboard." Miguel turned and told them.

"Over my dead body." Matt bit back, he was not going to let anyone get further than the water because there were too many people he cared about aboard.

XXX   XXX

While Mel had been talking to someone he didn't know he had tried the cells of her sister and his best friend again a few times, there still had been no answer and he was getting that feeling in his gut that their extraction wasn't going to be as smooth as they had thought it would be. As Mel stopped talking and closed her cell she didn't look to happy and his fears were becoming realized. "Who did you talk to?"

"Dumont, she's some female agent."

"I remember her from when Jamie was in." He stopped; they both knew where she had been those years before. "How the hell do you have her number?"

"I don't but I do have the number for Rob's desk. Dumont answered; I knew if she was there she would answer it. Rob used to say how when he was away he knew Dumont used his office because she hated having to share office space with twenty other people."

"Okay, so does she know what's going on?"

"She does, Nick is somewhere near, the plan was for them to rendezvous in Puerto Rico and while I was on the phone with her she said she was getting a call from Nick, there was something going on and he and the team were leaving to where the boat was."

Mel stopped and she took his hand. "Dumont thinks the reason my call was interrupted was because someone's trying to stop their boat from getting any further."

"I'm sure they'll be fine." He squeezed her hand. He hated that look on her face she had right then, he didn't know if it was her worry face or her 'oh shit I can't deal' face. "I'm sure they will be but knowing Jamie's pregnant and what happened last time that worries me."

"I probably shouldn't tell you Jamie told me about the baby." He was trying to get her mind off the bad side of what might happen and he hoped what he would tell her would stun her for a few minutes and let that angst pass a little. "Is there something wrong with it?"

"No, but its babies plural."

"Plural?" She shook her head. "Man is she having twins?"

"I believe so."

"Holy shit, are you lying?"

"Nope."

"That's so cool, carrying on the twin tradition, glad that's her and not me." She laughed slightly and Steve knew his distraction had worked a little.

"I don't know; the idea of twins sounds good to me." Steve watched her mouth fall open and her eyebrows rise just a little. "You want kids too?" She asked.

"You don't?"

"You just want everything don't you?" She joked sitting back where she had been when he had proposed on the edge of his bed. "I'm greedy enough yes. For years I wondered why the men on my team were so in to their families and kids and I never got it but the last time we were away all I thought about was getting back to you and having that life they had. When we were holding Izzy last week when I got home because your sister had fed her too much ice cream it felt right, perfect."

"I thought the same thing." Mel brushed a palm on his cheek gently. "I just thought I'd scare you off if I said anything." The sun was beginning to go down outside and as Steve savored the moment he knew Mel was holding inside the worry she was having for her sister.

CHAPTER THIRTY-NINE

Matt and Rob were either sides at the back of the boat and with the new light coming up the back of them from whatever was being pushed by the louder engine Jamie had given Beth her smaller hand gun to hold while she was getting closer to Matt as she scooched to them. He watched as his wife set the rifle on the edge of their own boat and quickly getting to her knees lined up the scope and fired, there was the soft sound of someone getting hit before a splash, whoever she just hit was now in the water. She came back to hide behind the ledge and pulling the chamber back and then forward again loaded the second of the ammo in to the chamber. She set the rifle up and a shot rang out shattering the glass of the cab not far from where Miguel was.

Getting the scope at her eye as she was hunched down she quickly came up spying the smaller power craft and got another shot off at the man holding a gun aimed right back at her before he even had time to respond to her being visible; he too fell to the water. "How many left?" He asked his wife knowing she would have gotten a view of the smaller craft. "One, steering, doesn't look like he's smart enough to shoot and steer."
"Think you can get him?"
"What do you think?" Her voice was filled with the smile her face wasn't showing. She had loaded two more rounds in and cocked the barrel ready, within seconds she fired again and they could hear the sound of the boat whirring as the throttle was released and it slowed down to a stop. Matt was able to shoot out the light and plunged them all back in to darkness again.

They could hear the sounds of the other boat better now as they moved further away from the sounds of the boat now running out of control. "We need to see where the other boat is and how many people are up there." Rob said from his side of the boat, his arm was throbbing and he was more concerned about making sure everyone else was okay first. "At least we took out the only way they can get to us from their boat." Jamie said positively. "How far away are we from anything?" Matt asked Miguel who was holding on to the wheel for dear life. "About fifty miles west of Basseterre, we're close to St. Croix."

"We need to know what we are dealing with." Matt opened the bench up again and took out a different gun and as Beth watched fascinated. He inserted some long item inside the barrel and she felt Rob next to her while Jamie remained up front. "Stay down." He told her. "Matt's letting off a flare; help us see what we are up against."

"Firing." They all heard Matt say and the green smoke streaked the night's darkness before exploding in a shower of green, both Matt and Jamie could see from where they were that the boat had four more men aboard but the good news it was half the size of their boat. With the light Jamie and Matt both got off two more men leaving the man at the controls and the one they knew was Vince.

Beth watched the night's darkness swallow everything again as the flare dissipated Matt was speaking to Jamie and as she came crawling back she took Beth's hand and together they went below, Beth took a quick last look at the men and both of them were still hunched below the edge of the boat. Jamie had her cell in her hand because when she opened it the blue light lit everything eerily. "Take this, call this number." She punched away. "Tell the man that answers who you are and what's going on."

"Sure." Beth pressed the call button and was shocked the call was answered so quickly. "Jay?" The man's voice boomed.

"No, this is Beth; I'm on the boat with Robert, Jamie and Matt." She began. "Jamie told me to call and tell you what's going on."

"You are being attacked by the bad guys." He said.

"How did you know?"

"Jamie's sister called my partner when their call was disconnected. Tell them a team and I are on our way, about twenty minutes out from your position."

"Okay."

Beth sighed as she closed the cell and Jamie was coming back with what looked like life jacket. "Are we swimming somewhere?"

"No, this is a combat vest, Matt needs something from it." Jamie went as far as the hatch and with ease flung it across the deck to her husband. Beth couldn't hear anything they were saying to each other but the men definitely had something they were planning on. "Did you get through to Nick?"

"Yeah, he said him and the team would be here in

twenty minutes."

"I'm just going to go and tell Matt stay here." She watched Jamie crawl over towards the men, speak briefly and then return. "We need to get down below, there's going to be a loud bang so don't worry."

"What are they going to do?"

"Try and blow up the other boat."

"Are you kidding?" Beth's mouth dropped open, that had been the last thing she had expected to hear. "Nope, out here it's either we do what we can to stop them or they could get to us. Personally I'm fine with it being them not us."

"Me too, so what team is this Nick coming with?"

"Nick is Rob's right hand man and I presume the team is either a bunch of agents or possibly the coast guard but we're in international water so it might be something else, we'll find out soon enough." Jamie checked her watch. "In about eleven minutes." A loud bang made Beth jump and she felt the boat lurch. The lights came back on and Matt appeared at the opening to the deck. "Do we have any marshmallows?" He joked.

"Direct hit?"

"Close enough." He smiled. "You should probably get a better look at Rob's arm." He stood up and walked over to Miguel. "You okay?" He asked the man who had been quiet for so long. "Yeah."

"Bring the boat about thirty more feet from their boat and turn so we can keep an eye on it."

"Sure thing."

"I'm going down for a few minutes." Matt told Jamie and Beth as the two of them came up. Jamie was carrying the medical kit Matt had picked up just in case this case scenario happened, it wasn't your usual Johnson and Johnson kit that you could buy in the food store. Beth walked over to the edge to look at the burning remains of the other boat as Jamie took the soaked through gauze and bandage from his arm, a stethoscope in her ears as she checked his blood pressure and listened for a pulse lower near his wrist. Beth realized she had Jamie's gun in the back of her pants still and took it out putting it on the bench next to her. She sat down and watched as Jamie did what she could as Rob gave her a sly smile.

Jamie did what she could cleaning out Rob's arm, she had given him a shot and was able to poke around a little in there and with the pulse good she didn't believe there was any serious damage and he was lucky the bone hadn't been hit. Stitching a few stitches, they were talking about something when Jamie heard something behind them, figuring it was just a piece of debris hitting their boat she didn't pay much attention and Rob had just said something to Matt. The sound of a gunshot made Jamie drop her needle and she looked to see Beth holding the gun like she had shown her, her face was white and her hand shaking. "What the fuck?" Jamie heard Matt swear, it happened rarely but it was always necessary when it was. "He." Beth pointed and all three of them leaned over the edge behind them to see

Vince face up with what looked like a bullet hole in his left eye, he wasn't moving and for good measure Rob fired again.

Matt walked over to Beth, took the gun from her hand and made her look in his eyes. "I owe you the life of my wife and my kids." He told her. "Beth, are you feeling nauseous?"
"How'd you guess?" She turned and leaned over the side of the boat and threw up. Matt rubbed her back and when Rob came closer he stepped back and over to his wife who was looking as white as Beth. He embraced her and made her sit back down. "Beth." Rob said. "Did I kill him?"
"No, I did, you just got him in the shoulder." Rob lied to her and he hoped she believed him, he didn't want her thinking she had killed someone.
"You're lying."
"No, no I'm not." He put her in his arms. "Ask Matt or Jamie."
"I will." She said loving the feel of him holding her tight.

XXX   XXX

Stepping in to his private jet he looked back to what had been home for the last fifteen years, his beloved Charlotte had been here, his family, they had all died here too, all but one, the one he had thought would make him proud and take on the magnificent family business when his time came. But that wasn't going to be the case; his son had disappointed him through weakness, his unlikely loyalty to his whore of a wife and bastard of a younger brother.

With all he needed packed inside his jet along with enough ready cash and account numbers for the rest in the Cayman's he let the pilot close the door as he settled in to the big cream colored leather chair. He knew where his son was and what would play out, back at the house he had been connected to Vince by voice and when the boat exploded he knew it was time for him to leave. He had made arrangements and was going to be flying back to the country that had once forced him out. He would set up a base, get new men and when his son least expected it he would show him just how things were supposed to be taken care of. He had told them all unless they saw that CIA bastard dead then not to presume they had finished the job. It had been sloppy, and Vince should have known better.

As the plane started its run down the tarmac he accepted the glass of scotch from the female he was bringing with him. She was a young piece of ass and pleased him well, she would be good for a while but he knew once he was settled in the states he would toss her for something a little classier.

CHAPTER FORTY

The sound of a new boat coming closer made all of

them on deck begin to worry maybe this was a second contingent sent to finish anything the first boat had been unable too, the boat was bigger and faster and the lights were blinding. "Agent Wakefield, Commander Buchanan, Lieutenant Commander Taylor." A voice boomed over the engine noise. And the three named held a hand up to their eyes so they could try and see who was coming closer. "SEAL Team Twelve here to help." The voice told them. "Steady your boat and we'll come close."

Matt took over the controls from Miguel and as he had been asked kept the boat as still as possible with the current from the other boat rocking them. The lights became less intense and the sight of their boat receiving lines was a relief. Jamie and Miguel started securing them and once done the leader of the new boat climbed down to be on their deck. "Commander Buchanan?" He saluted Jamie and Beth frowned. "Senior Chief Weatherly Ma'am. SEAL Team Twelve. I believe you and your husband are SEAL Team Seven."
"He is I'm just the team doctor."
"I happen to disagree Ma'am, heard all about you from an old friend of mine." He shook her hand after he relaxed from standing and saluting, Matt came up behind her. "This is my husband."
"Lieutenant Commander." The men shook hands. "Our team is based out of Gitmo, we got a call from a friend of yours asking for our help." He pointed above him and it was then they saw Nick for the first time.

"Thanks for coming, I appreciate it." Matt told the fellow SEAL who looked pleased to be doing his job. "Agent Wakefield and Ms. DeVeuve?" The SEAL asked.

"Just Robert please." The man smiled at them from behind his camies and baseball hat. "Ma'am." He shook hands with Beth. "I'm guessing we missed all the fun."

"Sure did." Matt laughed.

"Shame, the boys and I have been looking for something different to our normal routine. Don't get as much action as you boys out in San Diego."

"Can we get an escort to our destination?" Robert asked.

"We've arranged one better sir." The senior chief smiled. "One of my men will return this boat for you and you can all ride back with us; we can have you in Miami in under four hours."

"What are we waiting for then?" Matt asked.

Getting all their things together and Matt telling the petty seaman assigned to returning the boat to another SEAL back at Bequia what he needed to know, Beth stood with Jamie at the stern of the new ship, she had met all of the SEALs and they all had this respect for Jamie she had never seen but was told by Rob it was because she was the highest ranking officer aboard. Rob had disappeared with both Miguel and Nick inside and Matt was now talking up a storm with the other SEALs.

"Can you tell me the truth about something?" Beth asked.

"Sure." Jamie was taking swigs of water from the bottle given to her by one of the men because she was seriously hating the motion of the boat as they sped back towards the states. "Did I kill that guy?"

"You want the truth right?" Jamie made her sit down both hanging their feet over the edge and putting the thick steel rail under their arms.

"Please."

"You hit him in the shoulder, nothing serious but he wouldn't have been able to swim far. Rob just made sure he didn't do anything, so no. You did not kill him."

"Good, I don't know how you deal with it, just holding your gun was scary."

"SEALs call them tango's, not terrorists or by name, when you train you learn to put a mental wall up and see them as just that, a tango. Will I be able to deal with knowing I killed more men? No. When we get back I'll be assigned to so many hours of psych and you learn to live on after."

"I don't know how you do it."

"Neither do I sometimes but like I told you back on the island you find the strength to do what you have to no matter what. Knowing you, Rob and Matt would die if I didn't shoot them, now that makes what I did feel a little better."

"What will happen at Miami?"

"We'll get in very early Saturday morning, Matt and I are going to fly straight back to California, Rob has to escort Miguel with Nick to Washington,

Miguel will make a statement and then more than likely he'll be put in the witness protection program while they find his father so they can prosecute him."

"Find him? Isn't he back on the island?"

"No, he took a private jet to we don't know where a few hours ago."

"So Miguel is still in danger?"

"He'll be given a new name, a new place to live and most people in the program do great safely."

"And what about me?"

"Only Rob can answer that question." Jamie laughed. "But I'd like to keep in touch with you."

"I'd like that."

"Think you'd like Rob around too?"

"I think so, but it'll be hard seeing as he's in DC and I'm in Boston."

"No chance you would move?"

"I don't know; I've not put any thought in to it."

"No thought in to what?" Rob interrupted crouching down behind them.

"Well I have to go and call my sister, word is she freaked out enough when our call was cut that she called your office."

"I heard." Rob stood as Jamie did and whether she wanted it or not he gave her a hug. "Thanks."

"You're welcome." He let Jamie go and then sat down where she had been, he watched Beth watch Jamie as she went over and put her arm around her husband as she joined the conversation. She spoke for a few minutes before taking something from one of Matt's thigh pockets and made her way to the starboard side where there was no one and it had been a cell phone she had taken from her husband.

"She's an amazing woman." Beth declared.
"So are you, if you hadn't used that gun, or even tried but wavered neither I nor Jamie would be here now. You were very brave the entire time."
"Jamie said it perfectly, you do what you have to, find the strength when you can."
"True." He put his hand on hers and she liked the contact, he laced their fingers together and after he looked quickly down at them and back up she saw something in his eye. "That look can't be good."
"I'm just trying to figure out how to tell you this."
"Tell me what?"
"I love you Beth."
"I love you too Rob." She touched his cheek with her spare hand. "But I feel like you are about to say but."
"I am, I don't want to do this like this but I have to get back to Langley and take care of Miguel and my reports. I was hoping though we could see each other after."
"I'd like to think you would."
"Maybe I'll come to Boston, get a feel of what Collegeville is like."
"I don't think you'd enjoy it much." She laughed.
"As long as you are there I wouldn't mind."
"Good." She kissed him letting her happiness come in. "Think you'll make it before my vacation is over?"

"That's right you have a week left."

"I do."

"How about this for a better idea?" He leaned in and whispered in her ear, the feeling of his breath and his words made a shiver run down her spine.

"I like that idea."

XXX   XXX

"Mel." Jamie said in to Matt's phone. The line was much clearer now what with the aerials and other communications aboard the boat. "Oh man, you're okay, you are aren't you?"

"Yes, I have a small cut above my eye, our boat was knocked when I was on the phone with you and I dropped it and hit my head but I am okay."

"What about the others?"

"Rob was shot but he'll be okay."

"Thank God. Steve and I have been stressing out like you wouldn't believe."

"You can stop, we're on SEAL Team Twelve's boat headed to Miami, Matt and I should get in early in the morning. Could we get a ride from you?"

"Of course."

"By the way, I'm so happy about you and Steve."

"Well I know it wasn't much of a surprise to you, I know he mentioned proposing to you and Matt."

"He's lucky to have you."

"Thank you."

"Look, there's something we need to talk about, probably better done in person but I wanted to say something now."

"Oh, now this doesn't sound good."

"I'm sorry Mel, for if I ever kept you down, controlled you or made you feel less than you could be. It's not much of an excuse but after Mom and Rick died I felt I had to be the one to take care, chastise and teach you. I should have seen a long time ago that you didn't need that anymore; that you just needed a sister." Jamie could hear her sisters muffled sounds of tears. "Don't be Jay, without you I wouldn't be clean, getting married or the woman I am. You did a great job helping me over the years and I don't resent you for that."

"Good, because here's where you might hate me."

"I could never hate you."

"I can't hold you up anymore, I need you to be the big sister for a while, the one who holds me up, the sister I can talk to about what's going on below the surface. The one who comes to meetings with my shrink for support."

"You're seeing a shrink?"

"Out of all that, you pick out that one section?" Jamie had to laugh slightly.

"I just didn't know." Mel paused. "I'll help you, I would love to help you and not because I owe you for everything but because you're my sister and I love you."

"Thank you."

"I know what happened a year after Izzy was born, why didn't you ever tell me?"

"You were still getting it together."

"And you didn't want to stress me out." Mel sighed. "No more babe, from now on you are taking a big

354

sister break and letting me take care of you. I know you were supposed to have this weekend with just you and Matt, Steve and I were wondering if we could have Izzy over next weekend, he'll be home and I love having her. Give you and Matt a chance to catch up."

"That would be awesome."

"Good, now give me a call when you are landing, wake me if you have to, I'll be there."

"I hoped you would say that."

Jamie hung up her call and leaned on the rail the ocean looked calm but the motion was still making her queasy. Knowing she didn't have to worry about Mel and that Rob knew where they stood did feel lighter on her shoulders. Her job was stressful but not as much as say working aboard an aircraft carrier, her marriage was perfect, she had more than she could ask for in Matt and Izzy was her little pearl, so perfect and precious.

"How is Mel?" Matt put his hands either side of her and she felt him pressed against her back.

"Looking forward to taking the role of big sister."

"Good."

"She and Steve also want Izzy next weekend, she knows this weekend was going to be for us and she wants to let us still have that."

"You can take everything I ever said bad about your sister back." He kissed her cheeks. "Knowing Mel and Rob are taking care of themselves does feel a lot better already."

"Good, but I still want you to continue those

sessions."

"I have been and I will."

"I was thinking, maybe resigning my post." Matt felt Jamie spin around.

"Why the hell would you do that?"

"Spend more time with you and the kids."

"I won't let you." Jamie put her hands on his shoulders like she was preparing to shake him. "You are a great SEAL Matt; you spend a lot more time with us than some fathers and husbands. You being gone doesn't stress me because I know you do everything you can to stay safe and the team too."

"My commission's up in two years."

"Then we'll discuss it when that comes up but I don't want you giving up your dream for me."

"Don't you know I would give anything up to make sure you are okay?"

"Then you should know I won't let you do something that you would regret."

"Fine." Matt kissed his wife. "Did I tell you I love you lately?" He smoothed down the band aid on her forehead. "You just did."

CHAPTER FORTY-ONE

Having gotten in to Miami at 0340 and had after some thank yous and goodbyes got in to a cab and arrived at Miami airport a little after four-thirty. Nick had them on a flight to San Diego that left at 0-four-forty-five and got them in to their home town a little before o-eight hundred. Mel had been there to greet them and drive them both back to their house where she had left them all the fixings for Jamie's favorite breakfast. Waffle mix, whipped cream and a pint of clean and cut fresh strawberries.

They both got in the shower together enjoying the alone time and a little outside of the shower, Matt went down and fixed them both a late breakfast almost lunch. They had a whole day before their daughter was due home and they were both looking forward to spending some alone time together. Jamie had told Mel unless there was an emergency they would see them Sunday as they were going to be a little distracted with each other.

While Jamie caught up on some sleep Matt made a quick trip to the market for some fresh foods and cleaned out the pool where a load of leaves had started to settle in the bottom. When Jamie came down midafternoon in her bathing suit and looking all fresh and awake he had needed no encouragement to join her in the pool. As he held her on his lap on the steps in the water he had taken his first look at where she had hit her head. It was a long cut and it was looking a little bruised. She had declined anyone giving her stitches aboard the SEAL Twelve boat and instead had used liquid bandage to seal it, he figured there was a great possibility it would scar but it would just be another physical spot to tell sisters apart.

He cooked them her favorite meal for dinner, a

chicken dish with a creamy garlic sauce, and they ate it out on the back deck. Spending this alone time with her was the best thing for him and he knew it was making her relax more. He knew she didn't want him to resign his post but there would be a day when he would and he was fine with that. After dinner he had taken her back to bed where he made sure she was thoroughly sated and then held her for a while before pleasing her some more. He made her get up before dawn and drove them both over to where he had proposed so they could watch the sun rise together.

Getting only a few hours' sleep on their return they had been sitting outside eating breakfast on the deck when Matt heard the sound of his daughter shouting as she ran through the house. Jamie was first to get to their daughter picking her up and looking like a woman not wanting to ever put her down. Matt had spoken his greetings to both Richard and Margaret before joining Jamie as she hugged Izzy. Their little girl was wearing a new pink princess dress with a little silver crown and shoes to match.

Sitting on the back deck altogether as Izzy played with her new Disney Princess dolls beside them they enjoyed some coffee and conversation. Seeing as Jamie and Matt had returned earlier than expected Richard and Margaret were going to get back to Georgia after they stopped in to see Mel and Steve and get some stuff done at their own house. Matt was happy to see Jamie's growing relationship with her father and step mother.

"Don't you think you should tell them the good news?" Matt asked in the kitchen while they were alone, she was getting a fresh pot of coffee and he was getting a juice box Izzy had just asked for. "I completely forgot. How about we just show them the DVD I showed you."
"Sounds good, I'll get the lap top and disc if you take this out to the little princess in pink."
"Sure." Jamie laughed walking back outside. She continued her conversation while she waited for Matt to come back and then as she waited for the computer to start up she felt a little emotional and wasn't sure why aside from how nice it was to have her father there.

"We have something to show you." Jamie turned the computer around so her father and Margaret could see it. She watched their frowns turn in to smiles. "Are you telling me I'm going to be a grandfather again?" Richard smiled.
"Yes you are." Matt said as Jamie walked to stand behind them.
"See this." Jamie pointed to the screen.
"Is that the heart beat?" Richard asked.
"Yes it is but do you see this too?" She pointed with two fingers on one hand at the screen. "Two heart beats?" Margaret gasped.
"Twins?" Richard beamed.
"Yep, can you believe it?"
"That's the best news ever." Richard pushed his chair back and stood to give his daughter a hug.

"No, the best news is Mel is getting married." Jamie fixed.

"They are both equally wonderful miracles." His joke about Mel was not lost on any of them.

"What going on?" Izzy climbed up on her father's lap.

"Mommy's having another baby." Matt whispered in her ear.

"Can I have a sister?" She looked up to Matt and his heart pulled when she did, the look of a daughter who thought her father was the entire world.

"We'll have to see about that. I think Daddy wanted little boys." Jamie told her.

"I guess they're okay too." Izzy gave in.

When Richard and Margaret were getting ready to go, Margaret pulled Jamie aside and giving her a hug told her. "Now will you take it a little easier? Give yourself a rest?"

"I will." Jamie smiled. When she had suffered the miscarriage her step mother had come out for a week, she had taken care of the house and Matt and Izzy and had been the best thing close to a mother Jamie could ever remember, their relationship was part of the new connection to them and she cherished it so much. "I presume Mel knows you're pregnant?"

"She does."

"Then let her be your rock for a while, you deserve a little break."

"I will."

"Seriously you do and you know whenever you

need an extra pair of hands we are more than willing to help out. Your father is thinking of leaving the Senate at the end of this term and moving closer."

"I would really like that."

"So would he." She kissed Jamie's cheek. "I know you aren't my daughter, not by blood but you make me proud and I worry about you like I always have since you were a teen. I'll call you in a few days."

"Take care." She told her step mother.

"You too." Margaret stopped and hugged Matt telling him to take care of her step daughter.

Later with Izzy tired out from a long day playing with her mom and dad the three of them went to visit Steve. Not being able to help herself Jamie had to check out Steve's records from after she had left. When she came back in Izzy sat next to Steve on the bed resting on his chest as she told them all about what she had done at Disney. After about twenty minutes though she had yawned and fallen so fast asleep that the adults talking around her hadn't woken her up.

Mel walked over to Jamie's office with her leaving the men with a sleeping Izzy and Matt liked this new Steve, they'd been friends for so long but it was new to hear him talking about getting married and wanting kids of his own. "Just one little Izzy would be fine." Steve said stroking the little girl's hair so it lay flatter than the usual mass of unruly curls. "You may regret that." Matt laughed.

"Do you?"

"Nah, not ever." Matt admitted.

"I wouldn't either. Mel says Jamie's taking it easy for a while."

"She's agreed to finally let everyone else control stuff. It will probably only last a few months but that might be all she needs."

"Well, Mel certainly likes the idea of looking after Jamie, and me. It will be good for both of them."

"We are good for them." Matt said smugly. "Never thought I'd have you as a brother in law but at least I can handle hanging out with you."

"Yeah, unlike if Mel had married Rob right."

"I don't dislike Rob, he's just got a history with Jamie I can't compete with but I realized while we were away, they don't have as much as I do with Jamie."

"You are a strong couple."

"I like to think so."

"I wanted your help with something." Steve shifted slightly and Izzy still didn't stir.

"Anything."

"I want to put together a surprise party for our engagement, the team and everyone. I know I'm not officially a member anymore but you're all my family."

"You'll be back on the team; they won't be able to keep you down now."

"No they won't. I figured maybe we could have it in a few weeks, make everyone know it's official."

"I'll get on it; anywhere special you want to have it?"

362

"On the beach somewhere."

"A little vague but I'll see what I can do."

"Thanks." Steve paused. "I'm hoping my mom will come back for it."

"Getting along with her okay?"

"I was until she told me yesterday who she was having dinner with."

"Who'd she have dinner with?"

"Captain Fuller."

"Are you shitting me?" Matt laughed so loud Izzy stirred.

XXX   XXX

Mel looked around the office her sister worked in, the pictures of all the men in the teams on her walls. The intimidating framed documents Jamie had earned like her medical degree. She had been in that office a few times before and they had always seemed so impressive but for some reason this time they didn't. She waited while Jamie turned on her computer and typed something up and sent it via e-mail.

"Matt said he was going to resign his commission when it's up in two years." She said as Mel looked around the room. "Why?" Mel was shocked.

"Wants to spend more time with me and Izzy and the babies."

"He'll miss it though."

"I know, I told him he couldn't but I wanted to ask your opinion on something."

"What?"

"Once the babies are born, I was thinking about quitting myself."

"Are you serious?"

"Very."

"Then my opinion is don't."

"Why not?"

"Because you love this as much as Matt loves his job, unless you are really sure it's what you want I wouldn't. Your hours are good, your friends are here and you make us all proud."

"I guess you are right."

"I know I'm right. How long do you have left on your commission?"

"Eleven months."

"Don't do it, Navy life is what makes you happy."

"Yeah, it does."

"So, I wanted to ask you a favor."

"Anything."

"Will you be my matron of honor at the wedding?"

"Ah, sure, how come?"

"Because you are the best sister ever and I know Matt's going to be asked by Steve to be his best man."

"If you put it like that."

"You will?"

"Yeah."

"Excellent, then I need you to help me completely, I have no idea about this wedding stuff and especially the weird extra's they do because they're military."

"There's only a few extra quirks." Jamie smiled thinking back to her own wedding. "I know someone who would love to help you more than I can who has a lot more experience."

"Who?"

"Pat."

"She'd help me?"

"Are you kidding, she lives for this stuff."

CHAPTER FORTY-TWO

One week after leaving Miami;

"Anyone home?" Rob shouted coming in to the hall of his house in Falls Church, Virginia, it had been a hectic week since returning from Miami and only one thing had been able to put a smile on his face when he came home at the end of the day. "In the kitchen." Her voice called back and he sniffed the air as he threw his suit jacket over the back of the armchair and began rolling up his sleeves, he walked to his new favorite room in his house.

Arriving back at Langley with Miguel they had set him up at one of the safe houses on site and let him rest for a while. Rob went and spoke to his boss filling him in on what had happened including why things had turned out the way they did. After he had finished making his report he had started everything with Miguel. Between him and Nick they had been able to link Miguel's father to over seventy murders in the last ten years alone. The numerous disappearances of tourists and money laundering and weapons dealing were also things listed and proven and would add time to any sentence given to his father if he was ever apprehended.

After three days they had all they needed and they began getting Miguel ready for the idea of the witness protection program. He surprisingly wasn't as against it as they had expected and today Nick had left with Miguel to a location Rob didn't want to know.

He found Beth in the kitchen with food all over the counter and preparation island. "Are we feeding an army?"
"No, just us."
"Then what's with all the food?"
"I figured I'd make up a load of food, I'll put it in the freezer and you'll have something better than a hungry man frozen dinner to eat when I go home."
"You don't have to go home."
"I wish I didn't." She wiped her hands off on the kitchen towel and moved so she could wrap her arms around his waist. "Then don't." He nuzzled her neck.
"I can't be on vacation forever."
"Then quit your job."
"It's not that easy." She pushed his upper body away and had that stern look on her face that he just wanted to kiss until it disappeared.

"Come with me." He said taking her hand and leading her to the stools around the kitchens island. He waited for her to sit down like he was and took both her hands in his. "I had a really interesting day today."

"You did?"

"I quit my job." He said with a smile and he saw her face frown. "But I have a new job."

"Why would you quit your job?"

"Tired of doing it I guess. Nick's very happy because now he's head agent of the team."

"What are you going to do now?"

"I was offered a position in New York City."

"Doing what?"

"Teaching law at my old graduate school Columbia." He paused and looked down. "I was hoping I could persuade you to go with me."

"You want me to go with you?" Beth choked out. "I err."

"I understand if you don't want to, I just thought I'd put it out there."

After everything they had been through, the feelings she stirred in him were so intense and away from the danger they hadn't lessened. He had hoped she felt the same way back or maybe it was too much too soon. "When are you leaving?"

"End of the month."

"Three weeks?"

"I figured its half way between so even if you didn't want to leave Boston it's closer for you to come and visit."

"Where are you going to live?"

"There's a great three floor walkup on the upper west side they have for the dean of law, the position I'd be taking. I mean I wouldn't have to take it, I could live somewhere else especially if you didn't like it, you know if you came."

"Are you sure this is what you want? I once read a book where an agent never really left the CIA and I think Jamie is proof of that."

"You're right; I can't disconnect myself from the agency that easily. There may be a time when they need my help on a case I may have prior history on and being in New York and the ex-head of the terrorist team if something was to happen on American soil again then I would have to help."

"But it wouldn't mean you spent months away?" She looked away.

"No." He smiled shaking his head. "Is that your concern about moving in with me?"

"Partly, I don't think I could handle the, what if's, I'd also worry about you after experiencing what you do first hand that doesn't help."

"Well I plan on becoming a stuffy old lecturer, does that help?"

"It sure does." She paused. "So when can we take a look at this place they have for you?"

"We could go up tomorrow; it's a forty-five-minute flight and spend some time in the city."

"I could call my Mom, see if she could meet us for dinner, she asked about you when I spoke to her."

"That sounds like a good idea, so shall I go and make flight reservations?"

"Yes." Beth kissed him. "And after you're done we can eat."

"There's only one thing that can hold my attention right now."

"Food first then sex." The phone rang and Rob

reluctantly let go of her to go and get it.

"Hello." He said in to the phone.

"You quit?" The female voice said down the phone to him, since getting in to Miami he hadn't heard from her, he had called Matt to make sure they had arrived home safe and was giving her some space, letting her make any first moves. He had always kept a track on her, knew things about her personally that she may never like him to have found out through his connections but after him and Mel breaking up he hadn't done it as much and it wasn't until Matt explained her depression and stress with everything that he truly understood why she had blown up at him the way she had.

"I did." He laughed and mouthed Jamie's name to Beth who wondered who would be calling. "I'm taking a job in New York at my old law school."

"I don't believe it, good for you. Those kids will be lucky to have you."

"I'm the lucky one; I think Beth is going to agree to move in with me."

"That is so wonderful." He heard Jamie's true happiness in her voice and was glad, not that he needed her opinion but it did mean a lot to him just the same. "You know as long as you are happy and healthy I'm supportive of everything you do."

"That's good to know, thank you."

"I have some more good news for you."

"Go ahead."

"I went to the doctors for a checkup; I'm actually further along than we thought which you know is great, less chance of anything bad happening like last time." She paused. "But Matt and I were able to find out the sex of the babies today."

"And?"

"Boys, Izzy and I will be outnumbered."

"That's great for Matt though."

His heart tightened as an image of years before when she had found out she was pregnant with his child came to mind. They had just got back from the first assignment together where she had killed Atwa's son, on their arrival back she had been ordered to do four months of psych. She had lived with him and not long after they had returned they had both felt something and ended up in bed together, he knew she had never liked the idea but an abortion had been the only answer, she had her life in the navy and he was still headed up the fast track inside the CIA.

"Matt must be so happy."

"More than you can believe, all the way home he could talk about nothing more than how to decorate the nursery and that he wanted to get little Padre shirts and chill out and watch a game with them at his side."

"He'll get his chance."

"How does it feel to be free of the agency?"

"A little weird but it will be fine, I have no doubt in my mind that this is the right thing to do."

"Good."

"Are you going to renew your commission next

summer?" Jamie had mentioned something to Beth and he couldn't believe she would leave the Navy. "I was thinking about not. Matt's is up in two years also, but we both agreed, we're Navy, career Navy. I'll continue for a few more years, my family and friends are here."

"Speaking of family, I heard Mel is getting married."

"She is; she also has a new career starting in a few weeks when Steve's a little more mobile."

"Doing what?"

"The local high school was looking for a peer counselor, full time and the pay is great. They loved that she knew what she was talking about and had experience in the areas they were seeking no matter that it was a personal experience. She'll make some good strides and she's having fun running around playing big sister, she's coming to take Izzy for the weekend soon, hold on."

He heard a muffled something on the other end of the line and then a voice he hadn't heard in a very long time. "Uncle Robbie?" Izzy asked.

"Izz." Robert felt his skin tingle; since she could talk she had always called him Robbie. "Are you coming to see me soon? I have a new princess dress it's...." He listened as Izzy went on and on for ten minutes before suddenly announcing. "Gotta go." And passed the phone back to her mother.

"The minute Matt told her who I was talking to she was pulling on my shorts dying to speak to you."

"I bet she's grown so much since I last saw her."

"She has, you and Beth should come and visit

when you get settled."

"We will."

"Oh, is she there? Could I speak to her?"

"She is, hold on." Rob walked the phone back in to the other room and held it out for Beth.

"Hi Jamie." Beth said balancing the phone on her shoulder.

"I wanted to ask your opinion on something."

"Sure, what is it?"

"You know its Rob's birthday next week right?"

"No I didn't." She looked at Rob watching her and smiled.

"Well its next Thursday and Matt and I happen to be off for another long weekend and he thought maybe we could fly out for a few days, bring Izzy with us I wondered if we should just arrive as a surprise or tell him."

"The first choice." Beth grinned wickedly.

"Great, I'll call you in a few days when we have something set, you can tell Rob it's to do with Mel's wedding and he'll ask nothing more." Jamie sighed. "Speaking of Mel, she just arrived to take Izzy for the weekend. Tell Rob I said goodbye and I'll speak to you both in a few days."

"Take it easy."

"You too Beth." There was a sly laugh thrown in as the line disconnected and she wondered what it was for. "What did Jamie want to talk to you about?" Rob asked opening a bottle of beer. "Her sister's wedding."

"So about moving to New York." Rob completely changed the conversation and with her back to him she was able to grin without getting caught.

EPILOGUE

Beth felt the bitter sting of the wind as it hit her coming up from the subway that had warmed her a little in the city that was freezing everything it could. She had lived there now for four months and she was still loving every part of her life.

She had found a job working with a women's shelter. Wasn't too far from the life she had been living in Boston but she wasn't in a position of telling someone why they should leave their partners, having the usual argument because the women in these shelters had already been through every case scenario and were just looking for a place to start fresh, a safe place.

The brownstone Rob had been given as an incentive for the job had been a dream, three floors of beautifully built high walls and hardwood floors. There were four bedrooms and a kitchen she just loved, his kitchen in Virginia had been spacious but this one was modern. She enjoyed cooking for him and now that the entire house was full of their personal effects it felt like home.

Stopping in at the bodega on the corner from the subway stop she picked up some fresh items for dinner and walked three blocks to her new home, their home. "I'm home." She shouted putting down the brown grocery bag and her shoulder bag. She had not only her heavy wool coat to get off but the other pieces that kept you warm in the wind. "How was your day?" Rob shouted back as she heard him walking on the hardwood floor towards her. "Busy but I think I made some progress finding Erin a new place."

"Good." She turned to see him leaning on the door frame to the living room, his hair had grown a little longer and the new stubble faze was suiting him well along with the jeans that made his ass look too good and the roll neck black sweater he had on only made him look sexier. One of the kids from his classes he had chosen to be his TA had told her Rob was the hottest thing on campus in decades, every female student and female faculty member enjoyed having a good look and of course it being New York City even some of the men looked. She had to agree with them, out of the stuffy suits he wore the week she had been in Virginia and the clothes he had worn on the island, this new relaxed look was definitely agreeing with him.

"Your Mom called a little while ago, she's going to look for your brother tomorrow and wanted to know whether you were joining her and also wanted to know if we were going to spend Thanksgiving with her."

"What did you say?" Beth had finally removed everything and picked up the brown bag passing it to him and leaving her other bag where it was.

"That you would call her."

"Chicken."

"Why don't we invite her here?"

"We could." Beth laughed following him in to the kitchen. "How was your day?"

"The usual." He smirked and she knew what it was for. When he had started his classes one of the kids in his class had made a statement about something about federal agencies and how they take the law in to their own hands. Rob had set him straight and the kid hadn't liked being shown up in front of his class mates. He asked Rob how he knew, he was probably spouting out the blah, blah, blah that anyone would who didn't know what went on behind closed doors. Rob had told Beth he had laughed, the students all frowning at the reaction, he had walked around the lecture hall so he could stand next to the kid. Leaning down he said very plainly and evenly stopping his laughter instantly. He gave him that agent look that Beth had seen once. The kid had shrunk back and with his even voice he had said. "Last month I was the head of the counter terrorist team at Langley for the CIA, unlike you I am fully knowledgeable of what does and doesn't go on inside the walls of the CIA so before you make a fool of yourself any more than you already have I suggest you shut up."

Rob had laughed about it later that night but she also knew he missed it a lot. He not only gave classes on first year law but also a special class for those students looking to go in to criminology and not some law firm. He had said he wouldn't have to leave unless something came up at either the CIA or in the city to do with terrorism. So far he had done one such evening when he had to meet with an agent, she didn't know what it was about and she hadn't asked. She also knew he still had his ID and gun in the locked drawer of his desk and she was fine with that.

"Emily is coming by Early in the morning for some class notes for Monday." He said about his TA. "On a Saturday?"
"Yep, you know she wants to join the CIA or the FBI, she doesn't seem picky."
"Think she could do it?"
"Yeah, I do, she has stones and she doesn't take a lick from anyone." He put the bag down on the counter and grabbed her and held her. "I had an idea about Christmas."
"You did?"
"I wondered how you would feel about going away."
"Depends where and if there are any bad guys?" She ran her hands through his hair, the thick dark hair that ruffled at the back of his neck. "No bad guys but there might be a few people you know."
"Where do you want to go?"
"That depends on your answer."
"To what?"

His hands slid down her arms as he got to his knees, the moment he set one up and let the other stay on the ground her own knees began to feel weak. She watched him take something out of his back pocket and with the other hand take her left hand. "Would you be able to live with me forever and become my wife?" He said smiling from ear to ear. He was holding the other hand closed and she couldn't wait to see what it held. "Yes." She said sinking to her knees and he kept holding her hand as he slipped on the prettiest diamond ring she had ever seen. "Oh, my." She said not noticing the tears coming to her eyes. "Is it okay?"

"It's more than okay, I love you so much."

"I love you too." He picked her up and carried her one flight to their bedroom where he thoroughly adorned her with his love and made her moan when she was there.

In the soft afterglow, wrapped up in the thick comforter Beth realized she had no idea where Christmas was going to be. "So where are we going for Christmas?"

"Colorado, Jamie and Mel's father has a huge house there so for the week of Christmas the Buchanan clan including Mel and her new husband and some of the other SEALs are celebrating Christmas together. Jamie said she really hopes we can make it and if you had any reservations about leaving your Mom we can bring her too."

"All those young people, she'd hate it."

"Jamie and Mel's parents are going to be there as well as Steve's mother and her new boyfriend and I think there was another parent of someone on the team."

"How big a house?"

"I did say huge right? And it's on the bottom of a private ski slope."

"I love skiing."

"I know you do, so you want to go?"

"Of course." Beth beamed.

"Then you can call Jamie later and tell her to count us in."

"Not until you let me show you how much I love you." Rob laughed as he felt her mouth leaving a trail of kisses down his chest.

COMING SOON

Tawnie - America's Favorite Sweetheart

"And in entertainment news." The CBS news at five am anchor said. *"Late last night America's favorite Thursday night actress Tawnie Rowe was involved in a routine traffic stop as her current boyfriend Ted Sanders was arrested for being three times over the legal alcohol limit."* The screen showed a recent picture of the actress and then a split screen as the bad boy guitarist from the latest alternative band had his mug shot shown for everyone to see.

"Sanders was released on bail this morning and no charges were brought against Rowe; this is the third scuffle with the law since last season's show wrapped. Their summer hiatus is about over and rumors the studio heads are considering a replacement for her are rife all over town. Has this actress gone down the same road that many before her have taken? Is stardom too much for this twenty-nine-year-old? Stay tuned for our Good Morning California show at nine when Stacie and Bob tell us more about the latest rumors about Tawnie and other CBS stars."

www.ingramcontent.com/pod-product-compliance
Lightning Source LLC
Chambersburg PA
CBHW062002170626
46813CB00001B/10